Susan

Also by C. E. Poverman
The Black Velvet Girl

Susan

by C.E. Poverman

The Viking Press   New York

First published in 1977 by The Viking Press
625 Madison Avenue, New York, N.Y. 10022

Published simultaneously in Canada by
The Macmillan Company of Canada Limited

LIBRARY OF CONGRESS CATALOGING IN PUBLICATION DATA
    Poverman, C.E.   1944–
      Susan.
      I. Title.
pz4.p875su [ps3566.082]   813'.5'4   76–49931
isbn 0–670–68521–6

Set in Linotype Caledonia
Printed in the United States of America

For you, Patricia, with love always

Susan

*I*t was getting harder to breathe. Susan took another deep breath as the close air in the cabin went on pressurizing. She felt her cheekbones grow leaden, her body begin to swell against the tight uniform, the edges of the wide belt cut into her stomach. Someone was watching her. She smiled over the faces in the cabin. One of them staring at her, which one? Pressurization. A traffic delay, they were waiting for clearance. Pressurization. Pressure in her ears, deep inside her head, the voices, the faces with big eyes and no features, people talking in the distance, she could feel someone, one of the passengers, still staring at her.

After a moment, Mickey's voice, but not like Mickey. Mickey's stewardess voice. Cool. Everything under control. Mickey's idea of slightly musical:

Aloha, ladies and gentlemen, welcome aboard Polynesian Airlines DC-9 Royal Fan Jet Flight 181 from Honolulu to Kahuului, Maui, then on to Hilo. In command of your flight . . .

Susan followed the introductions:

In this cabin to serve you . . . Miss Gale Lopez, Miss Susan Wilson, and, speaking, Mrs. Michelle Chun. . . .
We're experiencing a slight delay due to traffic. . . .

Automatically, Susan went through the motions with Mickey's voice, pointing out the emergency exits, holding up the Mae West, raising the oxygen mask at the right moment.

. . . Please feel free to call on us at any time. . . . Have a pleasant flight. Mahalo.

The airplane lurched suddenly, Susan lost and recovered her balance, the airplane turned onto the runway.

In a few moments, they were climbing steeply and Mickey was back on the microphone. Susan fought to tune it out:

Ladies and gentlemen, we're presently flying along the southern coastline of Oahu. In view now are . . . areas of Honolulu . . . Punchbowl Crater . . . covers a hundred and twelve acres . . . resting place for World War Two and Vietnam . . . Ala Wai Yacht Club . . . One of Oahu's most famous landmarks, Mount Leahi. . . . Diamond Head . . . English name from British soldiers . . . found crystals in the slopes . . . took them to be diamonds. . . .
. . . ahead, Koko Head and Koko Crater. . . . Hanauma Bay . . . once a volcanic crater until the sea broke through one side. . . .

Susan could still feel someone watching her as they pushed the cocktail cart up against the steep incline of the aisle, Mickey taking the money, Susan bracing the cart with her legs and pouring the drinks. Aloha, cocktail? Good morning, sir, may we offer you a drink?

For a moment, she felt an ache, for him, gone back to the mainland, hadn't written; she couldn't make an image of his face, just the feeling. . . . Jack . . .

Good morning, cocktail?

Maybe a letter today, some word.

Susan could feel her body swelling. Pressurization. Her feet starting to tighten in the white shoes, the elastic of the support hose getting tighter across her stomach, cabin pressure. . . .

Couldn't remember his face, today, but the feeling. Too many faces in here, someone watching. Mai Tai, scotch on the rocks, Bloody Mary . . .

Good morning, sir, cocktail?

Susan leaned over, the smell, something wrong, the hands spread on the tray, waiting, something about these hands, familiar, delicate, almost female hands, the gold ring, the Mason's ring, and the smell, cologne, remember the cologne, Susan felt herself starting to sink out of sight, Mickey, she wanted Mickey to reach across the cart, grab her the way she'd done that night in Hilo, help her, the rush of the engines, the air vents, these hands on the tray, his hands could do that to me and survive, lie here on this tray, neat, manicured, the nails pink, waiting for me to serve him, am I going to serve him?

He was looking at her. Susan looked away. A newspaper . . . *Star-Bulletin.* . . . Senate Watergate Committee to be nationally televised. . . . Daniel Inouye . . .

She knew she was going to be sick, she panicked, suddenly looked down at her legs, no blood, no blood, of course, no blood, she could barely restrain herself from reaching around to feel the seat of her skirt, no blood, of course, no blood. . . .

Scotch on the rocks.

Did he recognize her? After all this time? He seemed to be smiling. She looked down at her stockings, hesitated, set the ice-filled glass in front of him; she felt herself go lightheaded, nauseated, the squares of sunlight on the carpeted aisle fade and brighten at once, no blood.

The plane was leveling off, she put the miniature between his hands on the tray, careful not to touch him in any way, turned away, she felt herself still smiling, she had not stopped smiling the whole time, the belt and support hose were cutting into her waist, a cramp was spreading out. . . .

3

If she could just make it through serving the drinks . . .
Susan took another deep breath, sweating, could they see she
was sweating? the pressure in the cabin was tighter, she didn't
know if she was going to be able to move her arms and legs . . .
if she could just make it through serving the drinks.

In the buffet, Mickey looked Susan up and down.

What kind of stockings you wearing, Susan?

Hanes. . . . Gentlemen Prefer Hanes, don't you know? Susan
tried to joke.

Yeah, prefer Hanes on you. Your legs lookin terrific. Should
see da guys turn and look at choo! Long legs!

Mickey slapped Susan lightly on the arm. Susan tried to
smile, suddenly said, Mickey, would you cover for me a few
minutes, I've got to go to the lua. . . .

Mickey nodding, go ahead. Susan hesitated before she
stepped out of the buffet, she would have to pass him again,
had he recognized her? What difference could it possibly make
after all this time anyway? She walked down the aisle, her
head high, smiling over the heads of the passengers, the door
in the tail coming closer. . . .

At the door, Susan saw that the lua was occupied, supported
herself against the last empty seat, the cramp felt worse; in
panic, she looked down at her legs, again nothing; I know, I
know, she said, but couldn't get over the feeling; she stared out
the window at the puffy trade-wind clouds below, their shadows, far below, cool and dark islands on the water, speck of
white, a boat, she closed her eyes, felt the nausea rising.

The door opened, she stepped back, smiled, entered the lua,
locked the door, engines louder in here, the rush of the ventila-
tion system; she turned and saw her face in the mirror, the
surgically white light, under the false eyelashes, eye liner,
eyeshadow, make-up, rouge, she could still see her face was
pale, the nausea worse. Then Susan saw her face tense, freeze.

Suddenly it was her mother's face, she saw her mother looking back at her, middle-aged, Japanese, her short hair dyed too black, her mother's eyes crafty in perpetual terror of something she couldn't understand. Susan swayed, put her hands over her face in the mirror. Even though Susan's father was white, a haole, she could still see it was her mother's face. I am turning into my mother, was it the only face she'd ever really know? I am turning into my mother, she repeated out loud, I have turned into my mother. . . . She fumbled for a towel and vomited delicately, dabbing several times at the corner of her mouth, trying not to smear her make-up. She blinked at the tears, I'll ruin the make-up; she wondered vaguely where she'd left her kit. She reached up and touched a small mole at the corner of her upper lip.

After a moment, she washed her mouth out, looked at herself in the mirror—a little better, not much, still like her mother, but more now the way her mother had looked when she'd been young, back during World War II, the old snapshots, her mother smiling, tough and confident.

In one of the snapshots, her mother stood on the beach wearing a Japanese halter top, a silk print, they were coming back into fashion again; her hair, long and black, hung loose over her shoulders, it rose in the trade wind, the ocean behind her. Her mother had been a South Seas beauty. Beside her, beside my mother, her sister, my Aunt Jane, also smiling, the identical halter top, her long hair rising in the wind, the two of them smiling, the two of them beautiful, and, as Uncle William had said, Ruthie and Jane, inseparable, you look like her, Susan, your Aunt Jane. . . .

Jane, the girl on the gravestone, smiling, always smiling. . . .

Susan studied herself in the mirror, if she were in the snapshot, would she be her mother with her arm around her sister Jane? Or Jane, with her mother?

She wondered at the missing face a moment, there was only

one face looking back from the mirror, hers, which one? myself she said out loud, unsure, seeing her face tense again, my mother, I am turning into my mother . . .

Frank Sinatra had once given her mother a fifty-dollar tip. He'd invited her to a party with him. Back during the war. Or just after. She had been working as a cocktail waitress then. At the Blue Grotto.

Had she gone with Frank Sinatra to the party?

Susan wasn't sure. She knew her mother would deny it anyway, even if she had. Her mother denied everything.

The close antiseptic smell, traces of perfume and cologne were bringing back the nausea, Susan watched her face tense again, her mother would deny it anyway. Susan saw the hands on the tray, her own hand reaching over and placing the drink between his manicured hands, his face slowly starting to turn back toward hers, the smell of his cologne, his hands could do that to me and survive, pick up a drink . . . and I would serve it to him as though nothing had happened, as though nothing made a difference, any person could do anything to any other person. He was out there now, out in the cabin on the other side of this door. Susan hated herself for having to serve him.

Someone was knocking on the door, Susan slid back the latch, Mickey's face, her eyes, small, almost black, cunning, concerned, looking in.

You don't look so good. You okay, Susan?

Airsick.

You need something?

My make-up.

Susan started to close the door, Mickey jammed her foot in. Pushed the door wide open. Puffy dark bags under Mickey's eyes. Several oily brown pigmentation spots on her cheek, birth-control spots.

Ey, Susan. One second. You comin to da house blessing tonight, right? You not forget it?

Susan hesitated. She didn't want to say no. Mickey would take it personally, Mickey took everything personally. When Mickey received a notice she was three pounds over flight-weight, Mickey would say, see, I told you, airline going to dump me now, dey tryin to get rid of me, dey use me up, den dey discard me like some used piece of Kleenex. Mickey would rub the tips of her fingers together. Kleenex! You see, dey tink first dey going ground me, den dey going dump dis broad. You tink da fuckin airline like one old slant-eye buddha-head like me flyin for dem any more. Nevah. But I going take it up wit da union.

Mickey's eyes would get bright. She would go on and on. Everything was personal with Mickey. People were out to get her. The airline, people. People didn't like Japanese. And she bore grudges.

An outsider, hearing Mickey speak English, might think that Mickey was ignorant or stupid, which was not the case. For Mickey, pidgin was the language of familiarity, of emotion. Susan remembered how Mickey, self-conscious with Jack around, would speak a kind of stilted, correct English for Jack, for her idea of Jack, who was both a mainlander and a haole. And, of course, whenever Mickey was flying, she could—and did speak proper English to the passengers.

Didn't forget da house blessing? Mickey repeated.

Susan shook her head, no, lost her balance as they slammed into some turbulence, Mickey held fast in the doorway, no, I'm coming, Mickey.

Good! Want choo dere! Mickey took her foot out of the door. You pull yourself togethah!

Susan pulled the door shut. When she'd first started flying, Mickey had been about as old as Susan was now, her face still smooth, she didn't have that look permanently in her eyes, those lines around her mouth, under her eyes, in her forehead, lines from smiling too much, lines from too much pressuriza-tion and altitude, too much worry about money, rent, mortgages, lines from being nice to rude and obnoxious passengers, lines from worrying about her looks, her job. . . .

Susan dampened a towel with cold water. Pressed it against her face.

If he would just break this silence and write me, some word, anything, I'd know where I was, I could make a decision, but this way I'm nowhere, I'm just hanging. . . .

She pressed her face with the damp towel, started thinking of what she would write him in a letter, couldn't think of anything more than, I love you. She tried to remember his face, but couldn't.

He hadn't been gone that long. Two months . . .

She took a deep breath, raised her eyes to the mirror; her mother's face? Susan saw her mother sitting alone across the room, her lips moving slightly, her eyes shifting, seeming to follow something invisible in the air, the smoke rising straight up from the cigarette into the stillness of the room. Her eyes moving back and forth. The cigarette smoke rising straight up, then spreading into plumes.

Susan turned away from the mirror.

Her mother, suddenly close, holding up her wedding ring, her engagement ring, her voice close, don't ever, ever give a man *that* until you've got *these* on your finger! At least three carats! Never!

At other times, her mother suddenly saying, if anything ever happens to me, don't accept it! My death might look like an accident, but it will not be an accident! Promise me you will investigate after my death! Susan!

Her mother grabbing her.

Susan! I am counting on you!

Then her mother's face close. Susan! Don't speak pidgin! Only ignorant people speak pidgin! Do you want people to think you are an ignorant island girl?

Her mother's voice suddenly overwhelming Susan. Susan!

8

Stay out of the sun! You want to stay fair, don't you? The sun will make you dirty!

Her mother said the word dirty in two fastidious syllables: dir-tee.

By the time Susan was in high school—before, really, but high school for certain—she knew there must be something wrong with her mother. With her mother, not her. The way she stood at the kitchen curtains, her face slightly back from the window to keep out of sight, one hand holding up a corner of the curtain. Staring out at the neighbor's house across the street, her lips moving.

Her mother hardly let her leave the house, except to go to school, much less go out on dates with boys. What did she think would happen to her anyway?

In the afternoons, it had always been a relief to get out of the house and work in the drugstore. She liked school, and school was out of the house, too, but Aiea High School was dangerous for her, she could never relax for long, the school was filled with Samoans who called her sharkbait because she was hapa haole—ey, shokbait! shokbait fockah! She avoided them when they sat cross-legged in a tight circle at lunch and pounded out Samoan chants. Several times she was followed by Samoan girls, ey, shokbait, tita, and finally, when her way was blocked, she'd had to fight, scratching, biting, pulling hair, punching. And winning. If anyone could be a winner at that kind of thing.

So afternoons, she was happy to work in the drugstore in Waikiki. High school or home. She could no longer take the bus to Kalihi and sit with Obachan; Obachan was gone, she was trying to accept that she would never ever have her grandmother to go to again.

But at least the drugstore was cool and quiet. For several hours each day she could be away from her mother, away from the high school, she could sit on a stool behind the counter and read paperbacks and library books all afternoon. *Tender Is the Night. Light in August. The Heart Is a Lonely Hunter.* She could read without the sound of a tv blaring in the next room, without holding herself tense, inwardly waiting for the sound of her mother's voice. Occasionally she might look up to check the aisles in the convex overhead mirrors, to ring up the sale of suntan oil or a beach mat, or, once, to her mild amusement, to look into the face of a man nervously buying prophylactics. The old Japanese druggist, Mr. Matsumoto, was always kind and patient with her, teaching her how to count out change so she wouldn't get confused; first to the nearest dollar, then the bills; and he left her alone to read quietly. She never had to go through the motions of looking busy—reading didn't seem to be a waste of time to the old man.

After work, she usually wandered through Waikiki carrying the book she had been reading, calmed by the order of the words and the hours in the drugstore. First, wandering down Kalakau Avenue, watching the tourists, wondering about their lives on the mainland. Sometimes thinking of snow silently falling and covering everything in a peaceful silence. Maybe Vermont. Snow covering everything. By now the sun slanting down, still high above the horizon, but the shadows between the hotels lengthening, deepening into blue. At Kapiolani Park, she'd wander under the spreading old banyans, listen to the doves cooing in the tall palms along the beach at Queen Surf. Even over here, she could hear the cough of a lion, the sudden screech of a bird over at the zoo. Then, at the natatorium, stopping for a moment to watch the volleyball game. It seemed to be the same volleyball game played with the same fury by the same beachboys, and it never seemed to have a beginning or an end. So pleasing, the pink pastel of the late afternoon sun on the concrete of the old natatorium. Always, Susan noticed the clock. It had Roman numerals and had been stuck at seven minutes to five for as long as she could remember. The clock stood alone on a fluted iron column, framed by the main arch of the natatorium. Behind the clock, the sea, shining in the late afternoon sun, filling the arch right up to the horizon; and the horizon of the sea ran behind the face of the clock at three and nine from where she stood.

Wherever she went, even down in the silence of the natatorium, she eventually overheard a radio—a car radio, a portable radio—and the radio always seemed to be playing The Beach Boys. Surfing music. Blond southern California surfing music. She would think of Obachan, the heat of the car, the smell of eucalyptus on the road back, the blue of the sky, and she would walk quickly to get away from the music.

Finally, it would be getting late, and she would have to catch a bus.

At home, her mother chain-smoking, the tv on loud. Her father back from the shipyard at Pearl Harbor, lowering his cup of coffee—he, too, a chain smoker and coffee drinker. Silently watching Susan come in. His thick heavy forearms on the table. Carol off somewhere, maybe in her room.

What took you so long to get home from work?

Nothing, Mother. I'm on time.

Did you stop off somewhere?

No.

She walked past her father, and her mother said, aren't you going to say hello to your father?

Yes. Hi, Dad.

He gave her a tight smile, raised his cup of coffee, drank, and she went to her room and closed the door.

Susan knew that there was something different about her family. Even the inside of the house was different. Except for the books she brought into the house, there were no books. When she'd been younger, and was sent to her room for punishment, she would just sit and read library books and, after a while, she spent most of her time reading in her room.

11

Once her mother got the idea that Susan didn't mind being sent to her room, she would come in and take away the book. If one was taken away, she got out another which she kept hidden under the mattress or in the closet.

Her mother didn't read. Her father occasionally read something technical on electronics. The tv was always on. No one seemed to watch the tv, either. It just seemed to be on, always. It was already on in the morning when Susan got up for school. Her father, dressed for work, stood smoking a cigarette and drinking his coffee, staring at the tv, yes, but not really watching it. In the afternoon, the tv was still on, and then, into the night, though still no one was watching. Susan might turn it off, but in a few minutes someone would turn it back on.

Susan couldn't remember ever having seen her father kiss her mother. They never talked to each other. They never talked about anything at all. She couldn't imagine them making love. She knew her mother always wore her bra to bed at night, that she slept in her bra, and somehow, she knew that her mother and father had an old quarrel from a time before she'd lived with them. It must have been more than money. When she had married him, she had been working as a cocktail waitress at the Blue Grotto and had been able to make more money than he; in fact she had all but supported him while she pushed him; she never let him forget that when she had met him, he was an uneducated merchant mariner.

Now he was a foreman at an electrical shop at Pearl Harbor and drank fifteen cups of coffee a day and she still hadn't stopped pushing. It had been her idea for him to sell insurance. Life insurance. Often, he came home exhausted from work, showered, and went back out to call on clients; he had a special calendar with the birthdays of clients and on those dates, he would send them birthday cards—the whole business was a turn-off to Susan. But it had brought in money, a language her parents understood; her father had gotten far enough ahead to begin making lucrative investments.

But still, Susan knew it would never be enough for her mother, whatever he did would never be enough. She saw her mother sitting at the table, her eyebrows plucked into a thin line, her hair dyed too black, her skin waxy, shining, the pores under her eyes large, her hand resting on the table, the diamonds of her ring glittering conspicuously.

Susan couldn't understand what kept them together and why her father worked so hard. Money was the only thing that mattered. Why should he care about money when his wife never kissed him, slept in her bra, when there was nothing to enjoy, no books, they never went anywhere. . . .

Their idea of a good time was going to the drive-in up in Aiea and watching some Elvis Presley or Frankie Avalon movie. Or maybe a Western.

She would sit in the back seat trying to read and her mother would say, put the book away and watch the movie.

What was it all for? For this?

The only evidence she had of her father's life—no affection or talk or interest between her father and mother—was his work. The shields. Each time the shop completed one of the submarines at Pearl Harbor, the navy awarded him a heavy wooden plaque in the shape of a shield, the boat's coat of arms cut in bas-relief, the escutcheons painted in bright enamels; each shield was a submarine sent back to sea. The *Skate*, the *Triton*, the *Thresher*. . . .

At first, he had hung the shields on the walls of his den. He took pains to center a shield exactly in the middle of the wall. His insurance certificate, framed, hung above his bare desk. To the right, he kept a small safe and a metal filing cabinet which he kept locked. Eventually, he would bring home another shield, and take down the old shield, and again take pains to hang the new shield, trying to center them both according to some inner cartesian symmetry.

Finally, there had been too many shields and her father, seemingly overwhelmed, gave up hanging them symmetrically, and simply let them stack up anywhere, either laying them on the floor, or trying to lean them against the wall; because of the point at the bottom of the shield, they usually tilted to one side or the other, and eventually, fell over.

Getting up late at night, walking through the house to the kitchen, Susan would see the shields, some hanging, some leaning at crazy angles against the walls, and think of submarines —silent, dark, menacing—moving somewhere out there in the black oceans, miles and miles of wire and fuses, whispering with electricity, leading to fire-control boards, to missiles, to torpedoes, think of her father, sleeping beside her mother in the next room, her mother in her bra, her father asleep, lost somewhere in those endless labyrinths of wire.

Her father had once brought home an arm patch taken from the missile-control board of one of the big nuclear subs. It had a missile streaking in flight. Above and below the missile it said: For Those Who Care—We Send the Very Best. The arm patch filled Susan with horror.

Susan knew he'd been handsome. Some island ideal of haole good looks—blond hair, blue eyes, tall and broad shouldered, not like the Oriental men, but big. And back then, her mother the South Seas beauty—the long black hair, the open face, the smile. Susan knew her from the snapshots.

Well, her mother had gotten what she wanted, the ring, the handsome man, the house; and she was no longer a South Seas beauty, her father was no longer handsome, the house had nothing in it.

Susan finished patting the streaked eye liner and make-up. She studied her face in the mirror. Looked at her hair. Parted a lock. Was that a gray hair, or the light? Blond southern California . . .

Tried a little in her hair. Blonde. A bottle of peroxide home from the drugstore. A little. Not much. A little each day. An experiment. Just to see what would happen. Then she'd forgotten about it.

Reading. Her mother across the room. Then something odd. Her mother staring at her? Somehow odd. Susan looking up from the book.

Mother, what are you staring at?

Her mother slowly getting up out of the chair and crossing the room. Staring.

Mother?

Your hair . . . your hair, what have you done to your hair?

Taking hold of Susan's hair and jerking her head into the light.

Mother! You're hurting me! Mother, you're pulling my hair! You've bleached your hair, haven't you? Haven't you?

Let go! It was the sun!

The sun! Don't lie to me! I know! Then her face close, screaming, you are a Japanese girl, I am your mother, I am Japanese, Japanese girls have dark hair—grabbing her own hair—like mine, are you blind, Susan, like mine!

Let go! You're pulling my hair!

Black like mine! Do you want to be a little blond whore?

Then her father had been there, he had hold of her mother's wrist, he was prying her fingers back one by one, let her go now, Ruth! Carol only thirteen then, crying, the look on her face, and Mother screaming, I know what you're up to, I know!

Let her go, Ruth!

Take her side! I know you, Susan! I see everything you think and do! Everything!

Her sister Carol. The look on her face. Then. And just a couple of months ago. Carol walking toward her at Ala Moana. Hair snarled and full of broken ends, so overweight and pasty faced, Susan didn't recognize her at first.

They stopped for a drink, and Carol relaxed a little and started talking about herself—always facetiously.

Yes, she was going to graduate in a few days, but a lot of good that would do her, where would she find a job with a B.A. from the University of Hawaii? Things were just the same at home, a new place now, a condominium, two-inch rugs on the floor, but the same atmosphere, Mother and Dad impossible, Carol wanted to move out, they were driving her crazy, but she really didn't have enough money, where would she go anyway . . . well, she had saved a little money. . . .

Susan was looking at Carol's face—the heaviness in the cheeks. Remembering the fat dresses . . .

Suddenly, Carol said, I'm thinking of having my eyes done. She looked at Susan. Her eyes were gray, clear gray. She wore too much black eye liner and eye shadow. Trying too hard to make her eyes look big.

Then, in a while, I could save up money for contact lenses.

Carol took off her glasses to show Susan, gazing at her across the table, her eyes out of focus.

Susan didn't say anything, she didn't know what to say.

After a moment, Carol said, maybe defensively, it's a simple operation, Susan. Cut the folds . . . it only takes an hour or two in a doctor's office. It's not supposed to hurt much.

Susan nodded.

Carol said, I am seriously thinking of doing it. Why not?

Susan still didn't know what to say, finally agreeing, why not? Susan would have been embarrassed to suggest Carol lose twenty-five pounds.

After a time, Susan asked, does Mother ever say anything about me?

Like what?

Oh, like . . . anything, anything at all.

Carol thought about it. No, not really. Maybe she was worried when you were living with Jack, but she never says anything to me about you. You're lucky, Susan, you've got a good job, you're out of that madhouse. They're driving me crazy.

Susan touched the folds at the corners of her eyes. Would she? She studied herself in the mirror.

Carol would graduate from college. Had graduated with honors.

Susan remembered she'd gotten good grades too, not that it meant anything at Aiea High School, but she'd gotten straight A's. She'd studied.

What else had there been to do anyway? She'd get home from the drugstore, have dinner, go to her room, put cotton in her ears when she couldn't stand the sound of the tv any more; she'd stay in her room most of the night and read. Carol was still really too young to talk with about—about her feelings. . . . There was a big difference between seventeen and thirteen.

Her adviser urged her to go to college. It's the place for a girl like you, you'll find so many interesting things. . . .

But college seemed a waste of time to her parents. It would be worthwhile if Susan knew exactly what she wanted to study and if it would lead to a job after graduation, yes. Maybe then they'd consider helping pay her tuition. But only if she'd live at home. Her mother insisted on that. She had to live at home.

But to Susan, more important than college, was just that— moving out, so the summer after high school, Susan took a job at Sears, hoping she could begin saving enough money to get her own place, start in second semester; and then, by proving herself with good grades, earn a scholarship.

Every day, the same thing, taking the bus to work in the morning, work all day, back home, back to the house, the tv, the tension between her parents, her mother watching her, that strange look on her face; her mother still wouldn't let her go out with boys.

Each day, a really nice-looking guy—it was hard to tell how old—came into the store, he had beautiful blue eyes and long sandy hair, he would disappear somewhere into the store on some business; then, after a while, when Susan had forgotten him, he would reappear, and smile at her, and, finally, one day, he asked her out.

She was embarrassed, she certainly couldn't say her mother wouldn't let her go out with boys—at seventeen! so she finally said, I can't go out . . . in the evenings. . . . I have another job.

Well, that was all right, he'd take her to lunch, how was that?

That was wonderful.

So each day—after the first time—they had a standing date for lunch. He'd come by in a beat-up Fiat and they would drive somewhere new for lunch.

Never the same place twice—at least not in the same week, he'd laugh.

They lunched at Canlis, the Willows, the Hau Tree Lanai, the Royal Hawaiian Hotel . . . wonderful places, expensive places, unbelievable places with white tablecloths and soft-spoken people and beautiful views of the ocean, or else set back in quiet gardens like in some book.

He never seemed to mind that she couldn't go out in the evening; she remembered he would just hold her hand, and smile, and she didn't think much about it except he was something to look forward to during the day.

One day he dropped by in an old Chevy and at lunch he seemed different—nervous and . . . just different, somehow.

Toward the end of lunch, he suddenly said, Susan, I've got to go back to the mainland tomorrow—on business. To Idaho.

She felt disappointed, asked if he were coming back again.

He shook his head, no. No, I won't be able to for some time, but Susan!

He looked at her. Will you come with me? I mean . . . he reached into his pocket and took out a ring, I mean, come with me, stay with me . . . marry me?

18

He reached for her hand and started to slip the ring onto her finger, but she pulled back.

Marry you? You want me . . . to marry you? Just like that? you're . . . kidding me . . . aren't you?

No, he wasn't kidding.

But Richard, I don't know you, really. . . .

Yes, yes, you do, Susan.

She looked at him. Richard . . . she felt confused. People don't just get married like this. Except in movies, maybe . . . I'm only seventeen.

But Susan, what's the difference? I love you.

There was something desperate about him, now, he was older than she, twenty-six, he should know more about love than she, but it still didn't seem right.

But why are you going away so suddenly? That it has to be done by tomorrow?

Susan, it's a long story. It's business. You trust me, don't you?

She looked at the ring on the tablecloth.

Yes, I trust you, but I'm too young to get married. . . . Why don't you stay and we can see more of each other?

She knew she didn't want to see him any more, either. She knew there must be something wrong with him, it didn't matter now, his beautiful blue eyes, his long sandy hair. . . .

He drove her back to Sears without saying anything and then, just before she got out of the car, he wrote down his telephone number and said, I'll be there until noon tomorrow. If you change your mind, call me.

He leaned over to kiss her good-by, and they kissed quickly and she went back into the store. She felt confused and amazed for the rest of the afternoon; it was hard to believe, really, and after work, not quite ready to go home, she walked quietly along the streets, thinking about him—his asking her to marry him. Just like that. What was wrong with him? people didn't—

She stopped and looked in a shop window. What beautiful dresses. Wouldn't it be nice to have the money to buy a dress like that one. Well, she did have some money saved, but that was for moving out, for college.

She looked at the dresses, and then abruptly decided, it won't hurt to buy one dress—I'll still have enough to go second semester, one dress . . . all of the clothes she had were so high-schoolish, so kiddish, she *was* seventeen, she saw the way other girls dressed, they didn't dress like kids . . . she went into the store. . . .

At home, she held the dress up in front of her.

Do you like it, Mother?

Her mother looked at the dress a long time, then stared at her.

Do you?

Her mother turned and walked out of the room and said nothing.

After dinner, her father pushed back from the table, lit a cigarette, and said, I hear you went out and bought yourself a new dress today, Susan.

Yes, she had. Something fat and self-satisfied about him with his after-dinner cigarette. Something in his tone—condescension, but Susan tried to ignore it.

Why don't you let your father have a look?

When Susan was standing in front of him with the dress, he looked at her a long time. She pressed the dress against her shoulder and waist, and smiled.

Do you like it, Dad?

Isn't it a little short, Susan?

It's the fashion, Dad. Good Lord, this is 1965!

That may be, but I still think it's a little short for you, girl. Why don't you take it back and try something a little bit more ladylike.

Ladylike? This is ladylike, Dad. It's beautifully cut—

Susan, this is not a debate. I'm telling you to take the dress back.

There's nothing unladylike—

Mother in the doorway. Carol at the other end of the table finishing her dessert. Mother speaking, her voice high, quick.

Really, Susan, you may think that looks smart, but you will just look silly, people will laugh at you, you will attract the wrong kind of attention, it's very exhibitionist, you wouldn't want to get pregnant, would you? Only a slut would wear a dress like this. . . . If you behave this way, Susan, you will get pregnant. . . .

Pregnant? Pregnant? What are you talking about?

All right, Ruth, I'll take care of this. Susan, I'd like you to take the dress back, that's all.

I bought it with my own money.

I thought you were saving your money for college, Professor.

I am, but I can buy a dress once in a while.

Susan, take it back.

Can't I dress the way I want to?

Did you hear me?

I'm not taking the dress back!

You'll take the dress back, Susan. And watch that temper, girl. I don't like your tone of voice. I am your father.

I feel as though—

Suddenly, her father leaned forward and slapped the table so hard Susan winced.

I don't care what you feel, Susan! I am your father and I said take that dress back. As long as you live under this roof, you have no feelings, you have no reactions, you do what I say, I am your father. Afterward, when you are old enough, when you have your own place, you can live in the gutter, for all I care!

Live in the gutter?

That's all, Susan! You've been nothing but a pain in the ass since—

21

He stopped himself.

Pain in the ass? I have no feelings? She felt herself flush, her lips begin to quiver. Pain in the ass? I have no feelings?

He stood up and walked out of the kitchen, turned the tv on loud in the living room, sat down, and stared straight ahead.

Carol looking at her from the other end of the table.

A pain in the ass?

Susan looked down. She realized she was still holding the dress pressed hard against her.

Her mother's voice from the doorway.

Now, take the dress back, Susan.

In a way, she'd known it would always happen. In the letter, she wrote over and over again, you're wrong, I do have feelings, I do have reactions, people who don't have your feelings and reactions don't have to be living in the gutter. I know I've always been a pain in the ass to you, I've known it without you telling me, I don't know why, I don't know what I ever did, Obachan raised me, loved me, she was my mother and father, both! not you, I don't want your love any more, you don't know anything about love, Obachan knew about love, I'm a pain in the ass to you, I've always known it! Always!

Susan remembered Obachan putting her hair into a topknot, the feel of her fingers in her hair, pressing her school dress, getting her ready for her parents; she would take the bus back over the Obachan and stay with her again. . . . But Obachan was dead, Obachan wasn't there any more.

At least her father had finally told her what she'd always known, always! it was out, a pain in the . . .

Her mother the instigator, her father . . .

She'd always known it.

Susan finished the letter, I do have feelings, I do have reactions, and there is someone who cares about those feelings and reactions!

What else had she done? A blur now, but she remembered

leaving the house before they were awake, having to walk a long way to a pay phone, calling Richard, who was still sleeping, saying into the phone, simply, I've changed my mind, Richard, I will marry you, can you come pick me up?

She couldn't remember, either, that much about Richard—later, more of what happened would make sense—why, for instance, he couldn't come pick her up, but called a cab for her, coming out of the house in a pair of shorts to pay the driver. His bare feet in the grass, the dew, leaving several tracks in the driveway. On the way to the house he stopped and kissed her and then she realized she'd never seen him without a shirt before—he was thinner than he'd looked, tan. Was he going to ask her what had made her change her mind, what would she say? she wasn't going to spend the rest of her life with him, was she?

In the driveway, she stopped and looked around. She'd never been to his house before and she realized they were halfway up Tantalus, surrounded by eucalyptus trees, mangoes, African violet, white ginger, guava trees; a beautiful view of the city, it was cool up here, the air felt lighter, easier to breathe and now that she had discovered him in his beautiful house, they were leaving.

Inside, Susan discovered Richard had a nice roommate who shared the house, and wouldn't it have been better to stay here, no one knowing where she was, not having to marry Richard, either, but just living here in her own room with the two of them—Richard and Barry—who looked too young to be a lawyer. And he was so nice, Barry. Just the way he looked at her made Susan feel as though he cared, was concerned about her. He almost looked as though he were going to take her aside and talk to her, tell her something special and important, the way he kept looking over at her.

As she sat sipping coffee and watching Richard pack, several times she wanted to say, Richard, why don't we stay here a few days? Just try it. Can't we?

But he kept taking out suitcases, filling them, snapping them shut, and she kept on sitting, wanting to say something to him, not being able to find the words, thinking, no, no, this is too much, too much, I can't really be on my way to Idaho to marry this man, spend the rest of my life ... I haven't even had a life, yet, I don't know him.

She heard her father ... you have no feelings, you have no reactions, you do what I say, I am your father.

The look on her mother's face, Susan closed her eyes, her mother's face came closer, her voice rose, SUSAN! she squeezed her eyes, pressure, the house squeezing her tighter....

She stood up suddenly and took a deep breath.

Richard, she said.

He turned.

What?

Confused, not knowing what she wanted, what else to do or say, she smiled at him, feeling a sense of loss.

He looked at her a moment and smiled back. I love your smile, Susan.

Barry drove them to the airport, went to park the car, and when he came back, he had a big carnation lei. He hung the lei around her neck, kissed her lightly on one cheek. The cool wet carnations against her skin, soft. Susan looked around. All these people. She almost hoped to see her mother.

She was afraid when they closed the doors, the cabin started to pressurize, get close. She'd never flown before. And then, on take-off, looking down and seeing the island falling away beneath the plane's wing like something dropping away from her body and starting to fall slowly through space and drift away. How green it was, the mountains, how white, how orderly and quiet the city looked against the green bowl of the valleys— Manoa, Punchbowl, Palolo. . . . She watched the island float below, then behind until it hurt to turn her neck. Then the other islands started to come up, Molokai, Maui, the Big Island, come up and fall behind; then the ocean opened up, endless.

She fell into a feverish sleep, voices, voices getting louder, coming closer, she awoke with a start, grabbed Richard's arm, asked him where they were going to live, where they would go when they got to Idaho, and he said, don't worry, we'll stay at my father's apartment until we find a place. He's away for a few days and we'll have something by the time he gets back.

She fell asleep again, fell back into the voices, the faces getting closer, voices talking in a language she had once known, could almost recognize, had forgotten, but she was getting closer to one of the voices, she could almost understand the words, just a little closer, she called out. . . .

She woke to his hand covering her mouth, she pushed at his hand, felt tears on her face.

His voice, it's okay, Susan. He took his hand away, you're awake now, you were crying in your sleep, calling something like oba—chan. . . .

She noticed the people across the aisle staring at her.

And the stewardess was leaning over and smiling.

Can I get you something?

Susan couldn't say anything, she had lost her voice, she just stared, finally shook her head, no, but Richard ordered her a Seven-Up, something to settle her stomach.

When Susan picked up the glass, she saw the ring on her finger, he'd slipped it on while she'd been sleeping, she looked down at the ocean, endless, a huge empty space, and thought, we're in a different time zone, now.

Then she looked at the ring, and at Richard, who was reading a magazine, and thought, I'm going to have to sleep with him, maybe even as soon as we get there, she looked out the window at the clouds, wondered about birth control and the look of embarrassment on the face of the man when he had come into the drugstore to buy those things; maybe Richard was one of those men, but . . . maybe we won't have to make love. When had she had her last period and how many days after the period was it safe? She remembered seeing something like a spectrum of days and the spectrum flared up a radiant red when there was danger and cool blue when there was not, where would she be on the spectrum, and where had her father gotten that about living in the gutter anyway?

She would ask the stewardess, the stewardess looked cool and confident, she would ask her about the safe days, but then, what would be the point if she couldn't remember when she'd had her last period, and besides she'd feel like an idiot, asking a stewardess something like that. She realized she didn't really know anything about sex—not real sex, not the kind Richard was going to want.

She remembered kissing James Clark—a hapa Japanese boy in her class. He'd come over several times and while Carol kept watch at the door, they held hands. Then he'd gotten up to go, she kissed him, he lurched, and suddenly passed out on the floor. Carol looking in. What'd you do to him? He was coming to. Just kissed him. They'd—Susan and Carol—laughed. But that wasn't what Richard was going to want. Just kissing.

The plane suddenly slammed into some Kaiwi Channel turbulence, Susan grabbed hold of the sink, braced herself, if Mickey would bring back her make-up, she could get cleaned up, put on her face . . . Richard. Landing in the dark at Boise. The cool light air. A strange apartment. His father's. The suitcases in the hall.

She'd been so scared, but now when she thought of Richard, she felt sorry for him. The first two or three nights they slept in his father's bed and he was so nervous, he couldn't do anything. Which was all right with Susan. All the time she was wondering if she were getting closer or farther away from the red days in the spectrum. When he had finally gotten over his nervousness and made love to her, she hadn't felt much of anything. Just relief when it was over.

During the days they looked for an apartment, wandering

through strange rooms with strange smells, different people leading them, looking at her a bit curiously . . . because she was so young? Oriental?

There were voices raised in the next room, a high-pitched voice—Richard's? but it didn't sound like his voice, and a deeper voice, a man's voice. In her sleep, she thought, Dad and Carol?

She felt around in the bed. Felt next to her. Cold. Wet. She pulled back the sheet. A faint acrid odor. After a moment, she realized he'd wet the bed.

Dressing, then she was in the living room, there was a tall man with white hair and Richard's beautiful blue eyes, Richard's father. And Richard. And both of them looking at her; and then she was alone with his father, scared, but he was soft-spoken, he asked her to please have a seat, and could he get her anything, no, and then he asked her how old she was, seventeen. He looked at her for several moments and repeated, seventeen, and then seemed sad; he crossed the room and said, may I sit down? She nodded. He sat down beside her and said, I'm going to tell you a few things about Richard.

And he did. He told her that Richard was already married. He was in the process of getting a divorce. And that he'd been married once before and had a child, a little boy, had he told you these things?

No.

Yes, and that he had been under a psychiatrist's care before he had left for Hawaii, that he had been under a psychiatrist's care for several years. . . .

He spoke quietly and as he went on, all Susan could think was, I'm going to have to go back. . . .

He's my son, yes, but I'm telling you these things for your own good, don't marry him, he'll ruin your life, you're a beautiful girl, you look very intelligent, go back home; Richard will ruin your life.

For a moment, she felt relieved and then she thought of going home, of her father slapping the table, you have no feelings! a pain in the ass! her mother, her face, her voice . . . Maybe she could get back to Hawaii without anyone finding out, get a job. . . .

Richard's father was saying, you know, he doesn't even have enough money to pay for your ticket back, he has no money, he really can't hold a job, I don't know what he thought he was going to live on. I'll pay for your ticket back.

Then he held out his hand.

May I see that ring?

She slid it off her finger and dropped it into his hand.

He looked sadly at the ring for several seconds, turning it over in his hand, and then said, did he give you this ring?

She nodded, yes.

He turned the ring over several more times and then said, quietly, if he gave it to you, then it's yours now, but may I ask you a favor?

His voice so soft.

She nodded.

Will you give the ring back to me? It belonged to his mother. I gave it to his mother.

She tried to say yes, but then suddenly just put her face in both her hands and nodded quickly, hearing herself choke.

He put his hand on her shoulder and said, I'm sorry.

He booked her flight back and then, the arrangements made, and the rest of the day still left, Richard acted as though things were the same, as though she weren't leaving. They drove up into the mountains above Boise, parked the car, walked down from the road through a field of long grass and daisies to a stream, where he assembled two fishing rods. With the stream rushing, the sun warm on her face, and the smell of the mountains, Richard, quiet and patient, taught her how to cast with a

28

fly rod. They fished quietly for several hours, Richard gently helping her with the fishing rod, changing a fly, pointing to a pool and showing her where to place the fly in the current, how to float it down into the pool. They caught several trout, he said they were rainbow trout, they were beautiful, jumping out of the sunny water, splashing at their feet into the net, then lying on the grass, gills moving in and out, finally lying still. Then casting again. Susan looking at Richard. His eyes so blue. The sunlight on his hair. She stared at him. Suddenly, she put down her fishing rod, and waded over to him, held him tight, burst into tears, pressed her face against his chest. He held her tight, smoothing her hair, the stream rushing around their knees.

At the airport, he took her hand and said, I'll see you . . . see you soon, Susan.

Was he pretending? For her? For himself? Did he believe he would see her again?

Keep this.

He slid a ring off his finger.

She shook her head, no.

Please. Suddenly, his eyes wild.

He pushed the ring into her hand. Closed her hand about the ring. Then she felt afraid for him and knew she had to keep the ring. For him. Maybe to keep something bad—or worse—from happening to him, she didn't know what.

She kept the ring in her hand. Then she stepped out into the darkness, looked back once at him staring at her, turned, and walked toward the waiting plane.

On the plane, she looked at the gold wedding band. It had his initials. And another set of initials. His wife's. One of them.

She kept the ring in her jewelry box as a memento of something, exactly what, she didn't know. But she had kept it. She still had it.

She stood in the terminal. The close humid air of Hawaii. She walked back and forth in the terminal. Where would she go? She bought a Coke. Watched the people. Back and forth. So many people. Arriving. Departing. Hugs. Kisses. Leis. The carnation lei, soft against her cheek. Barry. She dug in her purse, found the number. He'd just gotten home.

Stay right where you are, I'll be down in a few minutes.

On the way back, Barry swung by a gas station, pointed at what was left of the Fiat, said, if this makes it any easier for you . . .

Richard had cracked it up before they'd left.

At the house, Barry sat her down at the kitchen table, made her a cup of coffee, returned with a shoe box full of bills, notices from bill collectors.

She reached into the box and absently shuffled through the bills. This is why he had to leave so suddenly?

Barry nodded.

Barry sat down at the other end of the table. Don't feel bad. He fooled a lot of people. He fooled me for a while and I was his friend. He's not vicious. He just doesn't know. Something's missing. I almost told you the morning you left for Idaho, but I decided it wasn't for me—my place—to tell you. Don't feel bad. I should have—

He thought about that for a minute.

I don't feel bad, Susan said. He didn't really fool me, either.

They talked at the table for a while, and then Barry got up and made her something to eat. She ate slowly, feeling old—impossible to believe she had been gone, come back, and only six days had passed.

She ate the food without tasting it. When she finished, she looked up and said, his father sent me home or maybe I'd still be there.

After some time, she said, did you ever see him fish?

Barry shook his head.

We went fishing. We went fishing up in a stream. He taught me how to cast.

Barry nodded.

She knew he wasn't getting it.

She didn't know exactly what she was trying to say. She reached into the pile of bills. Gently sifted them through her fingers.

I mean, I know. I saw the car. All right, he left because everyone was after him. And his father told me about him. I know. But he did have something. She stood up from the table. She was having a hard time swallowing. She was tired. She wanted to sleep. He did have something. I saw it up at the stream. She swallowed again. She looked at Barry. I'm trying to tell you something, but I don't know what. I . . . knew . . . when he asked me to marry him . . . not to . . . but . . . he wasn't so bad. . . . I saw something up at the stream I hadn't seen before. . . . He's not so bad, she heard herself repeating as she walked into Richard's old room, lay down on the bare mattress, and fell asleep in her clothes.

Susan didn't know where she was. A sleeping bag thrown over her, a pillow under her head. After a time, Barry stuck his head in. Susan? Awake? A few minutes later he brought her a cup of coffee. He sat on the bed and watched her sip the coffee.

How do you feel this morning?

A little better.

He nodded. Good. Susan . . . I've . . . called your parents.

She tried to set the coffee down, spilled it on her hand, placed the cup on the floor.

She heard herself say, I thought I could trust you . . . I thought . . . I could trust you.

You could. You can trust me . . . Susan . . . I didn't do the right thing before. . . . If I had done the right thing before, none of this would have happened to you.

You called my parents.

You'll make it up with them and everything will be all right. . . . You shouldn't be running around like this. For now, your place is with your parents.

Something familiar. Long ago. Susan, girl's place is wit her mothah and fathah.

. . . being given away . . .

You don't know what you're talking about. . . .

Look, everyone feels like this at sometime. . . .

You don't know them. She sank back in the bed. Stared at the ceiling. When are they coming?

They said right away.

Did you tell them . . . where . . . I've been . . . what's happened?

He nodded. I thought I could make it better for you if I explained it to them first.

She shook her head. You don't know what you've done.

Her father was staring straight ahead, his hands on the wheel, his large forearms rigid. Susan was shocked when her mother finally turned to look back. Her thin black eyebrows, her lips—bright red, overlipsticked; her eyes, glassy and penetrating, seemed to stare right into Susan, but through her. When her mother raised the cigarette to her lips, Susan saw the bright red fingernail polish. Smoke streamed thickly from her nostrils, her lips. Her father was smoking, too, the ash getting longer and longer on his cigarette.

No one said anything.

Then her mother was speaking in disconnected phrases: I told you . . . I told you so . . . what have I been telling you? . . . I told you this would happen . . . it's my fault . . . I knew this would happen . . . it had to happen. . . .

Her father's thin lips were pressed together. Once she saw him form a word with his lips.

They drove back toward Aiea.

Her mother kept turning around, startled, suddenly looking at Susan, she seemed surprised, she shook her head, I told you. . . .

It didn't seem like her mother's voice to Susan.

In the garage, her mother got out. Her father sat with his hands on the wheel a moment, still staring straight ahead, then turned slowly and laid his arm across the seat. She thought he was going to hit her and flinched.

He stared at her. Then said, if you only know how sick at heart you've made your mother.

Carol was standing in the door, looking through the screen.

The three of them stood just outside the door looking in at Carol.

Then Susan said, hi, Carol.

Her mother suddenly turned, yes, Carol, say hi to your sister, take a good look at her, this is your older sister, take a good look at her now that she's gotten herself pregnant.

That's enough, Ruth!

The tv was on loud, her mother was still talking by the kitchen table in that high quick voice. . . .

See, Carol, see your sister. I told her not to wear those dresses, not to show herself . . . only a slut would . . .

God! Will you shut up with that! Susan heard herself shouting.

Don't you dare raise your voice to your mother after what you've just put us through, young lady!

What are you all talking about? A slut? Pregnant? Show myself? You're crazy!

Don't use that word! You will close your mouth!

I will not close my mouth! I am tired of being shut up, I'm a person, I do have feelings, I do have reactions, I will have them!

You will shut up!

Her father's face was getting red.

You would like to shut me up, I'm a pain in the ass, you

33

don't love me, you don't care about me, you left me with Obachan and then you took me back when you felt like it and didn't care what I felt, the easiest thing has been to keep me shut up, well I am not shutting up! I have been dead in this house, dead, dead, dead. ...

Susan, I'm warning you!

Her mother, standing by the window, staring, her hand held at her throat.

Dead!

Susan was staring into the next room at the submarine shields tipped at crazy angles on their points, their bright escutcheons. For Those Who Care, We Send the Very Best. ...

The shields.

Dead, dead ...

Susan! Shut up!

No! No! No!

There was just the beginning of a quick movement in her father's direction, she felt her head snap back, the room grow light, a moment later, far away, a distant thud as the back of her head hit the floor.

Susan came to on the floor, her mother kneeling over her, her father's feet close to her head; she got up slowly, walked, staggering once, to her room, closed the door quietly and lay down on the bed. She got up, pulled down the shades, lay back down holding her eyes, her head throbbing. The light in the room was dim, faded.

After a time, the door opened very quietly. Her mother. Susan lay still, eyes closed, holding her breath. She heard her mother step into the room, walk slowly toward her, the floor creaking. Susan held her breath. Her mother stopped several steps away from the bed, stood still, she knew her mother was staring down at her. She could hear her mother breathing in the warm, dim room. After a long time, her mother turned, went back out of the room, and closed the door.

Susan dozed. Her eye was throbbing. Her face. Obachan, she said to herself, Obachan, where are you? I wish I were wit you. Once she thought Obachan was in the room, was standing at the foot of the bed.

She was at the foot of the bed.

She was coming toward her. Smiling.

Obachan . . .

Obachan always keep da house neat and full of flowahs. She keep da floor scrubbed. On da wall she get one picture of da man she call General MacArthah. On da othah wall she gotta differen picture of almost da same girl who she call my mothah. I ast her if her name is Jane Hondo, too. Obachan, she say no, dat Ruth, her name no longah Hondo. My mothah, she look like da picture of da girl on da gravestone cept she no smile. Obachan and me and Uncle William, we go see da girl in da graveyard almost all da time.

Obachan say my mothah go to da mainland wit her husband, 'as why her name not Hondo eithah, she change her name and go to da mainland, live far away in one place call Florida. Obachan say one day she going come back for me, she going take me from her, break Obachan's heart.

I tell Obachan I nevah going leave her, I love her more dan anybody, dan my mothah.

Obachan look happy and sad when I say dat, she say, girl's place is wit her mothah and fathah, but nevah mind dat now, and she hug me.

Obachan always treat me good, love me, kiss me, she brush my hair nice and put da ribbons in da braids or put dem on da topknot.

Every day she take my nose between her fingahs, squeeze em tight, but not so tight I no can breathe, squeeze my nose jus tight enough between da thumb and fingah, she smooth my nose out good, da tip, she say, you get one nice nose, I gonna make em even nicer, she smooth da tip out good, she say, you my sweetheart.

She always treat me good; only time she do anyting is when I bad, den I run fast, get behind Obasan, he sit in da big chair, read da paper get da writing like on da stone, I run fast, get behind Obasan, he always laugh, lean forward, make room for me between em and da chair, den I safe, I know I safe for good when I hear Obachan start to laugh.

All da time I learn to read English so good in school I da best in da class. When we go to da graveyard, I always can read half da stone jus like dat.

One day I start tinkin what happen to da girl, my Aunt Jane, on da stone, how come she dead and how come dey put her in da graveyard all da way up in Waipahu when we livin down here in Palolo?

I tink bout all dis real good, long time, and den I ast Obachan, what happened to Jane Hondo, da girl on da wall here and on da stone dere, how come dey put her up dere in da graveyard? Waipahu?

Den Obachan she looked so sad I feel bad I say anyting, and I take her hand. It take Obachan long time before she say to me, she was in one acciden.

I say, she was in one acciden? What kine of acciden?

Obachan first start to say one ting. Den she stop. Den she start to say someting else. Den she stop. Den she take one long time and finally say, one car acciden. She went away one day in one car and nevah come back.

One car acciden put her undah da stone? I ast. She go in one car and nevah come back?

Obachan shake her head and no say more. She hug me good.

Den I tink, what make da acciden? I ast Obachan, what make da acciden? Den I ast her in Japanese. What make da acciden?

Den Obachan start to blink like in da graveyard, so I feel

bad, I scaid I going make her cry, she no say more and I no ast more cause I no like make her cry.

One ting I know for sure, I no like da smell of da plumeria tree, da flowahs, dey look real pretty, but get close, da smell make me sick.

Den one day, Obachan takin all my clothes outta da drawers and put dem in da box, she very quiet, she no say nothing, she get one lettah she keep lookin at all da time, she lookin sad.

Den she take me on her lap and say, your mothah, she comin back from da mainland wit your fathah and you going go live wit your mothah and fathah.

I tell Obachan, no, I going-stay wit you, but she say, girl's place wit her mothah and fathah.

I tell her, she my mothah and fathah, I no going-go.

She hug me good and say, you going-go.

I feel bad lookin at my clothes in da boxes and I start to cry. She tell me no cry, but now I angry, I know she no wan me no more.

I cry and she try to hug me, but I push her arms away, but she still hug me and den I tell her, you no love me no more!

Den Obachan, when she hear dat, she start to cry, she tell me she love me, but dat girl's place is wit her mothah and fathah.

She say to me, no cry, you going come visit me, I still going be here.

Den I tink bout dat, she here and me dere, I tink bout sleepin some place else and I start cryin again.

Den Obachan cryin, only time I evah see Obachan cry cept ovah da girl on da stone, Jane Hondo.

Den I feel bad.

Den, before my mothah and fathah come, Obachan say to me, no ast your mothah bout her sistah.

Da girl on da stone?

Yes, da girl on da stone.

How come? I say.

Obachan say, cause dat her sistah—it makes her sad tink bout—you no like make her sad, do you?

No, I no wanna make her sad.

You my good girl, she say. My good, sweet girl. Obachan's girl.

Yes, I tell her, I Obachan's girl all da time. Always.

Den she dress me up good for when dey come. Put ribbons in my hair.

I scaid.

Dey come in da car and put em out front da garden, same place Uncle William put da car when he come.

Da lady and da man get outta da car. When I see dem, I scaid.

I run back in da house, run to Obachan, I put my face in her dress, I tell her, no let dem take me, please!

She hold me tight. No let dem, I say.

But she gonna.

We going back outside.

Dey come up da path through da garden. I know den dat dey my mothah and fathah, I nevah seen one picture of my fathah, but I know my mothah from da picture, so must be my fathah.

First time I see da man, I no tink he my fathah, he not like my mothah or Obachan, he one haole man, he da only haole I evah see here in Palolo Public Housing, everyone else, too, dey stand out on da porches, everyone look em ovah good, even da Hawaiian crazy lady across da street, she da lady who hit Bubba, her son, she hit em on da head wit one hammah cause he no learn da alphabet, shoulda heard em cry, seen da blood, too.

Everyone, even da Hawaiian lady across da steet, dey all stand out on da porches and lookin at da haole man.

I scaid.

Den Mothah hug Obachan and da haole, my fathah, he give Obachan his hand, I see he no wanna kiss or hug her, he not know she good for kissin and huggin.

And den everyone look at me and I scaid, I wanna get behind Obasan and da chair.

I scaid. I know I going to cry. I no like Obachan cryin like at da stone, so I tryin not to cry.

I wearin ribbons, look good like at school, I hopin my mothah going to say someting nice like da teacher, my mothah look at me, come close, she smile, she kiss me on da cheek, give me one little hug, she smile again, but da smile no last so long.

She look at me long time. She starin and starin. Den she say, do you remembah me?

I say, no, I no remembah you.

She keep on starin. Den she say, well, you bettah! I'm your mothah!

I scaid.

I stand behind Obachan.

I like go wit Obachan.

Den da haole man, my fathah, he take da box of clothes in da car, den he come back, he come for me, he pick me up, his eyes blue like da sky and ocean, he get yellow hair, he get pink ears and nose, he get da biggest eyes I evah seen.

He carry me above da garden so high I scaid.

I lookin down at da garden, da banana plants, da hibiscus, da aloe plant. . . .

Da haole man get long hair on his arms, da hair yellow, t'ick like one dog. On one arm, he get one picture. Like Uncle William. Sometime I scaid Uncle William. Da picture bright blue, picture of lady and one anchor. It's in da skin. I touch da picture in da skin. Undah da skin. Blue ink.

My mothah talkin like da teachers—only she talkin so quick I no can understand everyting. My mothah talk differen. Obachan no understand everyting eithah. Den my mothah repeat it for her in Japanese, and den Obachan understand, but I no understand everyting she say.

We standin by da car.

Obachan take me from da haole man, my fathah, and hug me, one time, and I scaid, I no going cry, she look at me, I see her face, Obachan da one I love.

Den we get in da car and drive down da road.

All da time, I livin wit my mothah and fathah, I tinkin bout Obachan and how she press my dress good in da morning for school, how she huggin and kissin me. I tinkin bout how Sunday always one special day, Obachan take my kimono outta da trunk, get da white cranes on da red silk, get one blue obi for da waist, get da long sleeves, I tinkin how when I put it on, feel good.

So when I going live wit my mothah and fathah, all da time I tinkin bout my kimono in da trunk, I waitin all week for da kimono.

Sunday come.

On Sunday, my mothah, she no press da kimono. I no see da kimono no more.

Maybe da haole forget da kimono in da bottom of da trunk undah da picture General MacArthah.

I scaid ast.

Den, aftah more Sundays passin by, I finally ast my mothah, where da kimono, today Sunday, I like wear da kimono, but she not know nothing bout it, she no understand.

Den I say, maybe you forget da kimono at Obachan's?

She say, she not know da kimono, she tell me no worry bout da kimono, I get enough dresses. She say, you no wear kimonos. Kimonos are for Japanese. You American!

Den I start to cry. My mothah start shoutin, she yellin, you spoiled, she yellin dat Obachan spoil me.

Den I no say more. I wait until we going Palolo. Obachan get da kimono, dere, Palolo, I know.

Den one day, Sunday, too, we going Palolo. Obachan back from da church. Obachan huggin and kissin me, she start cryin, I cryin, too. Den I ast her for da kimono and she get da trunk, she get em out, she press da kimono good, den she hold it out for me, I put em on. Den I happy.

When Susan looked in the mirror, her eye had darkened and was almost completely swollen shut. She looked at herself, calmly, turned from the mirror, gathered up some of her clothes, put them in a bag, and pushed the bag back into her closet.

This time Susan did not leave a note.

She remembered a high-school friend, Rita Akida, who had moved into the second floor of a bungalow on Royal Hawaiian Avenue, down in Waikiki. Susan had visited her there once after work, and they had spent a nice afternoon, talking and joking around.

When she called, Rita said that of course it would be all right. Rita spent most of her time at her boy friend's anyway, so Susan could sleep in her bed when she wasn't there, the sofa when she was. It would be no trouble at all. Rita didn't think she'd be around much in the next few weeks.

The smell of the sun-dried wood reminded Susan a little of Obachan's old house in Palolo, the ocean was right down at the end of the street; a blue line above the sea wall down on Kalakau.

The first morning, she had seen herself, her eye swollen shut and puffed out, the black and blue streaking. She turned from the mirror. She felt calm. She put on a pair of sunglasses and went out for a long walk. The zoo in Kapiolani Park, the natatorium with the clock up on the fluted iron column, the clock stuck at seven minutes to five, the ocean and clouds behind the clock. She walked up toward Diamond Head and Black Point to look at the beautiful houses and gaze out at the ocean and the surfers paddling out to the coral reef. And then back down toward Queen Surf, where she stood by the sea wall and looked at the people lying on the sand. Running her fingertips along the concrete of the sea wall, she thought of Uncle William. Something about sailors? Around here?

Sailors. She remembered she knew her father had been a sailor. Had Obachan told her? She couldn't remember. She just knew. He was a sailor and he was away. She remembered as a little girl watching the sailors. . . . All sailors were Dad. Dad had a Southern accent. She'd known that, too. She wasn't sure what a Southern accent was, but it had frightened her . . . knowing he had a Southern accent. Would she be able to understand him?

She ran her fingertips along the concrete of the sea wall. Something else about sailors. Around here? And Uncle William?

Each day she put on her sunglasses and went for long walks, went to the market, shopped slowly, bringing the food home and cooking quietly, then watching tv for a while, game shows, soap operas, the late movies. Each day she checked her eye, once in the morning, once in the evening, resolving not to look during the rest of the day, keeping to her resolution.

A week after moving out, Susan turned eighteen. She spent the day alone, reading, watching some tv, feeling quiet and empty. She knew she was running out of the little bit of money she had saved for moving, for college, she didn't know where she would get more money. . . . Late in the afternoon, she went out, bought a pair of earrings and had them wrapped. Back at the bungalow, she baked a cake, a birthday cake, frosted it, watched tv a while, tried to think of someone to call and share the cake with, called Rita at her boy friend's but there was no answer, ate a piece of the cake, watched more tv, ate another piece, and finally, cut a large piece and put it outside on the porch railing for the birds. Then Susan put the gift-wrapped earrings on the bedside table, where she would see them first thing in the morning, and went to sleep.

After a time, the pressure eased, then the eye began to open, the black and blue streak turned to a pale yellow. When the eye was presentable, she went over to the old drugstore where she had worked afternoons, stepped inside, hesitated. No, they might come looking for her here. She would like to have said hello to old Mr. Matsumoto. She could see him at the back of the store, his head down behind the prescription counter. She turned and walked out. Without being able to put the feeling into words, she knew she would not do anything she had done before, she would have to put her life—her life so-far—behind her.

She found a job as a waitress at the Columbia Inn and worked for several days. One morning, clearing the breakfast dishes, she saw her tip had been left in the plate. Each coin carefully pressed into the cold egg yolk. Back in the kitchen, she took off her apron, walked out and bought a paper.

There was an ad in the paper, interviewing and taking applications for Polynesian Airlines. Stewardesses. If you were over eighteen.

Why Polynesian? Why not Pan Am? Pan Am flew all over the world. But after calling, Susan found the age requirement for Pan Am to be twenty-one.

Maybe Polynesian until she was twenty-one, then Pan Am?

Susan called the number in the paper for an appointment and an interview. Then, with the last of her money, bought a dress, shoes and make-up.

On the day of her interview, she washed her hair, made herself up, dressed carefully, looked at herself in the mirror. Well, she turned slowly, she thought she looked nice; at least okay. You can live in the gutter, for all I care! Susan thought she looked nice.

Susan stood outside the door, a sudden hollow feeling inside. There were at least twenty girls in a reception area of the hotel suite, most looking like models, most well dressed and beautiful. One she recognized as Miss Hawaii. She looked down at her dress, went back through the hotel corridor, took the elevator to the street, and stood outside for a few minutes. She started walking slowly. She reached into her purse for a cigarette, felt around a moment, saw the gold wedding ring in the bottom of her purse, reached in, turned the ring over slowly, dropped it back into her purse, took another couple of steps, turned, thought of the room full of beautiful girls, all good-looking, all well dressed, looked down at her dress again, she was sure there wasn't really anything wrong with the way she looked, she went back up to the hotel suite, sat, smoothed out her dress, watched as from time to time a girl would be called, listened to some of the girls talking.

When it was her turn, Susan stood up nervously, she felt the other girls looking at her, she took a deep breath, stood frozen for a moment. A small-boned girl with glossy black hair, large brown eyes, and a pretty Clara Bow mouth smiled at her and said, good luck, you look terrific. . . .

Susan smiled gratefully, walked across the room and passed someone who was holding a door open for her, stepped inside.

A tall woman in a chang san stood up from behind a table covered with applications, brochures. . . . Her name plate on the table—Miss Alice Pahoa, Chief Stewardess.

She smiled. You're Susan . . . Wilson?

Susan smiled, yes, uncertain for a moment, then Miss Pahoa extended her hand, aloha, and Susan stepped forward, suddenly aware she was being studied, though not in an unfriendly way.

They shook hands. Miss Pahoa smiled again, she had pale green eyes, black hair streaked with gray, she looked part-Hawaiian, part-haole, perhaps a trace of Chinese. There seemed to be some permanent sadness, but a toughness, in her eyes, something she had lost, but had made up her mind not to think too much about.

Miss Pahoa held Susan's hand a moment longer, smiled again, they smiled simultaneously and Miss Pahoa said, please, sit down.

Again, Susan was aware she was being studied. She sat, crossed her legs, pulled her skirt down over her knee, and placed her hands in her lap.

That dress is very becoming to you, Susan.

Thank you.

Miss Pahoa sat down behind the table and they spoke for several minutes. Things about Susan's life. Where she had grown up; oh, her mother was Japanese . . . yes . . . and her father worked at Pearl Harbor. . . . She'd gotten all A's at Aiea High School . . . very nice. Not college for an A student like you? . . . not now, anyway, yes . . . some of our girls manage it part time, but it does take them longer.

What made her decide to apply for stewardess?

Susan about to say, I like people, remembering one of the girls in the waiting room saying, when she asks you why, whatever you do, don't say you like people. That's the dumbest answer.

Susan smoothed her skirt, hesitated; finally said, I realize that it sounds dumb to say I want to be a stewardess because I like people, and that I should have some unusual answer, but the truth is I do like people. Well, I know that must sound dumb. . . .

Miss Pahoa studied her a moment, then smiled. I don't think it sounds dumb, Susan. It sounds truthful. It wouldn't be a very good job if you didn't like people, would it?

No.

Several times Miss Pahoa would stop after one of Susan's answers, look at her for a moment, and then her eyes would get warm and she would smile.

Miss Pahoa outlined the training program, there were no questions. . . . After a brief pause, Miss Pahoa stood up.

We'll let you know, Susan.

Susan nodded, thanked her, walked toward the door.

As she reached the door, Miss Pahoa called her.

Susan?

Susan turned.

Just stand there a moment.

Susan looked at Miss Pahoa. Yes?

Miss Pahoa gazed at her a moment. She smiled.

I just want to say that you look lovely.

Susan smiled. Thank you. She suddenly felt overwhelmed with gratitude. Thank you.

We'll call and let you know.

A week later, Rita left a note by the telephone:

A Miss Pahoa from Polynesian Airlines called. She wants to know if you want to be a stewardess.

That had been seven years ago. The training then had been three hours a night, three times a week, for three months. Ground school. Instruction in emergency procedures. The airplane as a machine. The airline as a business. Weather. Emphasis on the girls being the most important part of the airline. Each of them had been selected from over seven hundred and fifty applicants. Each was to be the face of the airline. It was the face of each girl, the voice of each girl, which would sell the airline.

The directress of a modeling agency had been brought in to instruct the girls in the proper use of make-up. A stewardess was always to wear make-up, but the object was never to appear made up. Rather, always to create the illusion of being natural. Likewise, the walk was to be with dignity, but never to be self-conscious.

Susan had been the only girl in the class of thirty-five who did not need her walk or use of make-up corrected. Miss Pahoa and the woman from the modeling agency had brought her to the front of the class.

This is the way to walk. Susan, walk toward me.

Embarrassed, Susan had walked toward Miss Pahoa, who had nodded and smiled. Just right.

There was instruction on how to stand, bend over, sit (crossed ankles, please), instruction on how to go up and down stairs properly.

Hair was to be above the collar, or, if longer, had to be worn up in a bun.

At all times, full make-up was required in flight. Full make-up consisted of false eyelashes, lipstick, manicured nails; nails, if painted, could have no chips.

High heels were to be worn, but in flight, flats were permissible.

One always had to have a change of nylons. Nothing looked worse than a run. Runs were out and would not be tolerated under any circumstances!

Legs and underarms were to be clean-shaven, deodorant was mandatory, mouthwash advisable; perfume was to be of a light scent.

In case of an emergency overnight—a mechanical failure, bad weather—a girl should always keep with her a toothbrush, make-up, a change of clothes.

Never say: sure. Say: surely.

Never say: I don't know. Say: I'll find out.

It was fine to be friendly to passengers, but never familiar. Be friendly, but distant.

It was fine to stand in a ladylike way in the aisle and converse with a passenger, but never sit on an armrest.

A girl was not to smoke in front of the passengers.

A pilot had come in and spent an evening explaining what went on in the cockpit and the general theory of the aircraft.

During the next session, Miss Pahoa had spent almost the entire class talking to the girls about the pilots, warning them to be careful, not to get involved with them. Not to get involved . . . It was rumored Miss Pahoa had been in love with a pilot who had married someone else after a long love affair.

Pregnancy was grounds for immediate dismissal, but the girl would have a chance to resign before being fired.

Evacuation procedures were practiced in the hangar. Opening the emergency door, inflating the slide. Each of the girls had then gone down the slide, while the mechanics and ground personnel had stood at the bottom to cheer and catch the girls.

Uniforms. Each of the girls was measured by a tailor for her uniform. Uniforms were always to be worn with a girdle, a full slip, of course, nylons—nylons were to be worn at all times. . . .

The uniform. The first time, Susan taking the uniform out of the box, holding it up, dressing herself carefully. The uniform a beautiful azure blue. First, the knee-length skirt, then the tailored military blouse, Susan's finger shaking slightly on each button. Then the matching three-quarter-length jacket.

Slipping her arms into the jacket, the snug fit, the pressure under the shoulder blades, for a brief moment, a sense of familiarity, putting on this jacket, from sometime in her life, when? sometime long ago, the moment gone, Susan stepping into the high-heeled white leather shoes, gathering her long hair into a tight bun, the military cap, feeling for the right angle, just off the center of the head, slightly up on the forehead, but not rakish, not to cover the forehead.

Miss Pahoa checking each of the girls, making minor adjustments, straightening a collar, a cap, coming to Susan. Looking her over, smiling, then reaching out and patting her shoulder. Susan, you look just perfect, you have something special.

Then Miss Pahoa was on the phone one evening. Explaining that there was a shortage of girls, and that Susan was needed, could she fly tomorrow? You can finish training in flight; I'll put you under one of our best senior girls, Mickey Chun, she'll help you; I know you can do it, Susan, I know you have the poise.

The next few weeks were a jumble of ten-hour days with Mickey always standing over her. All of the time Susan trying to remember announcements, regulations. Everything had to be done by the book, but by the book meant Mickey's way; napkins had to be folded Mickey's way; the air vents had to be checked Mickey's way; seat belts had to be straightened Mickey's way; literature arranged in the seat pockets Mickey's way. There were endless passengers asking questions Susan didn't have the answers for, men making embarrassing remarks which paralyzed Susan, made her blush; men with their elbows out, men constantly brushing against her legs as she walked by, men asking her out to dinner. . . .

Susan knew there was something strange in the way Mickey was treating her—the rages, the resentment. Why should Mickey rage at her? She had done nothing to Mickey. It came to Susan one day, as she watched Mickey glare at a haole girl in the terminal, that Mickey must be seeing her, Susan, like that—as haole.

That's why Mickey had at first spoken a correct, colorless English which still did not mask Mickey's fury and resentment.

Mickey would say, what's the matter with you! Don't stand there while men make dumb remarks. Turn them off. You've got to watch these guys! Give them an inch, they'll take a mile.

If Susan forgot a sentence in an announcement, Mickey would be right there on her back in the buffet.

I told you, learn these announcements, I'm not going to check you out if you don't learn; you've got to do more than have good legs.

Susan would get lightheaded, dizzy, nauseated, grab hold of the counter in the buffet, they flew Convair 640s, DC-3s and DC-6s then, the planes flew lower, there was more turbulence, the flights between the islands took longer, Mickey would be right beside her, face close. What's the matter? Sick? Stewardesses can't be airsick, if this job is too tough for you, you better get back on the ground and be a waitress or something, you've got to do more than stand around and look beautiful, this job is work. . . .

Mickey, face closer, skin pale, small black eyes, voice tough. . . .

A passenger would suddenly get airsick, start for the lua; get sick in the aisle. . . .

Mickey would point. Susan! Clean it up, that's part of the job!

Later on, when they had become friends, Mickey said in pidgin, it's true, I bust your ass, Susan, reason I make it so tough on you, first, dis da truth, I tryin to teach you! Make you good, make you tough . . . you look so innocen, you stand dere and you givin da passengers your feelings, men sayin all kine tings to you and you not know what to say, dey tryin to embarrass you, you know, so first ting I teach you I learn in dis job, you nevah let da passengers get close to you, nevah let dem get to your feelings, cannot show your feelings, once dey get to your feelings, den you gonna get mad, say someting. Tell someone to fuck off, den your job pau, you finished! Dis job is, people gotta give you shit, you gotta take it and take it and smile! So I tough on you, tryin to teach you to last. . . . See if you can last . . . make you into someting. . . . But it's true, I break your ass, Susan . . . ting for me is, I see dis good-looking haole bitch—I nevah know you was hapa haole—I nevah know you local until I heard you speakin pidgin to one of da ramp agents—but until den, I thought you one of dem stuck-up Punahou haole bitches . . . expect da world to fall at dere feet . . . how come you nevah speak like a local girl, Susan?

At the end of the day, Susan would take the bus, get home an hour later, take a shower, heat some leftovers, carefully press her uniform for tomorrow, and halfway through dinner, lie down and go to sleep. The nausea from the flight seemed to stay with her. Night after night, she dreamed she was just getting to the airport as the plane was leaving, that she was banging on the plane trying to get in and Mickey yelling, you late! or that she was making an announcement, but had forgotten the words and was just standing in the aisle, or she was looking down and seeing she wasn't dressed, she would wake suddenly during the night, look at the clock, fall back to sleep. Mickey's voice would suddenly be there, what do you think you're doing! I told you . . .

In the mornings, she would wake up nauseated, breasts aching, strangely sensitive, start getting ready, spend half an hour on her make-up, then out to the street, the streets still empty, catch the bus for the long ride out to the airport, still nauseated from yesterday's flight.

One night she dreamed she was a doll, a perfect porcelain-faced doll, and that she was both inside herself, and outside herself, and her mother was everywhere in the dream, shouting at her, go ahead, why don't you say something! and Susan, from outside herself, was watching herself, but was inside herself thinking, I'm not going to say anything, I'm not going to let her know what I'm feeling, I'm not going to give her a chance to yell. She was looking at herself, her face; the face was still perfect and beautiful, but she knew something terrible was starting to happen. . . .

She woke up terrified.

In the morning, she was exhausted and seemed off-balance and dizzy. She washed, then sat on the edge of the bed for a long time, nauseated. . . .

She stood up and saw her neatly pressed uniform on the back of the door across the room. She thought of her mother saying, don't wear those kinds of clothes, if you do . . .

Miss Pahoa reaching out and putting her hand on Susan's shoulder. You look just perfect. . . .

The breeze lifted the uniform, turned it slowly on the hook. If she could just make it into the uniform this morning. . . .

Susan! You will get . . .

She moved tentatively toward the uniform.

Pregnant! Her mother's eyes. Her voice, close. Susan!

She had to get into her uniform. She stepped across the room, touched the uniform, Susan, her mother's voice, the word pregnant, spoken by her mother, could make her . . . pregnant.

She took the uniform off the hanger. The girdle, the slip, the nylons, her breasts aching against the bra, she dressed, inspected herself in the mirror, walked away, returned, stood sideways, pressed her hand over her stomach, pulled in her stomach, lightly smoothed her hand over her stomach. Looked closely. She would have to do something.

Susan remembered Rita. Everyone knew that Rita had had an abortion—the word terrified Susan—senior year in high school. She would have to ask Rita.

Each day she put off calling Rita, and when Rita finally did give her a phone number, Susan went on putting off calling the doctor. Who would answer? What would she say? What a horrible word, abortion. And where would she get the money?

Each morning, Susan stood in front of the mirror, turned sideways, looked at herself in the mirror, flattened her palm against her stomach, said, I'll have to do something.

In the coffee shop in Hilo, Susan sat with one of the copilots on a short layover. He had been in Vietnam a year before and now he was back flying for Polynesian again, he was telling her about being an adviser and how after each mission, he would return, the plane shot up, and report to the commanding officer: Jesus Christ, I'm telling you they're shooting at us, can we shoot back, and the commanding officer would say, I know they're shooting at you, no, you cannot shoot back, we haven't declared war on them, Nick, and then Nick leaning forward in his chair, pushing his coffee cup slightly aside and saying, well, if we haven't declared war on them, I wish somebody would tell them that.

He laughed. After a minute he looked at Susan. What's the matter with you, Susan?

Nothing.

Well, if Mickey's getting on your back, don't let it bother you. I've known Mickey a long time, I'll talk to her. Her bark's worse than her bite.

She shook her head. It's not Mickey.

Well what is the matter?

She looked at Nick. She hardly knew him, but she was tired of worrying about it. And she had to do something. I need some money, Nick.

That's all? A long face over money? How much?

She told him.

Now he was going to ask her for what. But he didn't.

The next day he handed her an envelope. When she tried to say something, he just put his hand up and walked away.

She listened carefully to the man on the phone. He was local. Maybe Oriental. Was he the doctor? He gave her instructions in a quiet precise voice.

She was to leave a urine specimen off at the office during regular hours, just give it to one of the nurses. Then, she was to come in the evening, at nine o'clock, but not to go to the office entrance on King Street, but to walk through the parking lot, wait at the back door. She was to come alone, tell no one. If she brought anyone, he would not let her in, did she understand? Yes, she understood, but could she come at nine-thirty, it would give her time to get there from work. Yes, nine-thirty, exactly nine-thirty, she was to come alone, tell no one, and the money was of course to be in cash. Did she understand? Yes, she understood.

At the last minute, Susan panicked that she might be late and spent several dollars on a cab, getting off a block away from the doctor's office, still getting there a few minutes early. She waited under a banyan tree in the parking lot. A cat came up and rubbed against her ankles while she watched the door under the red EXIT sign.

At exactly nine-thirty, the door opened part-way. She could see a hand holding the door. She walked quickly toward the door. In an hour it would be over.

He didn't look back at her as she followed him down the deserted hallways of the office building, up two flights of stairs. In his office, she felt comforted to see the typewriters, the thick rug, the waiting room where she had left off the specimen. All as it had been on her earlier visit.

Behind his desk, there were his degrees from the University of Michigan Medical School, a Rotarian plaque. Dr. Moon. Korean. On the desk, a picture of his wife and two children. He sat down behind the desk, turned on the light.

She hesitated, moved closer, stood in front of the desk.

As he leaned into the light, she could see he was probably middle-aged, but looked younger in the way of Oriental men. He was wearing a suit and tie.

He leaned back out of the light and Susan could no longer see him clearly. He seemed to hover back somewhere behind the light.

After a minute, he said, no one knows you are here?

I've done exactly what you've told me. I haven't said a word to anyone.

I hope not. It would be an ungrateful way to return a favor, don't you think?

Yes.

I am doing you a favor and taking a risk. I hope you will keep that in mind and do exactly what I say.

She said yes again. Then asked, how did the test come out?

He didn't answer her.

I see you're a stewardess.

She remembered her uniform and nodded. She hadn't wanted to wear her uniform—not here. She'd brought a change of clothes, but at the last minute hadn't wanted to take the time to change.

Just starting out?

Yes.

Very nice. Very becoming. Of course, you'd lose your job. . . .

There was something odd in his voice. Maybe it was just her imagination.

But we'll take care of it. He waved his hand.

Something odd in his voice? Anyway, it would all be over in an hour or so.

When was your last period?

I'm not sure. Maybe nine or ten weeks ago. But they're not always regular.

She wanted to ask him about the test again, but decided she'd better not.

He said, you're familiar with the pelvic examination?

No, she wasn't.

If you'll step into the other room, you'll find a gown hanging on the door. Just undress—there's a hanger in there—get into the gown, and I'll be right in.

She hesitated, reached into her flight bag, brought out the envelope, placed it on the corner of the desk.

Did I tell you to do that?

No, but—

I thought you were going to do exactly what I said—

But you told me to bring the money in cash.

Did I say anything about money—yet?

No.

Susan reached for the money.

Did I tell you to take the money back?

She felt confused and frightened. She could just grab the money and run out of the office. . . . She looked up above the desk—University of Michigan Medical School . . . It must be her imagination . . . if she just did what he said, it would be over.

Well, what do you want me to do?

I want you to go into the other room and change, like I told you.

She left the money on the desk, walked to the door of the examining room. She heard his voice behind her: there's a light just inside the door.

She reached in, felt for it.

The light flickered, dim, less dim, bright.

She saw the table, the white sink, the stirrups coming up out of the dark, suddenly felt oh, no, I can't do this, I won't do this, I'll just have to quit the airline, go some place, have the baby. . . .

She stood there a moment longer.

Then she walked into the room, closed the door, found the gown, slipped off her jacket, and slowly began to fumble with the buttons on her blouse. Hanging up her skirt and jacket. Stepping out of her shoes. The linoleum floor. Cold.

She slipped the gown over her arms, pulled it closed, sat on a chair, stared at the table.

In a few minutes, Dr. Moon came in, his jacket off, his sleeves rolled up, went to the sink, and started washing his hands.

Without looking back, he said, if you'll get on the table, please. . . .

Susan got up onto the table, sat a moment, swung around, lay down, figured she should place her legs in the stirrups. After a moment, she pulled down the gown.

He was beside the table smelling of antiseptic and some kind of cologne.

She stared at the ceiling, closed her eyes, tried not to think of anything, opened her eyes.

All right, now, relax, everything's fine here.

She felt his hand under the gown and flinched.

Relax.

The heat of the lamp between her legs.

His hands pressing on her stomach, feeling her ovaries. The back of his head for a moment. Close. Over her.

Then the speculum, the sudden gasp of breath, the cold metal of the speculum like a knife.

Several moments later, his hand in her. She closed her eyes. She wished there were a nurse, another woman in here.

He probed inside her.

What was taking so long?

The examination seemed to be lasting forever.

She stared at the ceiling.

He went on feeling inside her. Probing in her. Moving his fingers inside of her. What was taking so long?

She stared at the ceiling.

Finally, he walked over to the sink, the water came on.

You can get up, now.

What?

You can get up now.

But . . . aren't you . . . going to do it in this room . . . now . . . tonight?

Get up, please.

He dried his hands and walked out.

Susan swung her legs down out of the stirrups, and after a minute, she stood on the floor, and still in the gown, walked into his office. She stood barefoot on the thick rug.

He was putting on his suit jacket.

I am pregnant, aren't I?

Change out of the gown.

Is there something wrong with me?

I thought you were going to do what I asked.

She went back into the examining room, dressed, returned.

Ah, here is our young stewardess again.

Is there a problem?

You need this?

She felt confused.

Yes, of course, I'm not married, I support myself, I would lose my job.

Come back tomorrow night.

But why? Why can't it be done tonight.

I thought you agreed to do what I told you to do. I am doing you a favor.

I know, but . . .

Come back tomorrow night. At nine-thirty. Come alone.

Am I pregnant?

I'll see you tomorrow night.

He was sitting back behind the desk, behind the light. She could barely make him out.

You can find your way out. And Susan. Not a word to anyone.

She stepped outside and walked down the deserted hall to the stairs.

She felt confused. Had he found something wrong with her, something he was afraid to tell her about; she remembered Obachan lying there in the hospital. . . . Maybe she wasn't really pregnant, just sick with something. She had left the money, she remembered, and she remembered it wasn't on the desk when she had come back out, she shouldn't have done that, maybe he wouldn't even be there tomorrow night, she shouldn't have done that, so stupid! but then what could she do? She reached the street, relieved just to hear the ordinary sounds of cars, horns, people. . . . Maybe he wouldn't even be there tomorrow night. If she hadn't left the money, it might be better not to come back at all, maybe she still wouldn't . . . but where would she get more money . . . the examination had taken so long, what had he been doing all that time?

All day, flying, nauseated, Mickey over her, Susan wondered, am I going back tonight, maybe there was another way to do it, and maybe he won't even be there at all, he had gotten the money! that's what he wanted, wasn't it? She kept trying to think of another way, maybe she could even ask Mickey.

Then she thought of the tip, each coin pressed into the egg yolk. The wedding ring in the bottom of her purse. And her mother . . .

She shook her head. It was something from her other life, her life before. This was the last thing and if she could just be rid of this, she could be a stewardess, travel, have money, have her own friends, wear the clothes she liked, be away from them. She would go through with it.

When the hand had pushed open the door under the EXIT sign, instead of feeling afraid as she had the first night, she felt relieved. Maybe she could rely on him. He had shown up. He wasn't a thief anyway.

It was much the same as the first night, the empty halls of the office building, Dr. Moon in a perfectly tailored suit, his strange, confusing voice.

Maybe it was her, maybe she was being overly sensitive. She would just stop being so sensitive and do what he said, go through with it. *Susan, you'll get* . . . Yes, she had to go through with it.

As Susan lay back on the table, felt the heat of the lamp between her legs, she asked, did you find something wrong with me last night, was that it?

He didn't answer.

She tried not to jump when he touched her. The examination . . .

Again, the examination seemed to go on and on.

She felt her cheeks starting to burn. She blinked.

After several minutes, she asked, what is it? Tell me.

He didn't answer.

There's nothing wrong, is there? Is it . . . the money? Please,

I can get you more money . . . I'm sure . . . please . . . just do what you have to do. . . . I'm not afraid of the pain. . . .

Relax, you're tensing up.

I'll get you more money if that's what you want.

He turned off the lamp, went to the sink, washed.

Get dressed.

Please! Do it tonight!

He turned and walked out.

After a long time, she got up and dressed. She stood in front of his desk.

May I have . . . the envelope . . . back . . . please.

She was afraid she was going to cry. Her voice quavered. She didn't want to cry in front of him.

You're being so emotional. Everything seems distorted to you now. Come back tomorrow night and try to relax.

You won't give me my money back and you won't help me. . . . Her voice broke. What do you want?

I'll see you tomorrow night. Remember, do exactly what I've told you and everything will be all right.

Keep the money!

Susan—

Keep it!

I'll see you tomorrow night.

At home, she took a long shower, washing herself thoroughly, then sitting on the living-room sofa. After a while, she got up, carefully pressed her uniform, pressed a clean blouse, laid out her nylons, polished her shoes and placed them together. She hung the uniform on a hanger and then called into scheduling, writing down her flights as she watched the hanger turning in the breeze—now this way, now that way. When she hung up, she wanted to get up, get into the uniform, look at herself, but she didn't. If there were a way to get the money back . . . and where, now that she couldn't, where would she get that much money . . . and then find another doctor? Where would she find another doctor? It would take time. Any day now, someone would notice her stomach—if someone hadn't already—Mickey would report her in no time; she knew Mickey was just dying to get her in trouble, exactly why, she didn't know. She didn't treat the other new stews that way. . . . Gale Lopez, for one.

She lit a cigarette and smoked it slowly in the dark. She thought of her mother. Her father. That was her other life. She would have to put it behind her.

She thought of going to the police. But where would that put her? She had no proof he was actually doing anything wrong, no proof she had even visited him. And the police might contact her parents. . . .

That sudden movement at the corner of her eye, then her head hitting the floor and Carol starting to cry far away. . . .

She crushed out the cigarette, too tired to walk over to the bed, lay back on the sofa, her eyes started to close; she would get it all figured out tomorrow.

Maybe if Nick would go with her. Or if he could wait outside. Or if she could tell Moon, somehow scare him, tell him that this time if she weren't out in an hour, and with the thing done—then Nick would . . . do what? But if she didn't do exactly what he told her . . . What would Mickey do? Several times, Susan looked at Mickey when Mickey was talking to a passenger, studied her face. . . . Mickey was tough, Susan couldn't imagine anyone ever getting Mickey into . . .

Susan lay in the stirrups, she stared at the ceiling; his hand was in her.

She would not give in. Whatever it was he was doing, she would not give in.

She stared at the ceiling.

The heat of the lamp on her.

She bit the inside of her cheek.

I will not give in to him, I will not. . . .

The tears were running down her cheeks.

I will not. . . .

She heard her voice, far away, quavering, please, I'm begging you . . . now . . . I'm begging you. . . . I'll do anything . . . please do it tonight . . . what do you want . . . please . . . I'm begging . . .

His face was close to hers.

She smelled the cologne. His heavy gold Mason's ring over on the sink.

For the first time she noticed he was wearing rubber gloves.

Please . . . I haven't told anyone . . . please . . .

She felt the cool dab of alcohol on her arm, the sting of the needle. She felt herself starting to get lighter.

Something shaking her. A distant voice speaking a familiar language she could almost understand, a face, closer, huge eyes, no features, suffocating, the voice cleared, Obachan's voice, leaning over her, smiling, holding Susan in her arms, something shaking her harder, her mother's voice sharp, Susan! Stupid! Speak English! Don't speak pidgin!

He slapped her again, harder. Come on, wake up!

She could see him above her, there was a pain in her stomach. She heard herself groan.

She reached down toward the pain, her fingers touched something wet.

His voice, far away. Yes, you're bleeding, you're all right. I've put a pad on you, it's almost soaked through, I want you to force yourself to get up now . . . sit up, walk to the bathroom, change the napkin . . . then I want you to get dressed. There will be a cab waiting for you a block . . .

He was giving her directions, his voice was fading, she felt him slap her again.

Come on! Wake up!

She felt him pulling her up, her legs hanging over the edge of the table. . . .

Her legs, numb, hitting the floor, swaying, pain in her stomach doubling her up . . . passing. She could feel something warm on her legs, splashing on the linoleum floor. . . .

She dropped onto the toilet seat, blood dripping into the water, trails like smoke. . . . She stared at the splashes of blood on the tiles, then slowly, her hands far away, she changed the napkin. Wiped at the blood on her thighs.

Then he was steadying her as she dressed. Handing her a box of sanitary napkins in a paper bag. And pills. Take one of these every four hours—for pain.

Okay, hurry up. One thing, though. He grabbed her hand. Drunkenly, she pulled back from him.

You will not repeat a word of this to anyone. Don't forget, Susan, you may not think so, but I've done you a favor . . . my way. But I have. I've saved your job if nothing else. You have no proof of any of this. No witnesses. It's just your word against mine.

I'm bleeding . . . am I . . . all right?

Yes.

Will I . . . still be able to have children?

Yes, of course.

She looked at the drops of blood on the linoleum.

Who will clean it up?

Never mind that, go on now.

She felt drunk, she couldn't keep things straight.

Why did you treat . . . treat me like this?

He put his hand on her shoulder to turn her around. She pushed his hand off her shoulder.

Will I be able to have children?

You asked me that.

But will I?

Yes. You're not the first girl to have an abortion.

But she was thinking again of her grandmother, she had been so close a few minutes ago, Obachan, what would Obachan think? . . . if she had been alive none of this would have happened, would it?

She thought of her grandmother's face in pictures when she was young. When she had just come from Japan and was living on Maui. She didn't smile in the pictures, but she was beautiful. Her hair was so black.

My grandmother was a picture bride . . . from Japan. She was a plantation worker on Maui. . . .

Very nice.

I'm a stewardess.

Susan, go home now.

Why did you treat me like this?

He looked at her. His face was set. She turned and stumbled toward the door.

He followed her into the hall. Don't take a bath for three weeks.

She walked unsteadily down the hall to the stairs.

By the time the taxi had reached Waikiki, the pad had soaked through her skirt. She paid the driver and walked drunkenly toward the apartment, slowly climbing the stairs, coming to a stop halfway up, holding on to the banister and staring out into the dark, smelling for a moment the cool night scents of the mock orange.

Inside, turning on the light, she stumbled, pulling off her clothes, she made her way toward the bathroom, don't take a bath . . . she stepped into the bathroom. . . .

Standing under the shower.

Then, half-awake, half-asleep, she lay on her back under a blanket. She lay still. She was bleeding heavily, she knew. After a while, she realized she was holding her breath. She just managed to reach the phone and call in sick.

When the sun woke her, she was lying in a pool of dried

blood. When she moved, the blood started to flow again. She got up, made herself some tea, lay down, dozed deliriously on and off. Whatever happened now, at least it was over. The next time she opened her eyes, the bright sunlight was gone from the window.

Later, in the afternoon, almost evening, there was a suddenly a deep pain in her stomach. She stumbled toward the bathroom, the pain worse, she sat on the john, clumps of blood, the pain in her stomach, days and days. . . . Five years old, Obachan picking her up in her arms; outside, the sun on the flowers. . . . Obachan's garden get da bananas, orchids, crocus, ti plants, maidenhair fern, elephant ears, hibiscus, aloe plant . . . we go inside da taxi, da taxi waitin, we drive in da taxi, go-stay in da taxi long time, follow da road up da valley, den dere no more road, we almost in da jungle, everyting green, get ti and long cane growin, everyting wild up dere, we drive up to da house, get dogs, chickens, pigs undah da house, dere some old cars wit da cane growin through da cars, we get outta da taxi, Obachan carry me in da house, da old tutuma, she back inside da house, she tell Obachan, put da keiki on da floor, dey put da blanket on da floor, den dey put me, da keiki, on da floor, den da tutuma and Obachan, dey get down on da floor. Da tutuma, she old, she get plenty wrinkles, she get wrinkled brown hands wit da spots on da back, she look at me and smile, she no have so many teeth lef, she pick up my dress, den she bend her head ovah, put her ear on my stomach, she listen good, frown, listen long time, den she nod and tell Obachan, one evil spirit stay inside dis keiki, da spirit get inside and turn da girl's stomach upside-down, 'as why she get da pain. Den da old tutuma put her hand on my stomach, she rub her hands ovah my stomach and den da pain gone, pain stay pau. I see my grandmothah she sittin lookin down at me, smilin, she reach down, she touch my face, I say her name, Obachan. Den I get up and da pain gone, I can walk by myself. Den we get in da taxi, we hele-on home.

After a few days, Susan put herself back on the schedule. She had lost weight, and it must have showed, because Mickey, ready to light into Susan, no doubt for being off the schedule, looked at her face, then looked away and didn't say anything. Susan's face was thin and gaunt, she could feel the skirt loose at her waist. As she walked down the aisle, or reached up to stow a piece of baggage, she would panic and suddenly expect to see blood silently streaking down her legs. She would reach behind her, pretending to smooth her skirt, sure she was bleeding, expecting the passengers to be staring at her. But none of that happened and, after a time, she knew she would be all right. It was just that now the passengers looked a little different to her. In exactly what ways, she couldn't say. Just that when she saw their faces, she knew there was more behind them than she had ever thought possible. And herself, too. To have actually begged him . . .

Susan opened the door; he was out there on the landing. He was sweating and looked nervous and uncomfortable.

Hi, there, Susan.

She stepped back. How did you find me?

I've been looking.

All this time?

For some time.

I have a job, I pay rent here, I'm not going home with you.

Can I come in for a minute?

Did you come here to knock me down again? Because you can do it right out here without coming in. Then you can turn around and go home—before I call the police.

I'm sorry about that, Susan.

She didn't say anything.

Can I come in? Your mother and I have been worried about you.

Oh, that's sweet. Why worry about me, I'm a pain in the ass. Why go looking for a pain in the ass?

Can I come in?

Oh, please do. She opened the door wider. Step right in. Make yourself at home. Well, here it is, the gutter, and here I am, in the gutter, remember?

He stepped in, looked around, hesitated, sat on the sofa. He had something that looked like a thick scrapbook full of pictures or clippings. He looked around, then placed the scrapbook within easy reach on the sofa.

Looks like you've lost a little weight. Are you okay?

Of course I'm okay. And I'm getting better and better, thank you.

Your mother's been very worried about you.

Sweet of her. Tell her to save herself the trouble. And I'm not going home. This is my home, now.

She doesn't know I've come to visit you. Susan, I'm sorry, I didn't mean to hit you like that.

Susan looked out the window.

Your mother has gotten worse since you've left.

Oh, of course, she's worse, now that she doesn't have me to blame for everything! Now that I'm out of that madhouse, don't call her my mother. Call her your wife!

A moment later, Susan heard the remark and disliked herself. Where had that come from?

Her father was looking more and more uncomfortable. He put his hand on the scrapbook. She could see he didn't know what to say next. What did he want?

She looked at the faded tattoo in the thick blond hair on his forearm. A girl entwined with an anchor over the insignia of the merchant marine. She remembered when it had been bright blue, the girl and anchor clear, right up there in the skin. He'd held her in his arms, Obachan on the porch, the distance growing between Obachan and herself, the car coming. . . . The girl and anchor were fading into his skin, his skin was fading, local haole skin, the sun year after year . . . Uncle William had tattoos, too.

She tried to imagine her father, young, a runaway in the merchant marine, drunk maybe for the courage, head full of blond hair, not grayed out as it was now, eyes bright blue, no stomach on him, big and broad-shouldered. The tattoo needle entering the skin, the pain, the girl starting to flow into the skin. She stared at the tattoo, then looked away.

Her father lit a cigarette and looked for an ashtray. Pulled one over to him.

Susan, there are some things you don't know . . . know about your—

After a moment, he seemed to change his mind about a word, said, about your mother. Things you don't know . . . some things . . . do you have some coffee?

She hesitated, then got up and put the kettle on.

You do look thin, Susan. Have you been sick?

No.

Do you know, for one thing, that your mother is hard of hearing?

What's that got to do with anything?

She's seriously hard of hearing—I think—and I just recently became aware of it. Before I thought she was kind of just off somewhere.

Maybe she is.

No, I think she is hard of hearing. That's what it is.

He said it stubbornly.

Susan didn't know what to say. She busied herself with the coffee, he looked at it, stirred it a long time, took a sip.

Susan didn't want to help him.

I got your mother a demonstrator hearing aid—a good one. A friend of mine is in the business. That big. He pinched out a space the size of a nickel between his thumb and forefinger. That big, he repeated. Flesh-colored. You could hardly see it, and if she wore her hair forward, you really couldn't tell it was there at all. But she won't wear it. As a matter of fact—he seemed to be talking to himself; he stared up at the ceiling— she got pretty mad at me. She thought I was trying to tell her she had gotten old. Plenty of people wear hearing aids. That hearing aid costs over a hundred and fifty dollars. She doesn't wear it.

Susan said coldly, you could always return it and get your money back.

He looked at her a moment. The worst he could do was hit her again—or try—and he'd already done that. And that was the worst ...

They wouldn't take it back. I haven't altogether given up trying to get her to wear it. Well, I have, but I leave it around and hope she'll use it on her own. She did wear it for a few days. But then she just stopped. She said she was hearing voices—lots of voices. You know, there's no talking to your mother once she gets an idea. . . .

Oh, I know.

I tried the hearing aid myself. I listened for voices. I told her maybe she was picking up a local radio station. I thought I heard a local radio station. Just faintly. I couldn't tell. But your mother just won't wear it.

He sighed. Without noticing he already had a cigarette in the ashtray, he lit another.

But by then, she was talking to herself and got the idea, maybe she really was hearing voices. He waved his hand impatiently.

Oh, it's involved, involved. Your mother has stopped going out of the house altogether, she stares at the neighbor's house across the street for hours on end! She keeps saying the Hawaiian woman who lives there is out to get her and we have to move. . . . You know, Susan, you can't talk or reason with your mother, she just makes up her mind one morning and that's it.

He sighed.

She's decided I'm having an affair with another woman. Your mother's decided that the lady across the street and I are trying to kill her and make it look like an accident.

Susan suddenly remembered her mother, eyes frantic: Susan, if anything ever happens to me, don't accept it! My death might look like an accident, but it will not be an accident! Promise me you will investigate after my death! Susan! I am counting on you!

He went on: I don't know where she gets it, but she is definitely worse since you've gone. One night, she actually chased me with a kitchen knife. I was behind her in the kitchen, luckily I was facing her, she turned suddenly, her whole face changed, she just looked crazy, her eyes went wild, she grabbed a carving knife and came at me. I had to run into the bathroom and lock the door until she quieted down and pushed the kitchen knives under the door to me one by one. I tell you, I was afraid to stay in the house with her. I really thought she was going to kill me.

He sighed, puffed on his cigarette.

So I talked to your mother about seeing a psychiatrist. He shook his head. The long and short of it was no. Along with something else your mother threw in. The psychiatrist was part of it. Part of what? She just said part of *it*! I said, well, pick your own psychiatrist! She said, it wouldn't make any difference. He would still be part of it.

He lifted his hands in the air and shrugged. Part of it! Part of what? She said, don't try anything, it wouldn't do any good —she'd already left instructions with several people, not just one, but several—and there was no point trying to find out who they were either! They would investigate after her death, I wouldn't get away with it.

He shrugged. Well, I don't mind saying it, and you don't have to be a genius to see that this business is crazy. After she came at me with that kitchen knife— he shook his head —not just for me, but I was afraid to leave Carol alone in the house with her. I wasn't just gonna let this alone. But I couldn't get her to do anything. She wouldn't see a doctor, she doesn't really have any friends she confides in.

Suddenly, he said, Susan, it wasn't always like this, you know, your mother used to be— He stopped. He thought about it for a minute.

Anyway, I thought if I couldn't get her to go out to see a doctor, maybe I could bring a doctor to see her. . . . So I got one of the doctors from Tripler—a navy doctor—to come home with me. He was in uniform. I was going to just introduce him as one of the men on some navy business. . . . Thought he might just come over to the house, have a beer, kind of observe her. The minute we walked in the door, your mother took one look at us, looked at him, went into the bedroom and locked the door.

He shook his head in confusion and disgust. I don't know, Susan. It's not a hopeless situation, but it is difficult.

Since I hadn't been able to get her to a doctor, I thought maybe I could dope some of it out myself. . . . So I started looking through her things—which believe me, I didn't like doing, a person's things are still their things—but I felt I had to do something before she hurt one of us. Or even herself.

He paused. I did find something. I found this. He picked up the scrapbook.

Do you want to take a look?

No. No. No, I don't. I want you to take that scrapbook out of here and go.

Susan, I'm trying to talk to you.

It's too late. Look, I grew up in that crazyhouse— No, no, that's not true, I grew up with Obachan, I just suffered through the last few years with you. I know she's crazy! You're crazy, too! You just don't do it with a knife! I wouldn't even know any better if I hadn't lived with someone sane first! I'd be just as crazy, too! Maybe I am! Maybe it's too late for me, too. . . . No, it's not. So why come here now? I'm out! And I'm staying out! I'm a stewardess, I've got a good job; there are people who like the way I dress and act! People who don't live with the tv on morning noon and night—

Susan—

People who don't think it's a cardinal sin to go out on a date—

Susan—

I'm talking! I work for an airline; I'm a stewardess now. I have friends, I'm sure, of course, we all belong in the gutter and are on our way to hell, but *they're* my family, now! Not you!

He held out the scrapbook.

Her hands were sweating.

Susan, the clippings date back through to the war—about 1945. . . .

She got up and walked quickly around the room.

You live with her! Leave me alone! Take your scrapbook and go! Obachan was my mother and father!

He got up, walked across the room, placed the scrapbook on her empty chair. He returned to the sofa.

She walked around the room again, stepped outside. People were walking down to the beach. Relaxed, normal people.

She wiped her hands on her jeans and came back in.

Why did you really come here, that's what I'd like to know.

I told you, Susan.

She again walked quickly around the room, avoided the chair, lit a cigarette, inhaled, dropped the cigarette in an ashtray, walked over to the chair, snatched the scrapbook in both hands, jerked it back, moved toward him, damn you!

He looked at her calmly.

She held the scrapbook a moment longer, lowered it.

All right. I'll look at your damn scrapbook. Then get out and let me go on with my life.

He didn't say anything. He lit another cigarette.

Again, she wiped her palms on her jeans, then sat down,

opened the book. Quickly leafed the pages, front, back, and middle. All newspaper clippings from the *Star-Bulletin* and *Advertiser.*

Suddenly, she looked up. There's nothing about her—us— in these clippings, is there?

He shook his head, no no.

She answered some half-formed reaction she was having, well, it's not so stupid, anything's possible with this family.

Then she turned her attention to the newspaper clippings. As he had told her, the earliest clipping went back to 1945, the most recent to less than a month ago. . . . The clippings were all about kahunas. Any article that had any mention at all of kahunas was clipped, dated, and heavily underlined.

Susan became absorbed and forgot her father sitting over on the sofa. Kahunas. Anyone who lived in Hawaii knew that a kahuna was a Hawaiian priest, or minister, or a sorcerer of kinds. But why should her mother have a whole scrapbook fanatically devoted to newspaper clippings on kahunas? Any time the word occurred anywhere it was underlined. Susan leafed the pages. There were many kinds of kahunas. Kahuna ho'oulu'ai, agriculture experts; in the olden times, there had been a kahuna hui, a priest who functioned in ceremonies for the deification of a king. Some of this was Sunday-supplement stuff. But there were a great number of clippings which seemed to weave their way from short articles on page one, on through to the back pages. They seemed to be a steady under-current that ran through the newspapers. These articles concerned kahuna lapaau and kahuna pulis—healers; then, there were three categories of article where Susan's mother had cir-cled the word kahuna and placed exclamation points in the margins: these concerned kahuna anaana, the priest who was reputed to practice a kind of black magic and who could pray a person to death. He was also considered the lowest form of kahuna. There were articles mentioning the practice of the kahuna kilokilo, whose work was reputed to counter or undo

73

the work of the kahuna anaana; and, finally, articles on kahuna ho'opi'opi'o—the kahuna who could inflict illness by a number of acts or gestures. Each article concerning kahuna anaana, kahuna kilokilo, kahuna ho'opi'opi'o was covered with exclamation points, as though her mother had become frantic with some kind of recognition. Here were accounts of balls of fire rolling mysteriously through the air, appearing, disappearing. Menehunes—the little people. And eight-foot-tall people—the dead, or *make*—walking. . . .

What did this have to do with her mother, why did she keep these articles?

Here was an article on Kukhie Kuhns, a makapu kahuna lapaau, who used the sharp-leaved wapini plant to make a tea for diabetics and for arthritics. Who could set bones. Who had herbs for asthma, ulcers . . . here were pictures of the stones she used, the walking stone—to absorb the birth defect of a club foot—with prayer! Kukhie Kuhns emphasized she did nothing, though, without prayer in the name of the Father, the Son, and the Holy Ghost; nothing without the sign of the cross and prayer. She said, prayer is like dialing His number. He is always listening, but you have to ring Him up. Herbs accomplish nothing without God; proper prayers and Hawaiian chants must accompany treatment.

Kukhie Kuhns . . .

Susan went on reading. To be sure, running through the newspaper clippings were accusations and counteraccusations of fraud, charlatanism, personal motivation for intimidation, and so on, but still, there seemed to be a core of experience which never had, could not be explained away.

The perspiration on her fingers was leaving damp shadows on the scrapbook. There was something she didn't like about this, any of this—what could it mean?

Here was a clipping headlined: *Kahuna Anaana—Spell of Death.* A Joseph Kaapu had bought a house in Lanikaula, a place rumored to have been the site of an ancient battle. He

74

had moved into the house with his wife, and before long a number of strange things had started happening—sounds of walking in the house, but no one there; a strange-looking black dog with *make* eyes scratching at the back door; a clothesline pole, the trunk of a dead tree, shaking in the ground—the maid, seeing the pole shaking up and down, then stopping; also, sounds like the tapping of a stick. More sounds. Before Kaapu would return home, his wife hearing sounds like firecrackers exploding in a can.

One day, Kaapu and a friend had been butchering a pig for kalua under the house when, from above, they had heard the sounds of money sprinkling onto the floor. Then the sound of a baby carriage being wheeled from room to room. They had gone upstairs to investigate, but had found no money, the baby carriage folded and hanging in its place on the wall.

Kaapu's keiki had run from room to room ahead of them saying, look! Look at that big man!

But they had seen nothing.

Then Joseph Kaapu's wife had given birth to another child, but the baby had gotten sick and died, and soon after, the woman, too, had gotten sick. She had become weaker and weaker.

Joseph Kaapu heard of a Hawaiian preacher up in Honomu and went up to find him—Andy Ku—who had been up in the mountains, but who had come walking down out of the mountains to meet Kaapu, saying, I knew you were coming.

When they had returned to the house at Lanikaula, Joseph Kaapu's wife had been well. Andy Ku and Joseph Kaapu had walked from room to room in the house, Andy Ku sometimes reading from the Bible, until they had come to a window and stood there, looking out into the yard. Andy Ku said, there is a man out there in the yard, a giant. He is coming this way, he is wearing a feathered cape, a helmet.

Then Joseph Kaapu had felt something uncanny in the room —chills, like needles, tickled his neck, ran up and down his spine. There had been a breeze, the curtains billowing.

And a voice, booming. Andy Ku, eyes rolling, had read out loud in Hawaiian from his Bible, the voice had gone on booming, Andy Ku had gone on reading hard.

Andy Ku listened. The curtain became calm. Andy Ku's eyes gazed out the window, and he said, suddenly, *aloha, nui loa*: great long love to you!

Then Andy Ku turned to Joseph Kaapu and said, you have broken a taboo of the Hawaiian sacred dead—the spell of kahuna anaana has been placed upon you! You will be sick! You will live, but you will be very sick! You must leave this house immediately!

Then Joseph Kaapu had gone crazy. He had run through the streets and to the church in nothing more than his underwear. He had gone crazy and tried to kill his wife.

Andy Ku came back again, placed holy water in a glass, a red bandana over the glass, and then had prayed over it in Hawaiian from the Holy Book. When the water had foamed and boiled, Andy Ku told the wife, now give it to him to drink, but be careful he spills none on himself or he will be burned.

Joseph Kaapu had been given the water to drink, and had returned to sanity. Andy Ku told him, never return to that house and never trespass upon sacred ground. . . .

Susan suddenly snapped the scrapbook shut, stood up quickly, and handed it back to her father.

She lit a cigarette, sat down. All right, I get the idea; what about it, did you ask her why she collects all this junk?

What do you think of it?

I think it's creepy. Did you ask her about it?

I tried. But the minute I said anything, she flew into a rage, got up, locked the bedroom door, and wouldn't come out. I had to sleep in the living room. Susan, I really don't know what it's all about . . . if she thinks someone has put a kahuna's curse on her, or what. Or whom it would even be. Or why. I don't know what to think. But I do know she's a lot worse since you've left the house. . . .

Did you know my eye was closed for over a week?

I'm sorry.

Why don't you take her to a kahuna and see what he says?

He shook his head. I don't know what to do. . . . I don't think she'd go. All I know is she's acting crazy and nagging me to move and I can't just start moving right now. And what if I move and then she thinks another woman across the street is out to get her again?

Susan felt herself getting drawn in. She didn't want to think about it—any of it. Yes, there had been something strange, yes her mother was strange, how strange, she was just beginning to appreciate, now that she was no longer home. . . .

Look, what *do* you want?

He stood up. I came here to see if you were all right. And because I thought there were these things . . . you should know.

Okay, I know.

Should still know, Susan.

He seemed to struggle with something a moment. If your mother were all right, maybe she would tell you . . . maybe it wouldn't make any difference to you anyway.

What?

I hope it wouldn't make any difference . . . but it might.

Suddenly, Susan saw him lose all of his nerve. He picked up the scrapbook.

At the door, he hesitated. Then, in a quick movement he put down the scrapbook, Susan flinched, saw the hurt in his face, pretended not to.

He pulled out his wallet.

Here.

She looked at the money in his hand. She felt herself starting to smile.

What changes? Money and presents in our family! She shook her head. I don't need it.

Money is one thing people always need. Take it, Susan.

No.

I won't argue.

He placed it on the kitchen table, turned, and walked out.

Susan stood looking at the ashtray full of cigarette butts, the empty coffee cup, the money on the table—five twenties.

What had he been trying to tell her? He'd never ever behaved or talked like this before. It was always, I am your father! She touched the money. Had he known about the abortion? Was that it? No, impossible. Just his way of trying to deal with uncomfortable feelings he couldn't understand . . . money was.

She wandered nervously around the apartment. Kahunas. Her mother's eyes moving around the room. Following something. Andy Ku by the window watching something coming across the yard, a breeze, then a chill. . . .

Her father . . . she decided I'm having an affair with some woman. . . . Your mother says I'm planning to kill her. The psychiatrist is part of it.

And chasing him with a knife?

All right, so she's paranoid—crazy, whatever those words mean. But instead of calling it paranoia, she thinks it's a kahuna's curse, what was the difference, it all came to the same thing. But he had been trying to tell her something else, something more, hadn't he?

Whatever, he was gone now, that was the important thing. Somehow, even if only temporarily, she had defeated him.

She remembered a time when she had been eleven years old. He'd been trying to spank her for something. He kept trying to catch hold of her hand so he could pull her to him and turn her over his knee. She couldn't let him spank her and she couldn't explain, she didn't know how to explain she was having her first period; he kept grabbing for her hand and she kept struggling, and then she knew he suddenly understood why, and he had let her go. She had walked away from him, stood some distance away, and looked back at him; he was embarrassed and confused, and she knew she had crossed a divide and defeated him, defeated him in some way for good and always, just in her body's becoming a woman's body.

She caught sight of herself in the three-quarter-length mirror on the bathroom door and stopped. She saw her long slim legs, her tapered fingers. Thought of his thick hands curled around the scrapbook. She drifted closer to the mirror. Squeezed the skin between her eyes. Where his nose had a high bridge, she had no bridge. She hated having no bridge. If she ever had money, maybe she'd have plastic surgery. Where she had high cheekbones, he had none. He had a heavy jaw, a prominent chin, she, a slight chin. Her eyes were a light brown. Almost golden. No matter how much make-up she put on, or how cleverly she did it, her eyes never looked big enough. Some Oriental girls she'd known in high school had actually put fine strips of Scotch Tape on their eyes to hold the lids up, then had put make-up on over the Scotch Tape. She looked at her eyes. Golden. Carol's eyes came closer to his blue eyes—gray.

Susan saw her mother's face in her face, but then, Susan had light brown hair, not the black hair of her mother and grandmother. Yet in the length of her face, Susan saw herself as haole.

But still, she looked so Oriental . . . if she could do something to her face?

She touched the cheekbones—I'd leave the cheekbones—but wouldn't have my face so wide. And my nose? Gross. So Oriental. What could I do with my **nose?**

Not much. Nothing.

She stared at herself a long time.

There seemed to be no consensus on what she was or how she appeared. Mickey saw her as haole, that was clear. The mainland passengers always seemed surprised when they learned her name was Susan, and sometimes, they would show they were even more surprised when she spoke, saying, oh! you speak English? Or where did you learn to speak English so well?

As though they'd expected her to start speaking Japanese or Korean—all the same to them anyway! Just the other day a woman had said to her, why, you look almost American.

Susan looked at herself another moment, turned, and abruptly kicked the bathroom door shut. She paced the room.

Mother, Father, brown eyes, blue eyes, her nose, no bridge, where did you learn to speak English so well . . . why you look almost American. . . .

Mother. Father.

Mothah. Fathah.

So den I been livin wit my fathah and mothah for a while. Obachan say girl's place is wit her mothah and fathah.

Everyting differen.

I get one sistah, she youngah. She get gray eyes like da haoles. Carol no understand sometime when I talkin to her. I talk plain English like dis, but sometime she no understand.

Den I talk to her some Japanese, da language of da stone and Obachan, but dat make it more worse, she no understand none of dat talk.

Everyting differen and I scaid.

Get no more garden, no hibiscus, get no more banana plant, no vegetables for dinnah in back da house, get no more aloe plant growin, what I going to do if I bump da hot stove, da iron, get one burn? Get no more aloe plant in da garden.

My mothah going out before dark, she get dressed up good, put on da perfume, she going to one place called da Blue Grotto, she stay out, she nevah come kiss me goodnight, she going to da Blue Grotto, I sleepin, she in da Blue Grotto.

When she come home, sometime she come in da room, me and Carol we sleepin, but sometime I wake, I no see her good in da dark, but I hear her, I know she close, den she bend down, I no see her good in da dark, smell her, she wearin da perfume, she got da smell of smoke in her hair, smell like cigarettes, she get da smell, strong, sometime Obachan drink da same, call it whisky, smell strong, make Obachan wrinkle face when she drink whisky.

I no see my mothah good in da dark. She kiss me. I no like da way she smell, I pretend like I sleepin. She smell like smoke and whisky.

In da morning, everybody walkin around on tiptoe—we tryin to be real quiet cause Mothah been out workin in da Blue Grotto, now she real tired.

I try hard to be quiet.

Da haole man, my fathah, he going round on tiptoe, too. Everyone lookin at da door. Mothah sleepin behind da door.

Da haole man he try to move real quiet. Sssh, he always sayin, no wake Mothah.

Carol and I, we scaid. We no wanna wake her.

Da haole man, he scaid too, I can tell. He big, da biggest man I ever seen, but he still scaid, too.

We always lookin at da closed door.

Da haole man, he not real akamai like Obachan. He not know how to press my dress good. He no press it.

He not know how to braid my hair. He not know how to tie ribbons.

He not akamai like Obachan.

He put da milk and da cereal on da table, 'ats all. He no can cook da hot breakfast.

Everyone scaid and lookin at da door. Mothah sleepin behind da door.

When da haole kiss me good-by, sometime he scrape me wit his chin. He get one rough chin. Obasan get smooth chin.

We all quiet in da morning cause we all scaid wake Mothah.

One morning we make noise, we wake Mothah.

Den she come to da door and start shoutin. I never hear someone shout so loud cept maybe da crazy Hawaiian lady across da street in Palolo. She hit Bubba on da head wit da hammah.

My mothah, she shout at da haole man. She shout at all of us. She shoutin at me. She pointin her fingah.

She shout at da haole man cause he no have one job—she get one job—she no like da job. She gotta work at da Blue Grotto.

Den da haole man, he get angry, too. I see he scaid, but he get angry. He say he tryin for one job.

My mothah, she shout, he no try enough.

Den dey shout at each othah, some more tings.

Den Carol, she start cryin. I start cryin too. I no like it here, I like go live back in Palolo.

Den Mothah slam da door, it make a terrible noise, I scaid.

Dat day I glad leavin da house for school.

Everyone scaid of Mothah.

All da time, I livin wit my mothah and fathah, I tinkin bout Obachan and how she press my dress good in da morning, how she huggin and kissin me. I tinkin bout my kimono in da trunk.

I waitin all week for da kimono, on Sunday, my mothah, she no press da kimono. I no see da kimono no more.

Maybe da haole forget da dress in da bottom of da trunk undah da picture General MacArthah.

I scaid ast.

Den, aftah more Sundays passin by, I finally ast my mothah, where da kimono? today Sunday, I like wear da kimono, but she not know nothing bout it, she no understand.

Den I say, maybe you forget da kimono at Obachan's?

She say, she not know da kimono, she tell me no worry bout da kimono, I get enough dresses. She say, you no wear kimonos. Kimonos are for Japanese. You American!

Den I start to cry. My mothah start shoutin, she yellin, you spoiled, she yellin dat Obachan spoil me.

Den I say no more. I wait until we going Palolo. Obachan get da kimono, dere, Palolo, I know.

Bumbye, Sunday, too, we going Palolo. Obachan back from da church. Obachan huggin and kissin me, she start cryin, I cryin, too. Den I ast her for da kimono and she go to da trunk, she get em out, she press da kimono good, den she hold it out for me, I put em on. Den I happy. Like one rainbow.

Come time to go, I cry. I no like to leave Obachan. I like wear da kimono, too. Mothah, she angry. Obachan angry, too.

Dey angry each othah.

Obachan say Mothah not know how treat me.

My mothah, she sayin, I spoiled, she know how treat me, I belongin to her.

I like stay-go wit Obachan. Dey shoutin each othah. My mothah make me take da kimono off. Den Mothah takin me home.

Aftah dat, everyone shoutin all da time, everyone angry.

Sunday come an I no put on da kimono no more.

My mothah shoutin, all da time, workin in da Blue Grotto. I nevah see her no more, but when I see her, she shoutin.

She no like me. Obachan like me. Mothah, she no like da way I talk. All da time she shoutin, no talk like dat, I not know what she mean, she say, no talk dat pidgin, no speak no more Japanese, you speak English!

All da time she shoutin at me, stupid, speak English!

I scaid.

I not know what she like me say, so I no say nothing.

Den my mothah, she stare at me—she point her fingah at me, I starin at da big diamond on da fingah, she stare at me. I no say nothing.

She not like da girl on da stone, always smilin.

I scaid say anyting.

Den she shout, why you no say someting? I your mothah.

I like say someting, but I scaid. I know she going shout again.

Den she shout, you no love me? I your mothah.

But I no say nothing. I scaid.

All da time she callin me stupid. In school, I always da smartest, best everyting I do. All da teachers tellin me I akamai. Bubba no learn da alphabet. Bubba's mothah, she hit em on da head wit da hammah. Shoulda seen da blood. I akamai.

My mothah, she always shoutin, stupid! She shout it.

Aftah da fight wit Obachan, I no see her long time. One day I tinkin bout go-stay Palolo, stay-go wit Obachan, but I not know da way. All da time I tinkin bout Obachan. She love me.

Den I start havin da bad dreams. Da faces dey start out like da faces, den dey gettin biggah and biggah. Dey gettin closah. Dey comin closah, still. I no can see da faces, dey so close. De mouths movin up and down. Dey comin closah. Dey all talkin, I no can understand, dey all shoutin at me. Den I wake up, I cryin. I no like go sleep no more.

First time, den, I tink, I say, I stay-go for school now.

Den, I waitin a little, tinkin, den I make it up good, talk to my mothah like dis.

I . . . go . . . to . . . school . . . now. Good-by, Mother.

I going make her happy, she stop shoutin.

Den my mothah, she say, dis girl, she so stupid, listen to da way she talkin, she talkin so slow, she like one idiot.

Den da haole man, my fathah, he say, I no tink she dumb, I tink she scaid, not used to you.

Den my mothah shout, I da girl's mothah, I know da right ting for her. And you no take her side. Den she turn to me and she say like dis:

I . . . am . . . going . . . to . . . school . . . now. Say that.

84

I scaid. I tink I get it right, I right, but maybe my mothah, she right, maybe I stupid. I say:

I ... am ... going ... to ... school ... now. Good-by.

Den da haole man, my fathah, he say, stop tellin da girl she dumb, she not so dumb, are you, Susan?

I try answer, but I no wanna make mistake. I no say nothing.

Den my mothah, she say, I know da girl, she *my* child, I know if da girl smart or dumb.

Da haole man and my mothah, dey always angry wit each othah.

Maybe I dumb, but my mothah, she wrong bout one ting. I not her child. I Obachan's.

Nex time I see Obachan, she come my mothah's house. I happy to see her. I run ovah. She pick me up. She hug me close.

I like say someting, I glad to see her, I love her, but my mothah close, I scaid.

I say, Obachan!

She hug me and kiss me, she ast me lots of questions, each time, I scaid, I not know which way to talk, my mothah so close, I answer her slow.

Den my mothah and Obachan, dey going in da next room, start talkin. Dey talkin in Japanese and when Obachan talk, it get so I no understand da Japanese so good any more eithah.

Maybe Obachan forgettin how to talk, too. Maybe da shoutin makin her forget.

No one understand.

I understand when dey talkin English.

I hear dem talkin English, den Japanese, den English.

Obachan, say, now she talkin funny, haltin, you make da girl scaid.

My mothah get angry.

I not makin da child scaid. I helpin da child. Da child dumb.

Den Obachan, she get angry, she say, you no dare say dat

bout dat girl in dere, dat girl not dumb, dat girl akamai! She da smartes girl in her class in school, you know dat? You know dat?

Den my mothah shut up, but she angry. She say, you shounta let her speak dat pidgin.

Den Obachan say, she get use speakin differen, dis not da mainland here! People gotta understand each othah. You gettin high and mighty since you gone to da mainland! Dat girl, she akamai. She already read good English, she speakin what da people around her speakin so dey can understand.

Den my mothah, she say, I no wan her speakin to da kine people who understand dat pidgin.

Obachan say, den you not wan her speakin to da people of dis island. Dis island her home. Dis island your home, too. Da island been good to us. You not know. You nevah work in sugar cane!

Den my mothah not know what to say, she shout, I know what's best, I her mothah!

And I her Obachan. I raise da girl. Give her plenty love. You going be sorry for da way you treatin her. You no shout like dat at da child. Not dis child. I nevah shout at you like you shout at dis child. You no shout at Carol like you shout at dis child.

I her mothah!

Yes, you her mothah, you act like her mothah. . . . And you bettah tell her da truth.

My mothah, she get angrier, she stand up, she point her fingah.

But Obachan, she strong, she da only one not scaid of my mothah, she say, sit down now, you tell her da truth and you tell her now! You going be sorry if you wait to tell da girl da truth. You going be sorry for da way you treat dis girl.

Den dey talk Japanese. Dey get angry. Dey always angry wit each othah, but Obachan, she da only one not scaid of my mothah.

After her father's visit, Susan had moved. She and Gale—the black-haired girl with the Clara Bow mouth and cameo face; the girl that had smiled at her that day at the interview and helped her across the room by saying, you look terrific—they had become friends and had gotten a place together up on Wilhelmina Rise. Susan was glad to leave that place on Royal Hawaiian Avenue with its memory of the first lonely days waiting for the eye to heal, not knowing what she was going to do.

And Mickey had become friendly, too, although she seemed more friendly to Gale. But since Gale and Susan lived together . . .

Shortly after they had moved into the Wilhelmina Rise place, Mickey came in for a visit—Mickey used to live in Kalihi, back then, in a small white bungalow with her husband, Harry. Harry worked for United Airlines.

Mickey noticed the air plants on the window sill.

Susan, nice-lookin plants! Where'd you find dem?

Up on the Pali—I picked them.

Mickey had actually taken a step back, put both hands to her mouth. Oh! Susan! What choo do! Nevah move no plants, no stones, nothing! And nevah from dat spot! Don't choo know? Dat's a kahuna place, Susan! Put dem back! I'm not kiddin, Susan, put dem back!

Susan was surprised. At first, she'd thought Mickey was kidding. Just to be polite, Susan said, all right, Mickey, don't worry!

Mickey left a few minutes after that. And Susan forgot about the air plants; but a couple of days later, she looked at the air plants, snatched them all up, borrowed Gale's car, and drove back up to the Pali—where, with the wind funneling over the lonely rocky lookout, she placed them back as close as she could to where they'd been.

There was a sharp knock at the lua door. Susan?

Susan slid back the latch. Gale.

Hi there, fly-girl. Mickey said you were having a little trouble. How do you feel?

Okay . . . better.

You look pale. Here's your flight bag. Everything's quiet out here. We're going to start down for Maui in a few minutes.

Thanks, Gale. I'll be right out.

Susan closed the door, turned to the mirror, began applying eyeshadow and make-up, stopping momentarily to scratch at the burning in her palms, hold them up to the light, inspect them. Slight water blisters. Not noticeable, thank God. Nerves.

She had expected to fly for two or three years and then either have enough money to go to college or at least switch to Pan Am. But now she'd been a stewardess—it was already seven years, no money saved, no closer to college, though she had taken some courses at night, still flying endlessly from island to island.

All that time gone by. The apartment with Gale up on Wilhelmina Rise. Such a long time with Duke. Jack. And now Jack gone back to the mainland and no word . . . and still locked up in this aluminum tube, face made up, uniform pressed, shoes polished, waiting, waiting for something, something to change, move in her life.

Susan studied her make-up a moment longer, rubbed a little rouge into her cheeks, wiped some of it off, ready for the undertaker with make-up like that; she sighed, unlocked the door.

Mickey was already into the first announcement for Maui:

. . . in view is the town of Lahaina, Hawaii's first capital over a hundred years ago. Lahaina was also a center for the whaling industry, and had the oldest school west of the rocky mountains. Lahaina is presently a tourist town, along with the

multimillion-dollar resort called Kaanapali. We also have an excellent view of the west Maui mountains.

Maui is second largest in the Hawaiian chain. It has a population of approximately forty-five thousand, and its major industries are pineapple and sugar cane.

The passengers on both sides of the aisle were looking out of the windows, everything seemed quiet in the cabin. Mickey was back on the microphone:

We'll be landing shortly at the Kahului Airport. Please check to see that your seat belts are fastened and observe the No Smoking sign when it appears.

A moment later, Mickey walked down the aisle, looking from right to left, checking to see if the seat belts were fastened.

Susan smiled, thinking of Mickey: yeah, I check dere cocks!

Mickey turned, walked back to the buffet.

Ladies and gentlemen, the No Smoking sign has just been turned on; please extinguish all smoking materials. Mahalo.

Susan took an empty seat aft as the airplane began to shudder and bounce in its descent into the wind which swept Maui. The hard resistance of the landing gear, down.

Below, whitecaps. Surf breaking on the reefs. The water going from deep blue to lighter blue, then, turquoise in toward the shallows and beaches. The airplane bounced hard as they descended, flew over the beaches, still descending. Susan worked her jaw to loosen the pressure in her ears, descending, the ash-black lava, sugar cane bending in the wind, the shadow of the plane sliding across the lava and cane fields, the ground rising, taking on speed now, the green coming up, coming up, spreading out, the end of the runway, then the jolt of the landing gear touching down.

The pilot came on as they taxied toward the terminal:

Ladies and gentlemen, this is your captain. We have just landed at Kahului Airport. We have experienced a minor mechanical difficulty. There will be a very slight delay while we change aircraft and proceed on to Hilo. Mahalo.

In another moment, Mickey:

Please be sure to remember all hand baggage when you deplane. May we recommend that those passengers who are continuing on, step into the airport lounge while we are changing airplanes.

Susan tried to tune out the rest of the announcement:

. . . to the malahinis and the newcomers, we hope your stay will be a pleasant one; to the kamaainas, have a good day; to all . . .

Susan yanked the handle to unlock the aft door, cracked the door, pushed the button to extend the aft stairs. The ramp agent pulled up the handrails after him.

Howzit.

Okay. Howzit.

Susan took a deep breath of fresh air. Flowers. The smell of a recent shower drying on the hot runway. Aviation fuel. Burned tires.

She could smell the cigarette smoke in her uniform and hair; the close smell of passengers and liquor and perfume going out on the Maui trade wind. One of the baggage boys was trying to get a peek up her skirt.

She laughed. Ey! Howzit!

He smiled, embarrassed. Howzit!

The passengers were standing and separating loosely into two groups, one group slowly filtering forward, where Mickey and Gale were saying good-by to them, the others moving aft. Susan smiled at the first departing passengers.

Aloha, have a nice stay. . . .

Good-by now, enjoy your visit. . . .

She held her skirt down against the wind with one hand. Aloha....

Good-by now....

The cabin was emptying out. Suddenly, Susan looked down through the cabin. Which way was he getting off? Had he already gotten off? She looked at the backs of the passengers moving toward the forward door. Susan heard Mickey's voice, loud for an instant, one word she couldn't make out. . . . She felt her stomach tensing. She didn't see him.

Aloha....

Her palms moistened, started to burn, she rubbed them together, held down her skirt....

Good-by now, have a pleasant stay....

Her stewardess voice, sing-song melodious, somewhere out there, going out on the wind....

The last passengers were coming toward her. Would he even recognize her, what difference did it make anyway?

Aloha, please watch your step....

The last passenger.

Aloha....

She stood watching the last passenger heading down the aft stairs into the wind.

She looked down through the cabin. Only a few more moving forward.

Stupid to let herself get so upset. She sighed, leaned over the seat to pick up her flight bag.

The sound of a single seat belt snapping. She froze. She saw a man standing, his back to her.

She straightened up.

Maybe he would go out the forward door.

The wind gusted up the stairs, she held her skirt down, her heart pounding. Her palms burned. She stared down the stairs.

She waited.

He was coming toward her. He was carrying a briefcase. She realized she was holding her breath.

He was coming closer. Then he was next to her.

Susan felt herself starting to smile, hated herself, he was squeezing past her, he was so much shorter than she'd remembered, the back of his head over her, the gold Mason's ring on the white porcelain sink, the white lights overhead in her eyes, she still felt herself smiling, the way he kept her coming back, night after night, her legs up, his fingers in her, she could smile at him, serve him, endless, pointless, did he recognize her? She would just go on serving people, smiling, behind perfect make-up, a well-pressed uniform, shined shoes, walking on and on through this pressurized aluminum tube which had no beginning and no end and people would do what they wanted, say what they wanted, and no matter what they did, she would go on smiling, being sweet, being nice, with passengers saying, oh, what a darling girl, oh, I'd like to take you home with me. . . .

She heard her sing-song stewardess voice.

Aloha, enjoy your stay on Maui.

To think she had once cried, pleaded with him, please . . . I'm begging you. . . . Please . . . just do it. . . . I'll do anything. . .

He stepped past her and started down the stairs.

She turned away from the door. He stopped, turned slowly, looked back at her. He climbed back up the stairs.

He smiled. Don't I know you from somewhere?

She froze. Then smiled.

I'm afraid not.

He turned away. Then turned back once again.

Are you sure?

Yes, I'm sure.

She tried to smile again. Her heart was fluttering so she felt dizzy, her arms felt light, numb, and somehow bound to her body.

But I'm sure I know you from somewhere.

No, you have the wrong person.

Her flight bag was within reach. She would pick it up, turn, head up to the front.

He studied her face.

He was starting to smile. What was he doing? He was reaching toward . . .

This delicate little mole. . . .

He touched the mole above her lip.

She felt a heat go through her body, the cabin growing lighter, muffled, distant.

She felt herself convulse, felt her hand sting, heard something, saw him lose his balance, his hand go to his cheek, cover his face.

Heard her voice. Goddamn you! Don't you dare touch me! You fucking insect! Don't you dare touch me!

His hand was at his cheek.

She became aware of her own hand. She had slapped him. He stepped back, still holding his cheek.

He reached into his pocket and brought out a bright blue silk handkerchief. He wiped at his face. Looked at the handkerchief a moment.

She saw that she had spit on him.

He stepped back and spoke in a tight voice. You are going to regret this.

He turned and walked quickly down the stairs.

Then he was gone.

She stared down the empty stairs. She reached up. She looked at her hand. It drifted slowly up toward her face. She touched the mole with the tip of her finger.

She looked around the cabin. The cabin was empty.

She heard someone. Mickey?

Mickey stepped out of the buffet.

Mickey was walking toward her, a quizzical expression on her face.

I heard something back here. Swearing. A slap. Something. What happened?

Nothing.

I know I heard something.

No, I was just swearing at myself. I dropped my bag.

Mickey looked at her bag a moment. You sure?

Yes, I'm sure!

You look so pale. . . . Mickey shrugged. The quizzical look was replaced by a pinched expression—the strain of saying good-by to the passengers.

Susan stood very still. She looked down at her feet. She hadn't moved. After some time, she sat down, and stared down through the cabin. She reached over, dug out a cigarette, automatically checked out the window for the fuel truck and lit up. She smoked slowly. She felt very calm.

Ey! Come on, what choo doing sittin here, we gotta lay ovah, let's go in. You pale, you okay?

Susan nodded.

Well, what choo lookin at me dat way for? Come on! You really okay?

Susan nodded. I'm fine.

Mickey was talking about something, but Susan couldn't get herself to listen, make sense of it. Susan slipped off her shoes, reached under the table and rubbed her feet. In a minute, the waitress brought coffee and the Japanese tourists at the next table—the men freighted with cameras, several of the women in kimonos—looked over. A couple of them whispered something, smiled. Susan turned away.

Across the coffee shop, there was an older man buying coffee and Danish for several stews from another flight. Susan couldn't remember his name, but she'd once sat at the table herself. He was a stew bum. His trip was stews—which stews didn't matter. He would invite Susan and Gale to have a coffee with him between flights—order whatever you like. He never asked any of the girls out, he never objected to anything they said, he never seemed to want anything. He would just sit with a pleasant smile on his face surrounded by stewardesses and that was it, enough, whatever, for him. No more, no less. Susan could remember times when she and Gale had ordered two double, fresh-squeezed, orange juices, club sandwiches, side orders, salads, more, until there was no longer room enough on the table, and the waitress had to put the rest of the food on the next table, but still, no reactions from him. Finally, they got up to leave, not having taken a bite from one of the sandwiches, and the man just stood up, the pleasant smile still on his face, said good-by, and sat down again. Susan looked back, and he was still sitting at the table, the chairs askew, the table covered with plates of food and drinks; she had just shaken her head. Susan watched the stews as their drinks came. The stew bum wore the same pleasant smile.

There seemed to be a lot of noise and confusion, people crowding in, crowding out, loud talk at the surrounding tables. Now Mickey was saying, look at da tits on dat one! Da haole girls really get da tits!

A tall blonde in jeans and tank top, no bra, nipples prominent; her boy friend, sun-bleached beard, a surfboard wrapped in an unzipped sleeping bag outside the coffee shop.

Mickey shook her head. Look at da tits!

The Japanese men were looking, nudging each other nervously.

Mickey lowered her voice: you know, dey say da haole call girls can really clean up, da Japani men, dey get no tits like dat at home, dey come ovah here, dey go crazy for tits like dat wahine get, dey can make a mint wit dere tits!

Susan looked out the window. The Maui mountains.

Mickey took her gaze for disbelief.

Ey! Susan, I'm not kiddin! The Japani men go crazy, I tellin you, look at dem right here at dis table, dese guys fuckin wettin dere pants. . . .

Okay, Mickey, we get the idea.

Gale seemed to wake up and smile. Gale had either a slow

dreamy smile or a grin. Right now she had the slow dreamy smile.

That's what you should do, Susan. Go to New York, be a call girl. She grinned. The Oriental mystique. You've got it. No kidding, Mickey, take a trip to the mainland with this wahine and watch the haole men fall all over themselves. Cat lady! Gale made claws of her fingers, hissed. You should have seen them follow us in Europe. Gale mimicked, oh, my Oriental flower!

Mickey nodded. Hey, I seen it in Washington and San Francisco. We tryin to negotiate da contract and all da fuckahs hot for dis good-looking bitch! And da black ones! Ooh aah! Da big black popola, dey come walkin right up to her on da street—Mickey moving her shoulders in imitation of a cool black gait—dey walk right up close, hello, momma, where you headed, pretty babee?

No kidding, Susan, you could clean up in New York.

You like it so much, you do it Gale! That's your trip anyway! Oh, don't get so touchy, Susan!

I'm not touchy. I just think you might as well get paid, you give enough of it away. . . .

They stared at each other. Suddenly everyone laughed.

Ey, what happen to you on da way over, Susan?

Sick, that's all.

Gale and Mickey started talking about something, Gale was pulling a cassette tape recorder out of her flight bag, and Susan looked around the coffee shop again, sure she'd see Moon, but he wasn't around.

She touched the mole, lightly. It had just happened so fast. You are going to regret this.

She probably would, but she didn't give a shit, not any more. Yes, yes, she did. . . .

Susan thought for a moment. No one had been in the cabin, no one had seen it happen. It was her word against his.

Except, she knew, grievances with the airline never worked

that way. But still. And maybe he wouldn't do anything. What could he do? Complain, yes. Well, maybe he was bluffing, just trying to scare her. And if he did report her, she could always tell about his private little—

No, no, she couldn't.

She looked at Gale and Mickey at the table. God, they were irritating! What had changed? Had anything changed? Gale had been titillating herself about the call-girl thing as long as they had been flying together. Who had led a more sheltered life than Gale? Her father, good friends with one of the higher-ups in the Honolulu Police Force, had seen to it that a cop cruised by their place every night. It would just cruise past slowly. Gale always had a tear-gas pen in her purse, a present from Daddy. Gale's father seemed to know everyone on the police force, and so Gale had gotten used to doing anything and getting away with it—speeding, double parking, making a wrong turn, driving the wrong way up a one-way street. The minute the arresting cop saw her license, he would actually apologize. Gale would make a long face. Act contrite. The minute the cop drove away, she'd laugh: the asshole! There was something irritating to Susan about her—something girl-ish, lazy, impudent, no . . . insinuating, maybe that was it, about her walk, something so laconic in her speech.

Gale's father had a license to carry a gun—he ran his own business and would make several trips to the bank each week —either to deposit money or pick up his payroll. When Gale was still in middle school, he had been coming out of the bank and had seen a robbery in progress—a moke robbing a super-market. Without hesitation, he had shot it out with the moke. He had gone in, found the owner lying wounded on the floor, picked him up, and carried him outside in his arms to rush him to the hospital. A news photographer had caught Mr. Lopez, carrying the wounded man in his arms, the two of them splashed with blood. The picture had been on the front page of the *Star-Bulletin*. Somehow, that was it for Gale. Daddy would always be there to rush in. Lately, Gale had started going out with young boys—sixteen—and, for Susan, that was really getting off the wall.

Perhaps if there were a single part of Gale's body which epitomized her, it was her thighs. Gale was small-boned, even delicate, her neck, her throat, her collarbone, her wrists, but her thighs were heavy, soft, amorphous, even shapeless.

Mickey had brushed against her in the buffet. Reached around, grabbed Gale's ass. Look at dis ass! Like a babee, soft like poi!

Gale was fooling with the tape recorder, trying to get it to work, now breaking off to give her order to the waitress.

Susan, what are you going to have?

Nothing.

Come on. Have something.

No.

Gale shrugged.

Mickey ordered cottage cheese, debated having a salad as though her life depended on her decision. Flying fifteen years and still couldn't get past feeling the airline was going to dump her tomorrow: But choo not know! Dey no want no old slant-eye Buddha-heads like me!

It was pointless trying to talk to her.

Mickey hadn't changed either. She was tough. Had always been tough. Tough, angry, nervous. She had an irregular white scar on her upper arm—the sleeve covered it—a bite scar. Mickey was Japanese. Harry, Chinese. They had gone together during high school—before your time, Susan, you still lookin for your first pubic hair den! They'd married right out of high school, and neither Mickey's family or Harry's family had been happy. Japani marrying paké! Paké marrying fuckin Buddha-head? Nevah! Harry's sister, Iris, had never been able to stand Mickey; the feeling being mutual, they had just fought it out one day—Harry's sister leaving the bite mark on Mickey's arm, Mickey leaving a gash across Iris's eyelid—and the two of them had not spoken to each other since. Fifteen years! That was Mickey.

Susan thought of the way Mickey invited people over for dinner. Five courses! Cooking. Killing herself over the dinner so it would be just so. She set an elegant table. Flowers. Lovely dishes. Arrange the food. Make the food beautiful to look at. Everyone's mouths watering. The food on. She served each guest, almost ceremoniously. Next thing, Mickey would be telling shit jokes. The most innocuous conversational gambit turned into a shit monologue by Mickey, just as the first mouthfuls of food were being raised. Once Mickey and Harry had won free air-passes to Mexico at an Interline party. What luck! Two weeks in Mexico. What could be more harmless than asking Mickey if she'd had a good trip, how was Mexico?

Mickey sat up. Oh! How was Mexico? Disgusting! Filthy! Filthy people! Disgustin food! Harry got da shits! All da food contaminated! Flies everywhere! I go to da ladies room in dis restauran in Mexico City, I go sit on da john, I look down, dere's a fuckin turd in da toilet! Da Mexicans are filthy pigs, I'm tellin you!

Mickey now sitting up over the low black lacquer table, the guests pausing with their chopsticks raised, staring at Mickey, Mickey holding her palms a foot apart, da fucking turd was dis big, I swear to God, bigges fuckin turd I evah seen. . . .

Mickey looking at each of the guests in turn.

Dis fuckin big. I swear to God! Still, I gotta go to da bathroom, right? But I no wanta sit on da toilet in dere now, only toilet dey got in da filthy restauran, what am I gonna do? I wrap my hand in a handkerchief, reach ovah, I no touch nothing! I flush da toilet, but da turd so big it won't go down da toilet, catch sideways, catch every way, once I tink I got it, but it came back up, I just standin dere flushin and flushin, da fuckah no go down, finally, I get scaid da toilet going ovah-flow, I run out, Harry sittin dere at da table, I say, come on, Harry, let's get outta here, maybe dey tink I'm da one who do dat, Harry, he wanna stay, but finally we get da fuck outta dere.

Mickey shaking her head, still holding her hands apart.

Bigges fuckin turd!

And on and on.

Not a word about the churches, the pyramids, the university, just Mickey, having flown over two thousand miles, now standing in the ladies' room in Mexico City, trying to flush some poor turd which had staked its claim to be enshrined in Mickey's Shit Hall of Fame—while everyone sat watching five courses of Japanese food steaming, growing cold.

After Mickey and Harry had taken a conspicuous step up from Kalihi to Aina Haina, Mickey had become impossible. She would never be able to stop working. If she lost her job, there would go the house. So, even more fretting about her looks and weight. She even worried about her weight after three miscarriages. On the advice of the doctor, after the first miscarriage, she'd taken leave from flying for bed rest in the later months of her pregnancies—each day worrying about the money lost. Each time, the bed rest didn't help and she miscarried. Finally, the doctor prescribed birth-control pills and warned her not to try again, next time might be dangerous. She worried when she wasn't flying, worried when she was. Now, with the new house, Mickey would fly until they carried her out.

The waitress brought Gale's fried mahimahi, Mickey immediately reached across, cut off a corner, popped it into her mouth. Too greasy! Gale looked at her, then started eating quickly, tartar sauce gobbing at the corners of her mouth. The close odors of food, the noise in the coffee shop, it was all making Susan sick. She wanted to get up, get out, get away from the table, out of the coffee shop, but she was on the inside, she couldn't get out without pushing everyone back, pushing the table to one side, squeezing out. And now the waitress was putting down Mickey's goddamned cottage cheese. Susan sat. She looked at the tape recorder on the table beside Gale; there was a smear of tartar sauce on one of the buttons, but Gale was ignoring the tape recorder.

Gale. Mickey. Eating. The table a mess. Susan felt as though she had been sitting at this same table in this same coffee shop for years, forever—as though she had grown old at this table. She looked at Gale, her mouth full of food. Why didn't she wipe her mouth?

She remembered when Gale's face had been fresh, cameo delicate. Now, at times, more often than not, there were the traces of a double chin, a heaviness in the flesh of her cheeks. The corners of her dark eyes had become caught in a web of fine lines and her eyes covered over with a kind of glassiness, a sadness, a preoccupation—with what?—which seemed to be harder and harder for Gale to tear herself away from.

It had all been fun, once. They'd shared the house on Wilhelmina Rise, and though Gale had always been a slob, it hadn't bothered Susan. Not that much. They'd gone to Europe together on airline passes. Lots of trips to the mainland. Alaska. A short visit to South America. She'd always wanted to go to the Orient—to Japan—but she hadn't done that yet. Maybe soon. Susan felt afraid. What would Moon do? Maybe she'd never get to go now.

But it *had* been fun once. The fancy restaurants. Canlis. The Bistro. On their days off, shopping at Ala Moana, they would spend hours trying on make-up: Estée Lauder, Clinique, Charles of the Ritz, Germaine Monteil, Revlon. The perfumes: Maja, Norell, Joy, Givenchy, Chanel No. 19. And that stuff was a cinch to steal. It wasn't that bad to steal a small bottle—that stuff was way overpriced, and, anyway, the stores budgeted for petty theft, and it smelled so beautiful.

They would go to Carol and Mary's and try on the most expensive fashions. Halston, Anne Klein, Pierre Cardin; they would seduce the salesladies into exclaiming how beautiful they looked, how darling. . . . Bagatelle. Christian Dior. Valentino. Then one of them might steal a dress while the other kept the salesladies oohing and aahing. Well, they had it coming to them, all that phony flattery, just to sell their stupid dresses.

Later, they would get the dress home, maybe fight over who would wear it first, or make a grand gesture, no, you like it, you wear it, it looks good on you. The dress might be worn once or twice, then left to hang in the closet where it would finally just go out of fashion.

Just the other day, Susan had come across a box full of snapshots they'd taken of each other over the years. In them, the fashions invariably looked pretty ridiculous. The chic miniskirts were stupid and made no sense on the figure. Somehow, the expensive outfits all looked borrowed. There were some snapshots of them clowning, walking arm-in-arm down some street, waving, grinning—some street she didn't recognize. Snapshots of them in front of the old Wilhelmina Rise house. God, she had looked so young—so baby-faced. Her skin had looked better then. Maybe no one else noticed, but Susan knew.

More snapshots. One of Susan in a new dress, smiling, pretending to be waltzing with some invisible dance partner. She had a look of feigned bliss on her face, her eyes closed, her arms raised, one resting lightly on an imaginary shoulder, the other extending to hold the hand.

There were some snapshots Gale had taken of Duke and her. Duke was a copilot then. He didn't have the mustache either. He had drunk a lot then, too, but it hadn't started to show yet. That picture had been taken over on the Big Island—Hilo—on a short layover. Her arm was around Duke's waist, her cheek against his shoulder, he had his arm around her. She'd wanted nothing more than for Duke Hernandez to ask her to marry him. She'd been twenty . . . twenty-one. Which would make Duke . . . He'd been thirty-one, almost thirty-two; he had a wife—whom he said he couldn't stand—two kids; he'd asked her for a divorce. Mickey said, what choo want wit one old man like dat, he drink too much, I seen em drunk all da time, he been fuckin around on his wife for years. . . . Which would make Duke thirty-seven now. . . .

There were more snapshots. The uniforms changing every year or two. She remembered when they'd been new. The azure, the A-line skirts, the straw beret, still pretty military. New. Then old.

Then those mini-muus with flowers and bikini pants. Freebie beaver shots for all. Mickey had looked ridiculous. And Gale had had to lose a little over ten pounds. The passengers would make the same dumb jokes: ey, we got one X-rated flight today?

Then the knee-length dress, the slit up the side, the heavy necklace that was always flopping into passengers' drinks, that had been a bright idea of someone up in PR.

And after that? A full-length chang san with the Chinese collar, slit from ankle to mid-thigh, impossible to move in.

She discovered the box of snapshots a few days after Jack had gone back to the mainland and she'd had to move back in with Gale. She looked at the snapshots until she felt a kind of despair, shoveled them back into the box and walked outside, fighting a feeling of panic.

It had all been fun once. A dream. Some kind of dream.

Gale finished the mahimahi, looked at the plate, ate the pickle, sighed, wiped her mouth, sighed again. I'm still hungry, this is ridiculous. Began debating whether or not to have a hot-fudge sundae. Mickey shook her head. Oh! Should not, Gale. Should not!

Gale sighed. You think so?

Of course not!

Gale sighed. I know. She waved the waitress over and ordered the hot-fudge sundae. The sundae came, Mickey snatched the cherry, Gale looked at her, hey, I wanted that! And then began to eat quickly, her face close to the sundae, her upper lip darkening with fudge.

Gale held out a spoonful of sundae.

Have some, Susan.

Susan shook her head.

Come on.

Some fudge dripped on the table.

No thanks.

Gale ate the spoonful.

Well, I wish you'd stop looking at me that way.

I'm not looking at you any way.

What's the matter with you?

Nothing.

I'm going to start a diet next week.

Susan put her hands against the edge of the table.

Can you let me out?

Gale sighed. Can you wait till I finish?

Susan took a deep breath and sat back.

No, four or five years ago it hadn't been so bad—the house a mess, the sink full of dirty dishes, the trash bag spilling on the floor, coffee grounds flecking the sink, Gale's dirty underwear tangled beside the bed where she'd stepped out of it. When Gale's clothes got dirty, she would just start wearing Susan's. Once Gale had worn Susan's clothes and given her the crabs. That had been nice. She hadn't even known what the hell they were until Gale had come in and said with exaggerated contriteness—I've got something to tell you. . . . No matter how often Susan cleaned the place, Gale would leave a mess. Eventually, the house a total mess, Gale would just disappear and stay in her old room at her parent's in Manoa until she was sure Susan had cleaned it up.

It had been hard to tolerate, then. Impossible, now. Later, she had lived with Jack for two years in the beach house. There had been order in that house, no one would think of leaving a mess; Roy, who shared the house with them, never left a mess, any one of Roy's girls who would come, stay however long, joined in the spirit of the place and kept things clean.

She stared across the coffee shop. She couldn't understand it, but for some reason, she just couldn't see Jack's face today. She could feel him, his being gone. . . .

Sometimes, now, she would wake in the middle of the night, reach for him, feel the empty bed, not know where she was, feel panicked, start trying to piece together where she was, become aware of someone breathing, Gale? It was Gale, right? Of course it was Gale, but where were they, they were on Wilhelmina Rise . . . no, that was five years ago, wasn't it, yes, of course, she had lived with Jack, she was just sharing this apartment the last couple of months. . . . But then she would start to fight panic that none of it had been real, that she had just been lying in this same bed on Wilhelmina Rise and that time had been going by and she had been getting older, lying here in the dark. For years!

Sometimes Susan was awakened by Nathan. He would come to see Gale as he had five years ago. Now he was married to the haole girl, but he still came. Always in the middle of the night. And Gale always let him in, though she'd have sworn she wouldn't—that, too, was the same. Now, instead of a Triumph, Nathan had a white Mercedes sedan which, like the Triumph, he would not permit Gale to drive.

Susan would hear the Mercedes slowly winding up, around the curves of Sierra Heights, then stop. A light knock at the door. Then Gale stirring in her bed, getting up, the door opening.

Susan could hear them talking softly. Though Nathan was local Japanese, he spoke without a trace of an Island accent. It was some phony East Coast, vaguely English accent.

They would talk at the door and maybe Susan would hear Gale say several times, please, Nathan, I have to get up early. . . .

Then there was the creak of the bed springs across the room, the beginnings of soft, almost surprised gasps from Gale, turning to a kind of sobbing desperation which would build to a whimpering climax.

Susan would put the pillow over her head. Several times, it was too much and she got up and went out to sit on the cool grass, look up at the stars, clear and close from up on the heights, look down on the lights of Honolulu and Waikiki.

The next day, Gale's mouth would look soft, the circles under her eyes like bruises.

Across the coffee shop, a couple of stews were joining the girls already at the table, one was leaving, the stew bum, the pleasant vague smile still on his face, was raising his hand to signal the waitress.

Gale dampened a napkin in her water glass, dabbed at the fudge on her lips, looked out the window, sighed, then, nothing else left to do, she punched the button on the cassette.

It was a woman's voice—far away, dreamy, trancelike.

The three of them listened.

The voice went on, but Susan couldn't make much of it and asked.

She's a medium . . . lives up near Punchbowl. She's a Portuguee.

What's she talking about?

She asked for the names of ten people important to my life. She's talking about them. About their previous lives.

Ey! You give her my name?

I gave her your name, Susan's, Nathan's, my parents. . . .

You believe that stuff, Gale?

Gale nodded.

Susan sighed in disgust.

Since when?

I always have.

Yeah, almost. How much did you pay her for this?

Fifty dollars.

Fifty dollars! What about the money you owe me for the phone bill?

I'll pay you.

Fifty dollars . . . one-fifty for the encounter group . . . seventy-five for your shiatsu—

I'll pay you.

Susan listened to the voice. She sounds stoned.

Mickey was listening. What was I in my previous incarnation?

Gale smiled sweetly. A turd, Mickey.

Not funny! Mickey stabbed her middle finger at Gale. Not funny! You tink you Sigmon Frood?

Listen, she's coming to it.

The tape went on playing.

Will you turn that off!

Susan, I'll pay you, don't worry.

It's not that! It's just so stupid! An insult to a person's intelligence. Like my mother and her kahunas—

Ey! Don't joke about kahunas, Susan!

Susan, you ought to hear yours. It's not bad, really.

Gale advanced the tape. Stopped it. Started it.

Susan's hands were damp and burning. She punched the stop button.

I don't want to know!

It's not bad—good, as a matter of fact—don't be afraid, listen.

Gale punched the start button. Listen.

No! Why should I have to take your dumb trip?!

So touchy, Susan. Let me tell you what it says, judge for yourself, you were supposed to have been—

No! No means no! Cut it out!

Oh, she is so touchy.

Gale looked hurt.

What's the matter, Susan?

Mickey punched the start button.

Susan pushed against the table.

So touchy! Touchy all the time now.

I'm not touchy!

It's Jack, isn't it? Well, it's not my fault he went back to the mainland.

I'm not touchy. You two are carrying on like a couple of Aiea titas and I'm touchy!

Susan pushed at the table spilling the water. Let me out. Jesus! Between you and this airline!

She stood up, wobbled into a shoe, sat back down, wobbled into the other shoe, stabbed at the stop button.

And turn that thing off!

Excuse *me*!

Ey! Susan! Mickey stabbed her middle finger at her.

You always were a no-class tita, Mickey!

Mickey half-rose in her seat.

Sit down, Mickey! You don't want to lose your job, do you?

Fuck you!

Yeah, you'd probably like to, tita!

Outside, she walked down to the lower level of the terminal, sat. Hawaiian music played over the p.a. periodically interrupted by the announcement of arrivals and departures.

She reached into her flight bag, got out a notebook, wrote:

Dear Jack,

She stared out at the runway, looked at the pad.

Dear Jack,

She wrote:

Here on short lay-over in Maui. Strange day. Started with a man I haven't seen for years getting on the flight. Horrible man bringing up things I haven't thought of for years. Jack,

I've wasted my life. Ruined it. It's a waste. A nothing. Jack, you're the one part . . .

She stared at that, then crossed it out.

Jack, I'm in trouble now. I've done something I've never done before.

She crossed that out. Wrote:

I'm not glad I hit him, but at least I had it left in me to hit him. . . . Jack, maybe it wouldn't have happened if you were still here with me.

She crossed that out, too.
She started a new letter.

Dear Jack,
I think about you all the time.

She slammed the notebook shut, put her head in her hands, held her head tight.

The Hawaiian music. The voice interrupting. Arrivals. Departures.

A DC-9 took off, shaking the terminal.

It must have been something about her love—her kind of love—that had driven him away. Maybe something desperate. Had he sensed something desperate? Was there something desperate in her?

She knew there was something missing in her, hollow, empty, and she had been trying to fill it with his love, and he'd known and she hadn't been able to hide it. She wasn't whole, wasn't aggressive, not like the haole women. Even their fucking tits were bigger!

She lit a cigarette.

She just wasn't good enough. She didn't know why, but she just wasn't.

Even her own mother wasn't good enough. Wasn't that what

they were talking about—just her father and his mother when she had come out for a visit. A big blond woman from Georgia. Bleached blond.

Susan had been in the next room, and the big bleached blond—a bleached-blond grandmother!—kept saying, she's just not up to you, I've always told you this about Ruth . . . and you *know* what I am talking about. . . .

That's the way they felt.

She opened her notebook again. Suddenly she was angry. She would write it. The truth.

Dear Jack,

She would write him the truth, is it because I'm Oriental, is that what it is, really? You can tell me the truth. I wouldn't want you to feel guilty.

She rubbed her hands together, the slight blisters in her palms. She would write it. But had she loved him for the right reasons? Or because he was haole? From the mainland? If she really loved him, why couldn't she remember what he looked like, today?

Never, never give a man that until you have these on your finger.

The diamond.

Wrong, she thought, she's wrong!

. . . never give a man . . .

Wrong!

Then why hadn't he written?

Oh, what's the big fucking deal, she said out loud, let him go. . . .

She listened to the Hawaiian music. She knew the song. What were the words? One of Don Ho's . . .

Let him go, he will never write, he's gone, I'm just a stewardess, a dumb stewardess, that's why I've stayed a stewardess so long, because I'm dumb, why should he care about a dumb stewardess, that's all I can do, serve people, smile, I'm married to a DC-9, why should he care? I never went to college, I was never good enough. She reached up and touched the mole.

The music was interrupted to announce the arrival of a flight.

There was something wrong with her, she knew it. She'd had opportunities and she hadn't taken even a single one. . . .

It was Moon . . . his getting on the plane . . . he'd brought it all with him. . . . She would regret it.

But she'd had some chances.

After she'd been flying a year, Miss Pahoa called her into her office one afternoon.

Susan couldn't think of anything she had done. Miss Pahoa looked at her and smiled.

Susan looked nervously around the office. The model of a DC-6 on the desk. The picture of Miss Pahoa, stewardess class, 1949.

Miss Pahoa came out from behind the desk. Walked slowly around Susan. Looked her up and down.

Susan noticed a smudge on her shoe. Her hair and make-up, a mess.

What had she done?

Finally, Miss Pahoa said, do you know what I think?

Susan shook her head. No, but if you'll let me know what it is, I'll try to explain. . . .

There's nothing to explain. I knew you'd be the right girl to represent the airline and you are.

Oh, no, Miss Pahoa, no I'm not.

She knew she wasn't the right girl, there was something about her Miss Pahoa wasn't seeing.

Miss Pahoa shook her head. Why shouldn't you be the right girl? I've been a training stewardess for over fifteen years. I know when someone's right and when they're not right. You're right. You're tall, you carry yourself beautifully, you have the best of the island looks. . . .

Susan protested, but Miss Pahoa went ahead with the

photographers and PR men. Calendars. Newspaper and tv spots. Putting together a schedule of luncheons, promotional tours, trips to the mainland.

Just before the start of the campaign, Susan returned to the office, heavily made up. Miss Pahoa smiled, Susan stood in front of her desk, then suddenly said, I can't do it.

She'd tried to explain. Miss Pahoa sat her down, tried to calm her down, even asked her if she was pregnant, but all Susan could remember was her saying—it was like someone else had taken control—I can't do it, I'm not her, not that girl, not that girl, I'm not good, you don't really see what's inside of me?

Miss Pahoa said, tell me, I want to know, what is inside of you, Susan?

But all she was able to say was, I'm not good, not good. . . .

Then she cried and Miss Pahoa put her arm around her and said, all right, Susan, all right. I think you're fine, but all right, we'll find someone else.

At the door, Susan hesitated. She wanted to know if Miss Pahoa was angry.

Ask me to do anything for you and I will, Miss Pahoa. . . .

I know, Susan . . . it's all right. . . .

She'd started out the door.

Susan?

Yes.

Come in and close the door a minute.

She stepped back into the room.

Will you do something . . . not for me . . . for yourself?

Yes, what?

Will you consider . . . just think about it . . . seeing a psychiatrist? Don't give me an answer. Just think about it.

Yes. Yes, I will. Thank you.

And remembering now, she realized she'd had an even earlier chance—right back in the beginning. A couple of men on one of the flights kept watching her. They tried to give her a business card, but she didn't accept it. She was getting used to this from men, it was getting easier to handle. Just a firm, distant thank you, but I'm busy. As Miss Pahoa had said, friendly, but distant. It worked most of the time.

Several days after that flight, Miss Pahoa called her in. Some men had come to see her about Susan. They'd tried to give her a card, but . . .

I know, Miss Pahoa, I didn't take it.

And I can't tell you how happy I am with you, Susan. I can't watch you girls twenty-four hours a day. . . . I just knew I could count on you, you're one of my girls, but . . .

But these men were different. They were making a film called *The Sand Pebbles* and they were looking for a girl—a Eurasian girl. . . .

And they want you to try out, Susan. They think you'd be perfect. They'll fly you to the mainland, pay your expenses, they just want to see how you'd look on film. . . .

Susan was vague. But Miss Pahoa kept after her. Susan, what a chance for you! I'd be sorry to lose you, but . . . She kept after her for days. She offered to go with Susan. Reassured her that the men were fine. All Susan had to do was say yes, give it a try, what was there to lose?

Days and days went by. Time and again Susan walked to the phone. She would lift the phone, dial Miss Pahoa. . . . All she had to do was say yes. She would dial her number, then suddenly hang up. All she had to do was say yes. She tried. She wanted to . . .

Sometime later Susan came across one of the Polynesian Airlines calendars that had never been used. She studied it.

Her face superimposed across the island chain, the ocean. Her long hair rising in the wind. Her face tipped up toward the sun, a smile on her face, the months below. A white plumeria blossom in her hair.

After finding the calendar, she cut her hair. It had come

almost to her waist. She cut it to collar-length, thought of saving the hair, then threw it in the trash.

The plumeria . . . The photographer placing the plumeria in her hair, its thick sweet odor coming down out of her hair, the plumeria flowers overhead, the tree spreading out its branches, the flowers high overhead against the blue sky, Obachan now close to the grave, the sweet smell of the plumerias against the blue sky, playing under the tree, Obachan, quiet in front of the stone, and the other stones in the yard rising up the hillside, the sweet green grass, the flowers and the flowering plumeria spreading out, its thick sweetness—sickening in the heat, Obachan still in front of the grave, quiet, arms at her side, hair in a tight bun, the words, the picture on the gravestone, the feeling of the letters, fitting her finger into the letters in the stone, the girl in the picture, thick black hair, smiling, in a room right below the grass, playing under the plumeria tree, in and out among the gravestones, the other faces on the stones, now Obachan's arms no longer at her side, but lifted, opened, the way she does before picking me up, her arms raised, spread, now suddenly bending forward, Obachan making strange noises, howling, her hair suddenly loose, falling over her shoulders, down her back, bending forward again, throwing her arms up in the air, playing under the plumeria tree, climbing up into the branches, the sweet white flowers, the flowers in her hair, Obachan's face starting to shine, tears, her eyes rolling, bending at the waist, opening her arms, her hair covering her face, hanging forward and sweeping the ground, running among the stones, Obachan's howling coming through the stones, Obachan again, raising her arms, bending at the waist, Obachan letting out a scream, falling on her knees, now lying on the ground, sobbing, hair spread on the grass, the picture of the girl on the grave, still staring straight ahead, still smiling, Obachan sobbing, talking down into the ground, grass between her fingers . . .

. . . leaving, Obachan's hair bound up tight, quiet, dirt under her fingernails, the car, Uncle William in the front seat, quiet behind the wheel, the car winding down the road, the eucalyptus trees by the road, then the bridge, the bridge is coming, the car is going on the bridge, the car is on the bridge and the bridge starts to hum, to sing the bridge song, the vibrations in the car, in the stomach, the bridge-song vibrations, then the vibrations stopping, the eucalyptus trees behind, the sky empty and blue, the fields of pineapple. . . .

Forgetting, almost forgotten, the car, Uncle William, the winding road, the sky empty, fields of pineapple, then something coming, the bridge coming, the bridge starting to hum, the bridge song, the vibrations in the stomach. . . .

The girl in the picture, the sweet smell of the plumeria tree, Obachan quiet, hair in a tight bun, Obachan opening her arms, bending at the waist, starting to howl, the girl smiling, the girl always smiles, Obachan talking to the girl, the girl not answering, the girl only smiles, why doesn't she answer Obachan, something wrong with the girl, something wrong with Obachan, her hair over her face, tears, lying on the ground, get up, something wrong with Obachan. . . .

Dirt under her fingernails, her dress smelling of grass, the bridge starting to sing, the vibrations in the stomach, something wrong . . .

. . . almost forgotten, the empty part of the sky, the vibrations, something wrong, the girl always smiling, the smell of plumeria, and now, in school, able to read the letters:

J—A—N—E   H—O—N—D—O

And numbers:

1928–1944

And trying to read the other letters on the stone and finally asking and Obachan saying, they no teach you dat in school, 'as Japanese script, you and I, we going on speakin Japanese togethah like dis cause 'as da language I know best, I can tell you best I love you, but in school you learn to write English.

Still, trying to read the other letters on the stone, but they didn't teach Japanese reading and writing in school. They didn't teach pidgin, either. Pidgin was like breathing.

Each morning Obachan pluck one banana leaf from da garden, da front garden full of so many differen tings, get da papaya, bananas, orchids, da maidenhair fern, crocus, ti plants, fern, da jade plants, elephant ear, hibiscus, get da aloe plant; when I get one burn, Obachan run quick for da aloe plant, break one leaf, break em open, rub da sap on da burn, she say nevah get one blister dis way, say, be more careful nex time.

When Obachan get da banana leaf from da garden, she run da hot iron ovah da banana leaf, she say, dat way da banana leaf make da iron run nice and smooth ovah my dress. She press my dress good. She get everyting nice we need in da front garden—da aloe, da banana leaf—get da vegetables for dinnah in da back garden. Can see da back garden from da front garden, look right undah da house, da house up on stilts so da termites no eat up da house.

When she get da dress press good, she put da coins for my lunch in da handkerchief, pin da handkerchief to da waist of my dress, den she walk me by da hand through da streets to da bridge where da watah runnin fast. She kiss me dere on da bridge and den I walk da rest of da way alone.

One day it rain so much I no go to school cause when we get to da bridge, da watah rise ovah da bridge. I ast her, how come da watah get so red and she say, dat da mud from da mountains, rain been comin down outta da mountain.

I no go to da school when da watah ovah da bridge.

Dat jus one day or two. Most days I go ovah da bridge and go to school where da teachers always say to me, Susan, how nice you look, how good you dressed; dey tell me how lucky I am have one obachan who dress me so nice and love me good. Dey teach me in school da word for obachan is grandmothah in English. . . . All da teachers tell Obachan how smart I am, how I da best in everyting I do, I da smartes. I make Obachan love me, she proud, she hug and kiss me.

When I home from school, I hear da manapua man. I hear em callin, manapua! Manapua!

Oh, jus da sound make my mouth watah.

I run outside. He in da street. Kids around em.

He one old paké, get one pole on his shoulders, get one bucket each end.

Manapua stay inside.

He take em outta da buckets, dey always hot, like magic in da buckets.

I bite into em—da white dumpling, inside, get pork or black bean.

Eat em up.

Poor old manapua man. He so old. Feel sorry for em.

Sunday, I no go to school, Sunday special day, Obachan, she pluck da banana leaf, run da hot iron over da leaf, den she take out my special dress from da trunk and she press da dress slow slow slow. Press da dress good. Da dress my kimono. Obachan, she made da dress herself—get da white cranes on da red silk, get one blue obi for da waist, get da long sleeves. We put em on, den Obachan, she look at me, she say you look like one rainbow.

When I dressed good in da kimono, we go to the Makiki Christian Church, where we pray. Obachan say da church look like one Japanese palace. Da church big, painted all white. Like da cranes.

Afterward, Obachan like to go play cards wit da ladies all like Obachan. Obasan and me, we leave em play cards, Obasan take my hand and we walk some place special—maybe da market. Buy me one treat. Sometimes, da people see me in da kimono, dey ast me stop, dey like take da picture. Den I put out my arms so dey can see da long sleeves good. I smile. One time we stop at Obasan's shop, all full of da broken shoes, smell good, da glue and leathah, Obasan fix dem, but I no like to play wit dem on Sunday in da kimono, I no like mess da kimono up.

Bumbye we go back to da church and get Obachan, she pau play cards, we go home, walk ovah da bridge, and Obachan take da kimono off, fold em up good and put em back in da trunk, I gotta wait one whole week before I get to wear it again.

One Sunday, aftah church, we go some place. Dere one man wit one big box up on legs. Obachan tell me, dat's da camera, da man gonna take one picture of you and me.

Den we get in front of da camera. I dressed good in da kimono. Look like one rainbow.

Obachan and me, we stand togethah and da man take our picture. When da picture come, we standin dere, smilin. Obachan got her arm around me.

Everyting Obachan do, she do good.

The p.a. system called out another departure. Susan smoked a cigarette and stared at the west Maui mountains, at paper lifting and floating in the wind on the runway. She rubbed the palms of her hands together, they burned, the water blisters on her palms were barely noticeable, but knowing they were there repelled Susan.

She thought of how on weekends when she'd gotten older she would go to visit Obachan—take the bus over to her two-room apartment, then just sit with her. By then, Obachan had moved from Palolo, was living alone down in Kalihi; Obasan—the shoemaker—they had parted ways. She hadn't seen him any more, although once she remembered he came to the back door and stood outside—Obachan wouldn't let him in, though he had brought some fish for her—and Susan went to the back door and looked at him and felt sorry for him standing out there. He had his fishing rod. He did not immediately recognize her, just bowed deferentially, until Obachan put aside whatever quarrel had parted them just long enough to say something to him very quickly in Japanese, and he got very excited, his eyes brightening, he smiled, and took Susan's hand in both of his, his hands were small—half the size of hers—and shapely, the palms and fingers were callused. He held her hand, nodding and smiling and repeating, Susan, Susan, Susan. . . . She looked at her hand in both of his and smiled and afterward she had looked at her own hands and wondered at their shape.

But aside from that time, Susan hadn't seen him any more and Obachan lived alone.

Then it seemed to happen all at once, Obachan grew old, was old—her face and her body. The bones came out through her wrists, her hands became bony, spotted, her neck curved and brittle—all at once.

Her black hair was suddenly gray, her hair had always been black, there were lines in her forehead, her face, which had been smooth, was suddenly wrinkled under the eyes and around the mouth, her mouth seemed pinched.

She had pains in her stomach. She disappeared into the hospital, they gave her tests in the hospital, released her.

Then she would sit in front of the tv, Susan beside her. Susan reading a magazine or book or doing homework while Obachan watched Oral Roberts. At the end of the program, Obachan often bowed her head and placed her hands on her stomach. Her lips would move, and Susan could see she was praying but tried to pretend she didn't see.

But the pain didn't go away, and Obachan went back in the hospital and this time when she came back out of the hospital, she looked thin and weak and walked slowly.

Then Obachan asked Susan to come stay with her for a week. The first morning, they got up long before sunrise and

Susan brought her a cup of tea and rubbed her feet and hands and massaged her legs—she seemed to be shrinking.

She helped Obachan out of bed—it was still dark—and they got in a taxi and rode through the cool darkness, the two of them quiet, together, in the back seat. They rode up to Aiea and got out at the Sumida Watercress Farm; it was still dark.

The taxi waited.

Susan helped Obachan out of the taxi, helped her down through the rows of watercress, the smell of water and earth coming up out of the dark; then Susan spread the burlap bag between the rows of watercress, helped Obachan get down, first slowly on one knee, then the other, and while Obachan prayed, Susan went off a little way, and prayed—prayed just to herself. Then the sky lightened, the dawn started to come, and as the sun started to rise, Obachan, on all fours, began to eat the tops of the watercress where they were wet with dew. Susan tried not to give in to her feelings as she watched Obachan, down on her hands and knees. She ate the tops of the watercress until the sun had evaporated the dew. Not long.

Then Susan helped Obachan back up, wiping the dirt off her hands and knees, helped her walk slowly back down the rows to the taxi—where the taxi driver quickly got out, opened the door, bowed his head slightly.

On the way back, Obachan squeezed Susan's hand, tried to smile, and said, no tell your mothah—she no understand. They did this every morning at exactly the same time and in exactly the same way for seven days.

After seven days, the cancer was supposed to be cured, but Obachan went back into the hospital again.

Susan went to visit her there after school and sat by her bed and held her hand. Obachan's hand grew thin in Susan's hand, they gave her drugs to kill the pain, but still the pain stayed in her stomach, wouldn't go away, the pain got worse, cancer, Obachan held her stomach and stared at the ceiling, her lips moving, and when she came back from where she was, she tried to smile at Susan, and Susan tried to smile back. Once Obachan reached over and gently took the tip of Susan's nose between her thin fingers and smoothed it out and smiled at Susan; once, in a great sweat, in pain, Susan saw Obachan's face, her eyes, sharpen into a look of terror and grief and heard her let out a cry like the one she had heard in the graveyard, and Susan knew she had seen the look of pain which she had never seen as Obachan lay face-down on the grave. Obachan was sweating and holding her stomach and Susan had turned her face away and looked outside the window where the sky was blue and where she could see doves and pigeons floating down into the palm fronds below.

Sitting by the bed, watching her writhe, Susan remembered a story Obachan had once told her, how when she had been a girl in Japan, a little girl small as you, Susan, I was your age, a snake, followin me, he followin me through da streets, I running, da snake gainin on me, I could not get away, and den someone threw open one window and yell down to me, zigzag! Zigzag! Dat's what I done, I zigzag, I get away.

Each day, Susan came back and it seemed Obachan was getting smaller and smaller in the bed, as though the bed were slowly starting to swallow her.

Once Obachan looked at her and recognized her, Susan, she whispered, dey will be sorry for what dey done to you.

Susan laid her head down next to Obachan's on the pillow, Obachan no longer smelled the same, of flowers, the garden, Susan lay there for a long time, her head on the pillow next to Obachan, Obachan's eyes unfocused in pain and lost somewhere, she looked into Obachan's eyes and whispered, please Obachan, don't go, don't go away, please don't leave me.

It was the same as Susan had worn, a kimono, so many years ago, only this time, instead of red with the white cranes, it was many colors, it had been Obachan's wedding kimono.

Susan looked at Obachan in the coffin—like one rainbow—
then turned away.

The sky empty, fields of pineapple, then the vibrations from
the bridge beneath the car and the feeling in the stomach, her
father driving, her mother staring straight ahead.

The grass torn up, the hole, the plumeria tree in blossom, the
smell of the flowers of the plumeria tree.

Uncle William, not much different than she'd remembered
him driving the car, now standing back a distance from everyone, alone. Susan looking at him and he nodding, slightly, just
once, at her.

No one crying.

Then her mother, stepping back from the grave, turning,
looking over her shoulder at the stone, reading the stone for a
moment and looking down at the picture, Jane Hondo.

The smell of plumeria and then Susan lingering a moment
by the open grave, then standing by the stone and looking
down at the stone and picture, running her fingertip along the
grooves. . . .

The stone so high above, Obachan, hair in a tight bun . . .

Susan looked at the grave-picture of Obachan resting on the
wreath. Just her head and shoulders. She remembered the day
they had gone to have the picture taken. She'd been standing
right next to Obachan in her kimono. Like one rainbow. Sunday. After church, they'd stood in front of the camera together,
Obachan's arm around her. Now it was just Obachan in the
picture.

The gravediggers were filling in the grave, people straggling
away down the hill, looking up the hill through the stones. . . .

Playing among the gravestones, the smell of plumeria, walking back to the car, the earth under her fingernails. . . .

The thud of shovelfuls of earth falling into the grave . . .

Susan reached out and touched the picture of Obachan.

Obachan, she whispered, I wish I were with you.

Susan walking back to the car, and the car starting to wind down the road, the radio on, the vibrations in her stomach, the bridge, her mother turning to look out the window, eyes wild, lips moving silently, Susan becoming aware the radio was on loud, she looked at her father, he would turn it off, who had turned it on? She still felt Obachan's frail hand holding on to hers, he drove on, the shadows from the towering eucalyptus trees, then, then the sky opening, blue and empty, the pineapple fields, she couldn't ask, he would turn it down, the Beachboys, he would turn it down, she stared out the window into the empty blue sky, she couldn't speak, she couldn't cry, she stared out the window into the blue sky, her mother's lips were moving silently, it was loud, she couldn't cry.

Susan had been a stewardess two, three? years it had been the year of the eruptions on the Big Island, yes, they'd been phasing out the Convairs and bringing in DC-9s, one by one, and yes, that had been the year—no, not sure of the year, but the time when she'd done a lot of ferry flights; Mickey, Gale, she, they would do them as a lark, though Mickey would always bitch.

Always, it would be the same routine. They left Honolulu for Hilo at 2:00 a.m., seats folded down, freight lashed in place—fresh bread, the early edition of the paper, on occasion, a corpse. In Hilo by 2:30, they drove to the hotel in a rented car; each pilot always got a room to himself; the girls shared. First thing in the morning, they flew out with passengers.

When they were in their room at the hotel—and all other times thereafter—Mickey brought out holy water from the Japanese temple in Honolulu, ti—tea leaves—and Hawaiian salt.

In the hotel room, Mickey sprinkled the Hawaiian salt and holy water in all of the corners and around her bed, the doorways and the windows. Then she put the ti leaves on the floor around her bed. Even then she was scared.

In her long nightdress, sitting in bed, knees drawn up to her chin, she looked around the room and said, Leilani saw a ghost in here, I don't like it. She picked up the looks on Gale's and Susan's faces. Really! I don't! Go ahead, make fun! You know dis da path to da sea! You know it! Leilani saw da ghost!

Mickey went on like that, sitting in her bed surrounded by ti, the rug still stained with the holy water and sprinkles of salt.

The hotel had been built on one of the paths to the sea, everyone knew that—they'd even done a story in *The Advertiser* about it, and very few locals would have stayed in the hotel, no one but tourists. Everyone knew the paths to the sea ran from the mountains to the ocean, and were to be left open so the dead could walk to the ocean during the night and then back up to the mountains again. Those who knew said the dead moved in a ball of fire and if they saw you before you saw them, you would die.

Mickey sat in the bed surrounded by ti and looked around the room.

Gale said, if you're so scared, why stay here? I mean if you really believe it. I'm not knocking it, but why stay here?

Mickey said, airline pays! You tink I gonna pay my own hotel room? Only dis dumb airline would keep rooms in one hotel like dis! And she looked around the room at the salt and holy water sprinkled on the floor.

Gale said in a flat voice, you know, Mickey, you're just like a paké, tight, Harry must be getting to you. Really, you're very Chinese.

Betcha ass!

Tight and superstitious.

That got Mickey excited and started all over again. Not superstitious! I just no gonna fuck wit da spirits.

Gale laughed and Mickey saw she couldn't explain, and Mickey, Gale and Susan knew, was poor at taking a joke, took everything personally; she cursed, hey, fuck you, and called Gale a banana, which only made Gale laugh more, so then Mickey called Gale a haole, Gale went on laughing, and Mickey said, no, no, not a haole, you'd like that too much, you jus one chop-suey fucked hapa-haole bitch!

That was one of the dividends of getting Mickey mad, she swore so nicely.

Then they laughed and went to bed, one in Mickey's sanctified room, the other in the room adjoining. They talked through the open door.

Gale shouted, oh, Mickey, look! A ghost! At the window!

Once Mickey had almost been asleep when she screamed and turned on a light, but there was nothing.

Mickey slept fitfully, moaning out the name of her husband, Harry, Harry, ooh, Harry, or, at times, talking quickly in Japanese.

If Gale and Susan were still up talking, they stopped and listened, and Gale answered Mickey, yes, Mickey, this is Harry, oh, Mickey, I love you, even though you are a tight, superstitious Buddha-head!

Then Gale and Susan went on talking until one of them didn't answer because she had fallen asleep.

Between their routinely late arrival in Hilo, Mickey's superstitions, and Gale's and Susan's clowning, they could usually depend on something weird happening to liven things up.

Coming into Hilo, 2:30 a.m., they flew over the eruptions, seventeen straight miles of lava and magma exploding in fountains, sending molten rivers down to meet the ocean and raise columns of steam that were visible only in daylight; in the dark, the pilot laid the DC-9 into a steep bank, laid it over on its side, darkening the cabin, the glowing magma light rising closer and closer, filling the windows, flickering on the dark bulkheads, and the plane shook, rose and fell, slamming in the superheated air. Silent, they pressed their faces to the windows and almost always, Mickey said—Pele, see her hair—and point into the magma.

Most of the pilots loved the new DC-9s, said they could outperform anything that had ever flown in World War II, and, sometimes, ferrying without passengers, took the opportunity to prove it. Dawn. They climbed steeply, Haleakala rising out of the ocean ahead, stars fading, the horizon lightening, pale gold, the trade-wind clouds turning purple, tops red; the pilots pointed the DC-9 up to where the sky was still deep blue and several stars were still shining, and then, leveled off, abruptly, and dove. Everything—pillows, books, anything not strapped down—went weightless and floated for about ten seconds. The first time it happened to Gale, she simply rose off the floor, pillows and books bumping around her, rose between the seats in the aisle, her eyes widened, she looked down, and suddenly, said, oh, oh, OH! The sun was coming up, the cabin was filled with sunlight, and Gale just floated above Susan and Mickey, oh, oh, oh . . .

As soon as they leveled off, Gale shouted up to the pilots, again, again! AGAIN!

They were looking aft through the cabin door. They were laughing.

Mickey shouted, no, no! I gonna report choo!

Susan unfastened her safety belt.

Susan! You crazy. Gale! Make em stop it!

Again, they climbed and dove, Gale and Susan floating together, Gale going, oh, oh, Susan laughing, Gale eyes widening, her face getting a strange look, and suddenly gasping, I think I'm going to come! Oh, OH!

Mickey, sitting, her face frozen, fingers dug into the armrests, Gale floating over, what have we here? A superstitious buddha-head? What's she doing strapped in?

Susan laughing, waiting for her pension.

Yeah, I wanna live to get it, too!

Gale? Gale? Susan turned her head on the pillow, listened, looked over at the doorway. She could see a strip of ti in the doorway to the next room. She could hear Mickey groaning in her sleep. Gale? Gale was silent, too. Sleeping.

Susan looked at the empty bed next to her, closed her eyes, dozed, across the room the curtain billowed, Gale? a pale light filled the curtain, drifted across the room, Susan watched the light drifting toward her, toward the foot of her bed, she felt a chill pass over her feet and rise up her legs, rise through her body, she tried to move her feet, her lips, but she felt unable to move, far away, she heard a phone ringing, the phone on the dresser, the curtain billowed, she was cold, there was a pale white light in the room, she felt herself walking, floating over the floor, she could not feel her feet touch the floor, the phone got louder, she stood over the phone, it went on ringing, she looked down into the dark coil of plastic, she did not want to lift the phone, the receiver was in her hand, the receiver was cold, Susan lifted it to her ear, someone was talking, asking her, Susan, something, Susan listened, she couldn't understand, it was another language, she kept listening, it was far away, but coming closer, then she heard her name, Susan, clearly, Susan, why you no cry for me, Susan, why you no cry for me, Susan. . . .

Obachan, oh, Obachan, your voice is so cold.

Why you no cry for me?

Obachan, your voice is so far away, where are you?

Why you no cry for me?

Obachan, oh, Obachan, when you went away from me like dat, dere was nothing left, you no want me no more, Obachan, da kimono, Obachan, do you have da kimono?

Susan, why you no cry for me?

Obachan, nothing left no more.

Susan, you no cry for me, why you no cry for me, Susan . . . ?

Obachan!

Susan, you no—

The voice tangled and started talking in another language, the words grew louder, a noise in the doorway, she's in a gown, stamping her feet and cursing, grabbing Susan, No! Let me Go! slapping her face, Me! It's me!

Louder, Mickey shouting, me! Mickey! Ghost had you! Me!

She felt Mickey slapping her and then heard herself sobbing and Mickey holding her, Susan, ghost had you, first I hear da phone ringin and ringin, den I heard your voice, so strange! I heard da sobbin, thought I was dreamin, nevah heard no one sob like dat, I come to da door, you standin, da phone in one hand, your eyes were open, I call you, you no hear, you no see, your eyes, da whites showin, you talkin Japanese, you talkin Japanese, I call you again, you still no answer, I see da whites of your eyes, den I know da ghost get you, I shout loud, I ast my neighbor, he's Hawaiian, hey, it's okay, now Susan, we going across da ti in here, dis room safe, I ast him, whatsa bes ting to do when you see one ghost, he said, stamp your feet and shout da Hawaiian curses at da ghost, oh, Susan, no cry like dat, you're breakin my heart hear you cry like dat, Mickey rocked her, okay, okay, now, Susan. . . .

Gale and Mickey pushed the two beds together and they took turns sitting up with Susan.

In the morning, before they checked out for their flight, they asked the manager of the hotel to check the switchboard for calls during the night, but the switchboard operator had nothing for them.

Susan? Where've you been, Mickey and I have been looking for you? The new plane is ready for boarding.

You've been looking for her, I haven't.

Didn't you hear the call for Hilo?

No, did they call us?

Yeah, come on.

Mickey was sulking. Being cold.

Oh, thanks, Really, Susan stood up, I'm sorry about what I said in there before.

Oh, that's okay, Susan.

Mickey didn't say anything. Mickey, I'm sorry.

Mickey stared straight ahead. This kind of thing could go on for months with Mickey and Susan wasn't up for it. Mickey, it was stupid of me, really, I'm telling you, I'm sorry, okay?

Come on, we gonna be late.

Well, I am, Mickey. I'm sorry.

Okay, Susan, okay, let's go, we all gonna be late, you know you shouldn't lose your temper like dat. . . .

Now Mickey would lecture, and Susan knew she'd be forgiven if she could stay contrite during the lecture, nod agreement, I know Mickey, and so on.

Gale said in a low voice, uh, oh, the pastry pilot, let's go.

But the pastry pilot was on them.

Hi, girls. Mickey . . . Susan, hi Gale.

He shifted the box. A local haole, forty-five or fifty, single and an excellent pilot, decorated in World War II and Korea; the only other thing he did, besides fly, was bake pastry.

He reached into the box, carefully unwrapped the tissue, and took out a croquembouche.

Oh, that really is beautiful. Puff pastry. That's hard to make. Oh, look at that, each little one, so delicate, how do you keep them from getting broken in flight?

I hold them on my lap. And land like a feather.

Mickey said, yeah, you make light landings.

The pastry pilot held up the croquembouche. His skin had the baked worn look of the local haole.

Who's going first?

Oh, I can't, I gonna get overweight, they already looking for excuse to drop me.

Oh, go ahead, Mickey.

No, cannot.

Gale smiled. Well, go ahead, Bob.

A pastry pilot veteran, Gale closed her eyes and opened her mouth. The pastry pilot eased the croquembouche up toward her nose, held it under her nostrils, Gale took a deep inhalation, the pastry pilot, after waiting another moment, brought one of the puffs to her lips and slowly eased it into her mouth. With her face still upturned, eyes closed, Gale chewed slowly, oh, unh, hun, ummm, oh, God, that's great, oh, the best, really . . .

Yes? Better than my vacherin?

Oh, god, yes, it's two different categories, chalk and cheese, you know, really, just incredible.

Susan, you next? The pastry pilot was already selecting another puff.

Susan nodded, opened her mouth, closed her eyes; the pastry pilot had to reach up to put the puff under Susan's nose. She was taller. She inhaled, almost started laughing, the pastry pilot hesitated. Susan?

Yes?

You're not concentrating.

You're right. Susan composed herself. Now I am, go ahead.

The pastry pilot slowly eased the puff into her mouth, she chewed slowly, eyes closed, oh, Gale's right, that's really something, the best yet, absolutely perfect, I could try for the rest of my life and never bake a croquembouche like that.

The pastry pilot nodded gravely, good? reached into the box, brought out a puff, and looked at Mickey.

Mickey?

Really, you know I can't, I gotta keep weight.

Come on, now, Mickey, you know, one bite isn't going to put you overweight.

Really, I can't, I'd like to, you know that.

The pastry pilot slowly picked one out. He turned it around slowly.

All right, Mickey, then why not take just one deep breath of it.

Mickey sighed. Worse, makes it harder.

Come on, Mickey, no harm in smelling.

But then I'm going to want to eat it.

One smell, Mickey.

Gale and Susan, nodding, come on, go ahead, Mickey, no harm in one good whiff, you gotta live a little.

Mickey nodded, okay.

She tipped back her head, closed her eyes, kept her mouth closed tightly. The pastry pilot raised the pastry to her nose.

Mickey took a deep breath, oh, that is so good, so delicate. Give me one little piece. Break off a piece.

The pastry pilot lowered it. We don't break up the pastry, you know that, Mickey.

I know, I'm sorry.

They looked at each other, apologetic and offended.

The pastry pilot drew himself up.

Shall we try again?

Mickey closed her eyes and the pastry pilot brought the croquembrouche back to her nose. Mickey inhaled.

Gale and Susan watched them.

Mickey slowly opened her mouth.

The pastry pilot held the croquembouche just beyond her lips for a long moment.

Mickey opened her mouth wider.

The pastry pilot waiting, watching Mickey's face. She opened her mouth wider.

The pastry pilot eased the pastry into her mouth.

Mickey chewed once, the pastry pilot watched, Susan and Gale watched, chewed again, a look of ecstasy spread over her face, the pastry pilot said nothing.

Mickey opened her eyes, wiped a crumb from her lips, slapped him lightly, you! Now I'm going to be overweight, you!

Gale said, what's the recipe?

The pastry pilot looked hurt and disappointed. You know I don't give the recipe.

Just a hint! One thing, tell us one thing.

The pastry pilot shook his head, no.

Susan joined Gale. Oh, come on, just a hint.

Mickey chimed in, oh, please.

The pastry pilot hesitated a long time.

Oh, please!

He waved them into a close circle and whispered, it's a special ingredient.

Tell us.

You know I can't. He turned and walked away.

Mickey said, you know, every time I see him, I tink he's wastin hisself on pastry, jus throwin hisself away, I could cry when I tink of da fruitcake he could make.

They were already leaning into the wind on the runway, walking quickly and holding their skirts down.

In a few minutes, they were greeting passengers, aloha, watch your step, glad to have you aboard ...

For a moment, Susan was afraid Moon would come aboard for the next leg of the flight. . . . She hadn't thought of that. . . .

The Japanese tourists from the coffee shop came aboard. Several of the men looked at Susan's legs.

You know, Gale, I can't stand Oriental men. . . . They're so fucking small.

Gale nodded.

An old Hawaiian woman came aboard and Susan helped her to her seat.

Aloha, Mrs. Makalii, how are you today?

The old woman nodded, smiled.

She got on the plane maybe once every month or two carrying a bottle of gin, a sack of silver dollars in her purse.

She would fly over to the Big Island, visit her daughter in

Hilo, then go on up to the Kilauea Caldera, where she would throw the bottle of gin over the lip of the steaming caldera, sprinkle the silver dollars into the steam for Madame Pele who lived in the pit.

Mickey took a head count, checked the manifest, the cabin began to pressurize. Susan took her place in the aisle.

It came to her from nowhere. The old manapua man. The manapua men. What happened to them? You never saw them any more. They had disappeared—where?

Mickey's voice came on the loudspeaker:

Aloha, ladies and gentlemen, welcome aboard Polynesian Airlines DC-9 Royal Fan Jet Flight 181 from Kahului to Hilo....

Moon had not come aboard.

In a few moments, they rose steeply into the wind and banked for Hilo and Susan went to the buffet and began to serve drinks.

After that night in the Hilo Surf, the phone ringing always made Susan nervous, her palms would sweat, she would walk to the phone, stand there, look down, she would hesitate, move her hand toward it, feel the chill in her body, hear the voice, insistent and faraway, Susan, why you no cry for me? why you no cry for me? then suddenly hear the tangle of strange language, feel the slaps, hear the shouts, Mickey cursing in Hawaiian, ghost had you! She'd stare at the phone and Gale would shout, Susan, what are you doing, pick it up, Nathan was supposed to call! Gale would finally grab it.

Sometimes, when the phone rang late at night, she would turn quickly, walk out the front door, the sound of the phone following, and wonder, as she walked and still heard the phone ringing and ringing, if she was really awake or if she was asleep.

She thought of the day her father had come to visit her, his arms on the table. The faded tattoo. How, the first time he had picked her up, it had been bright blue under the skin, not far away, then.

She'd looked at the book of newspaper clippings, kahunas. The clippings going from yellow to white and recent. But back into the forties.

Then there was Uncle William that day, walking away from the funeral by himself, and before, in the front seat, driving the winding road from Honolulu to Waipahu, Waipahu to Honolulu, the back of his head, the light through the windshield shining on his cheekbone and jaw, the glare of his eye moving on the road. He was always nice to her, but she had been afraid of him.

There were rumors that Uncle William was in the syndicate, but she had no feelings about that; she just remembered him driving.

Ladies and gentlemen, as we leave Maui, we see on its eastern end the Haleakala Crater—Haleakala means "house of the sun"—and it is one of the largest inactive craters in the world. It has a circumference of twenty-one miles, is ten miles long, two miles wide, has a trail that descends seven thousand feet from rim to floor. . . .

A hot Saturday, Honolulu deserted, everyone at the beaches, the streets empty and the pavement shimmering, the sky deep blue, as though a bright star might still be shining.

Inside, the place was chilly, and for a moment, she stood in the dark by the cigarette machine, then, slowly, she was able to make out the booths, the bar at the other end, the bottles and the mirror behind, dim, a pale blue light, and then she thought the word, blue, Blue Grotto.

She took a step toward the bar, stopped, had the feeling she might lose her balance, put her hand out for the back of a booth, looked around, were there other people in here?

134

She walked between the booths. In the last booth near the bar, two Japanese girls were talking over their drinks. They looked her over as she walked by.

She waited a moment at the bar, heard one of the girls walking behind her and then stepping back around behind the bar. She was wearing a pink sweater with sequins across the front.

Susan saw herself talking to the girl in the mirror, the back of the girl's head, and Susan facing her. It looked like someone else. The girl smiled at Susan with only her mouth, and asked with a heavy accent, yes, please?

She started to say, Uncle William, but corrected herself, is William Hondo here, please?

What choo want?

William Hondo?

The girl studied Susan. You want William Hondo? Who is dis speakin, please?

He knows me. I'm his niece.

The girl gave Susan a skeptical look.

We no need no more girls now.

Is he here?

What choo like drink?

Nothing.

The girl looked her over again, turned, stepped out from behind the bar, disappeared down a short hallway, Susan heard a door open and close.

After a few minutes, she came out and sat back down at her booth without looking at Susan. Susan heard them start to talk quickly again in Japanese.

She heard the door open, heard footsteps down the hall. Her heart pounded for a moment.

He stepped to the end of the bar and looked at her. His face didn't show anything. His hair was still black, short, combed back on the sides into an abbreviated D.A., she looked for the tattoo on his arm, but he was wearing a white shirt with long sleeves. She knew something about men, now, and could tell that although he was short, he was powerful. He looked at her. Did he recognize her? She had the feeling he was looking her over as a prospective bar hostess.

Uncle William, you remember me, Susan?

He nodded. Susan.

Was it . . . is it . . . all right for me to come in here like this?

Sure, Susan. You nevah come before.

Did you recognize me?

Sure I recognize you, Susan. You my niece, I recognize you. Long time, but I recognize you.

She felt relieved.

You passin by?

Yes, was passing by. . . . No, Uncle William, I've come to see you.

He didn't say anything, seemed to make a decision, then said, in a soft voice, dat's nice of you to come, Susan, nice of you to visit your uncle. Come on, den.

He waved her over to a booth, what you like drink, you take one drink now you grown?

She nodded, though she wasn't sure if she should refuse, if he'd want her to refuse. I'll take a Bloody Mary. He snapped his fingers at one of the girls, said something quickly in Japanese.

They sat down and looked at each other.

So, I hear you one stewardess now, nice job for you, eh?

Susan could see he was used to being careful about what he said.

She nodded. The girl brought them the drinks, Uncle William asked, you like some pupus, Susan?

Thank you, not just now, I'm not hungry, Uncle William.

But he had them brought anyway. Japanese pupus. Sashimi, salads, tempura. . . .

Susan stared at his gold watch; he had a large diamond on the little finger of one hand.

He watched her study him, he studied the way she studied him, waited. She sensed there was no advantage to be gained in waiting.

Eventually, she said, I've got to ask you something, Uncle William. I hope you won't get mad, please, if you don't want to tell me, that's okay. . . .

He still waited. She felt he was tough, she wouldn't have wanted him for an enemy, felt as though it weren't right for her to say, that's okay, not to him, she couldn't imagine anyone saying, that's okay to him. He would tell people what was okay and what was not okay.

She took a deep breath. Started again.

Uncle William, all those times we drove to the . . . she started to say graveyard, changed it to . . . Waipahu, with Obachan . . .

She waited a second, she knew he hadn't forgotten. but wouldn't help, either . . . When I was little . . . to the grave . . . of my aunt, Jane . . . and Obachan used to cry . . .

I asked Obachan once, what happened to her—Jane—and Obachan said she was in an accident. She told me never to ask my mother. Uncle William, I never asked my mother.

She paused.

Uncle William . . .

He looked steadily at her.

What happened to her?

She knew he knew.

He waited a moment, got up, and left her in the booth. She expected to hear the door close at the end of the hall and not see him again.

She stared at the tabletop while he was gone. Took a napkin and carefully wiped a ridge of water from the table. Folded the napkin. He came back with two more drinks and sat down.

Hey, you no eat nothing, whatsa mattah wit you?

Not hungry. That's what he was going to do, ignore her question.

He looked at the goosebumps on her arms.

You cold, 'as why.

He said something quickly in Japanese over the top of the booth and the girl who'd first met her at the bar came over, unbuttoned the top button of her sweater, and handed it to Uncle William.

He stood up, draped it over her shoulders, and sat back down. She could still feel the warmth of the other girl's body in the sweater. The sweater smelled heavily of perfume, she felt cold.

Thank you, Uncle William.

Why you want to know bout your aunt?

She didn't know what to say. She was confused. Her father bringing her the book of clippings on kahunas. Susan, your mother's worse, she chased me into the bathroom with a knife. The way her mother had always shouted at her.

Finally she said, because of Obachan . . . her crying.

She almost added, and Obachan visited me one night not too long ago, but she decided not to say that.

She repeated, because of Obachan.

What Grandma tell you bout dis?

She told me Jane was in a car accident. Is that right, Uncle William, one car accident?

One car acciden, he repeated. 'As what she told you?

She said, she went away in a car one day and never came back. Obachan always told me the truth about everything. She was the only one. She told me the truth, didn't she?

He took a sip of his drink, looked at her, then nodded. He had made another decision.

Okay, Susan, I gonna tell you. No, your grandma, she nevah tell you no lies, 'as true. She tell you da truth, your aunt, she go away in one car one day and nevah come back. Dat part is true.

Susan felt relieved.

Uncle William nodded. Dat part is true.

The way he repeated, that part is true, suddenly she felt afraid.

She go away in da car two, maybe three years before you born. We all livin down near Piako Street, den. Your mothah, she only fifteen, maybe sixteen, Jane, she one year older.

It was strange hearing Jane's name. She'd once been a real person. Alive. No one had ever actually spoken about her before.

Your mothah and Jane, day both very good-looking girls. Jane, she beautiful, she walk down da street, people stop and look aftah her.

He looked at Susan. You lookin like her, too, Susan.

Everybody love Jane, you know? She always jokin, smilin, your mothah and her, dey like dat.

Uncle William held up two fingers crossed over each other.

Like dat. Dey go everywhere togethah.

Dat time, during da war, dis island full of servicemen, army, up Schofield Barracks, navy, marines over at Kaneohe, everywhere you go, get GIs.

Your grandma, she say to da girls, stay away from da servicemen. Your grandma, she nevah like da girls to have no heartbreak. Jane, she one good girl, but she meet dis one GI, he one haole in da army, and oh, he love Jane, he fall in love wit her, take her everywhere, bring her flowahs, presents, he take her everywhere, come to da house in one car and dey going all around. All da time, he follow her around.

When he ast Jane to marry him, den your grandma, she tell Jane, no more, now 'as enough! I tink dis okay wit Jane, she like to do what your grandma say, she a laughin kine of girl, sweet girl. But Ma say to Jane, now 'as enough. So Jane do it, she tell da GI, 'as enough.

Den dis GI, he keep callin her and tellin her how much he love her. Every day he sendin her flowahs, he ast her to marry him, tell her he no can live witout her.

But no mattah what he do, Jane tell him she no gonna marry him.

Finally, den, your grandma, she get tired of it, she know Jane jus a young girl, have a tendah heart, she fraid maybe Jane gonna feel sorry for da GI and marry him anyway, so she tell da GI, you one very nice boy, but please now, stay away, you keep up like dis, you going to make Jane unhappy.

So da GI, he try to stay away, but every day, he send a lettah or some flowahs, or he try to call Jane. He tell her, he no can live witout her.

So den one day, he come to da house in one car. Everyone workin. Your grandmothah, she workin, your grandfathah, he workin, everyone dey work ten–twelve hours a day. No one home but Jane and your mothah.

Da GI, he ast Jane please to marry him.

But Jane, she say no, she tell him she like him, he one very nice man, but no more, now, please.

Den da GI plead wit her, tell her, he no can live witout her. Your mothah, dere, she heard it all.

But Jane, still, she say no.

So den da GI, he say, Jane, come for one ride wit me, we be togethah one more time, den I no going to bothah you no more.

Your mothah, she talk to Jane in da next room, say to Jane, bettah not go, bettah leave em go, you stay wit me.

But Jane say, I going talk to him a little, make em feel bettah.

Den dey going, dey walk out to da street, get in da car, your aunt, Jane, she smile, wave to your mothah standin on da porch, den dey stay-go.

When you grandmothah come home, dey still not back. Your mothah tell your grandmothah Jane gone off wit da GI and your grandmothah, she go walkin in circles, sayin to your mothah, why didn't choo stop em? and your mothah, she only fifteen, sixteen at da time, what she going say? She tell your grandmothah, I tryin, but your grandmothah, she upset, she walkin around; your grandfathah, he try to calm her down, but your grandmothah, she sure dat da GI going to convince Jane to marry him, dat dey gone off and already get married. She cursin Jane and da GI.

All night dey no come home and da nex day, your grandmothah—she been up all night—she call police first ting in da morning. She tell da police. Da police say dey going look. Your grandmothah ast if dere been any car accidens, but the police no have any.

So den your grandma, she waitin all day, she no going to work, she sure now dey married.

Police call da army base, Schofield Barracks, but nobody seen da GI—da military police no have him in jail, nobody knows where he gone, da GI AWOL.

So everyone lookin, da MPs and da Honolulu police.

Den, on da third day, in da evening, da detectives come to da house.

Dey tell your grandma dey found dem.

Uncle William didn't say anything more for several minutes. Susan could hear the air conditioner rushing. He looked at Susan a moment; he seemed to be thinking what to say, how to say it.

Dey found dem, he repeated.

It was the car? she said.

He shook his head. Your grandma tell you no lies—she say to you, dey went in one car and nevah come back. 'As true. Dey was found beside da car in da grass, da detective tell me.

He nodded.

So den some people—some neighbors—dey come to sit wit your mothah and your grandmothah and grandfathah and I going in da car wit da detective. Dey no like your grandma to go. I going. Da neighbors holdin your grandma, she on her knees wit her hair down shriekin. Your grandfathah, too—dey weepin. Dey stay at da house. I going wit da detective.

Dey take me to da morgue and we going in da room and da detective, he try to get me ready for dis, he say to me, no look at da GI, he's in one bad mess, jus look at da woman, tell us if it's your sistah, maybe it's not, da woman, she jus look like she sleepin, she was one beautiful woman. . . .

Den we go into da ice room. Freezah room. Dey been dead, two, three days, I remembah, dey were very hot days and dey been lyin in da grass two, three days. So dey in da freezah room.

He pushed his glass once in a circle on the table. I nevah like da heat anyway.

So we going in da freezah room and dey two bodies and da detective show me da woman and was Jane. I just stand dere and nod and I still standin dere when da detective gotta take my arm and lead me outside. I just standin dere.

Uncle William stopped then for a long time. Finally asked, You wanna nother drink, Susan?

Susan shook her head no, but he ordered two more.

He got up and went down the hall.

When the girl brought the drinks, Susan took the sweater off, but the girl shook her head no, without expression.

After a few minutes, Uncle William sat down again. He had a white envelope. He opened the envelope, carefully took out a clipping and handed it to her.

The clipping was dated August 1944.

Susan read the clipping. It couldn't have been more than five or six sentences.

Uncle William took a swallow of his drink.

Da detective told me, dey found dem lyin in da grass, dey tied togethah at da waist. Dere was a forty-five in the grass wit dem.

Da detective say it happens like dis: da GI get out of da car wit her, shot her once in da heart, den he tied hisself to her wit one long silk scarf, it was dere in da morgue, I seen it, it was white, part of it—most of it was dark from da blood. So da GI shot her, she dead now. He tie hisself to her and den he shot hisself through da head.

Susan looked at the clipping in her hand. All she could think of was not to get it wet in the circle of water on the table.

'As da way de found dem, lyin dere in da grass, tied togethah at da waist.

She handed the clipping back to Uncle William.

They sat for a few minutes.

Then Susan shrugged. Why?

Uncle William shook his head. I not know. I tink bout it plenty, but I not know.

Uncle William slid the clipping back into the envelope.

She shook her head. Poor Obachan.

Uncle William nodded. Aftah dat, she cry all da time.

And my mother?

She act crazy, cry all da time, too. Maybe she tink it her fault, she da last to see her going.

That's why my mother started with the kahunas?

Uncle William shook his head quickly. I not know nothing bout kahunas.

Susan remembered walking with Uncle William in Waikiki. He had been sitting on the sea wall near Queen Surf. She was playing on the beach. There were tall men, haoles, in white suits. With beautiful white hats. And red and blue stripes on their sleeves. One of them put his hat on her head, she wore it, the man gave it to her. A beautiful white hat. It smelled nice inside. Like perfume. Uncle William was still sitting on the wall. She ran back to him, smiling. He reached up, took the white hat off her head without saying a word, walked over to the man, and gave it back.

They got back in the car, she was watching the men in their white suits and white hats standing against the ocean, she wanted the white hat back. Suddenly, Uncle William reached across the seat and hit her, slapped her so hard he knocked her head against the car door, said:

Don't choo evah let me see you flirt wit no sailors, evah again!

Now, in the bar, she looked at Uncle William and sighed. She felt tired, she thought of all the things that had been said to her, by her mother, her grandmother, and had the unreal feeling that none of them had ever been said to her, but to someone else, that perhaps no one had ever really noticed her, Susan. She felt tired, exhausted, she remembered sitting in the car and crying after her uncle had slapped her, the sun glaring through the windshield.

She looked at him now. He was staring down at his glass, talking to himself in a low voice, something Japanese. She wondered if he even remembered hitting her. He looked up at her. She thought, he knows what I'm thinking.

But he started talking again about something else, not what she was thinking.

Aftah dat, da family come apart, your grandmothah and grandfathah, dey sad, dey no have no more life, dey get up, dey going to work, dey come home, dey going to sleep, nex day, dey get up and going to work again. Your mothah, she get strange, she cry all da time, burst out laughin, she going crazy, run here, run dere, say crazy tings, she run wit differen man, she nevah bring no man to da house, but she run wit dem, she hate haole men, but she always wit dem, servicemen, too, den she pregnant wit you. . . .

He stopped. Gave her a quick glance. Said something to himself in Japanese.

You, he started again, you stay wit your grandmothah aftah your mothah going to da mainland; dat de only time I see your grandmothah happy again. He nodded. She love you good. He

144

reached across the table and squeezed her cheek lightly.

She nodded. I know, Uncle William.

She knew her Uncle William had loved her, too. That's why he'd hit her.

Then he looked at her, seemed to study her face, and said, your grandmothah, she love you for yourself, Susan.

He put his hand on hers for a moment, patted her hand. I glad you ast me, your uncle. Nevah mind dis, now, you grown, you one beautiful girl, you get one good job, you forget it now. You deserve to know, you know your grandmothah, she nevah tell you no lies, eithah, but it's all ovah and done wit. . . . Nothing to be done no more.

He got up, she stood, slid the sweater off and handed it to him.

At the door, he said, Susan, you come back visit me from time to time, no forget your Uncle William, we talk bout someting else, have a nice time.

She wanted to thank him, she nodded, she took his hand. He patted her arm, nodded, she turned quickly and pushed through the door.

Outside, the heat was a shock, a solid wall that made her gasp for breath, the pavement shimmered. At the stop light, hers seemed to be the only car. She sat, the red circle of light in its black iron box against the deep blue of the sky, sweating, waiting for the light to change, listening to the remote-control switches clicking in their box. Then the light changed. Then she came to a stop at another light.

Several times she saw the ocean, a blue square at the end of the street between buildings, and turned in a different direction. Mauka . . .

Then she was winding up Tantalus, up the curving roads, round and round the mountain, the beautiful homes built on the hillside hidden in green, Richard had lived up here, then, higher up, the towering eucalyptus trees, their sweet turpentine smell, and thin shreds of bark in and beside the road.

It was cooler now, and cooler still as she got to the top of the mountain. She got out of the car. The wind was blowing, the grass on the hillside was shining in the sun.

She walked away from the car and down onto the grass. Below her, in front of her, she could see all of Honolulu, the buildings blindingly white, their shadowed sides a pale blue, like a mirage. Behind the high-rise buildings and hotels, the ocean, silver white in the sun, the sun now over in the west, and on the ocean, ships, half the size of her finger, some, farther away, almost on the horizon, the size of the moon on her fingernail, each leaving behind a shadowy wake on the surface of the ocean.

She thought of the white silk scarf.

She turned her head. She could see over and down into the green bowl of Diamond Head Crater—farther over, Koko Head. She could see Kahala. That's where her mother wanted them to move. Turning her head the other way, she could not quite see over to where they did live—Halawa Heights.

Kahunas, the woman across the street trying to get her.

Buying a house, waiting until it appreciated, selling it, always working, investing, moving up. And staying ahead of the kahuna, the lady across the street.

Planes floated beneath her. Taking off, landing. Higher up, overhead, planes from the mainland, from the Orient, high and still, descended into their approach patterns, flashed.

Ewa, the tip of the island stretched away toward the Waianaes, shimmering away into the distance in a line the color of ash.

The planes rose, climbed steeply, leaving heavy black vapor trails which would come apart slowly and disappear into the air.

She thought of her mother's eyes moving quickly. Her lips moving.

She went away in a car and never came back.

Her mother shouting, stupid!
Susan stared down at the city.

Ladies and gentlemen, we're presently flying along the south-
ern coastline of Oahu. Coming into view now is Koko Head
and Koko Crater. Koko Head's last eruption occurred about a
hundred thousand years ago. Also in view is Hanauma Bay—
once a volcanic crater until the sea broke through one side,
creating a favorite picnic and playground area. Coming up are
a few of Oahu's most famous landmarks, Mount Leahi, more
commonly known as Diamond Head. . . .

An ache in her ears, the seat belt sign on, and Mickey making the announcement for Honolulu landing.

In a few more minutes, they made a rough landing in Honolulu. . . . Susan unfastening her seat belt and walking to the
buffet, slamming up against the cockpit door as the pilot
braked hard. She caught her balance, whirled and banged the
heel of her fist against the cockpit door, turned, looked at
several passengers, and started walking aft.

The stew lounge in the terminal was the usual chaos—tv on,
too loud, girls playing cards, talking, knitting. Susan walked
quickly to her locker, checking the clock on the wall and
wondering if there would be time to run into Honolulu, up to
the house, and check the mailbox.

There was a note in her locker:

Susan, please see me as soon as you get in. Miss Pahoa.

Uh, oh, what choo did now, Susan?
Susan handed her the note. Here, Mickey, don't mind me.
Mickey shook her head. So touchy, Susan. Eh? What did
happen—da Maui flight, wasn't it? I thought I heard some-
ting—what choo did, Susan?
Nothing.

Dat's why you so touchy.

Because you're reading over my shoulder? That's touchy? Privacy not a word in your vocabulary?

Mickey suddenly gave her the finger, stabbed it at her face and walked away.

Gale approached. Should see the look on her face. Well, fly-girl, what was that about?

Nothing. Just dumb.

Gale shook her head. All the squabbles. You two are so childish. Will it never end?

Miss Superior here.

Gale laughed. Susan showed her the note.

Gale stuck out her lower lip. Probably nothing, what's the big deal?

Everything's a big deal around here.

Don't worry. I'll see you on the four o'clock. She turned. Spa'k you later.

Susan reached for her make-up kit, saw the notebook in her flight bag, took it out and leafed through the three or four attempts she'd made to write Jack a letter.

She looked at the beginnings, crossing outs, new beginnings. They made her feel stupid.

Why couldn't she just write him, say what she felt, that she loved him, she missed him?

That was what she felt, wasn't it?

There was something else she wanted to say, something she was trying to avoid.

She felt afraid.

She wanted to write, come back, when will you be coming back? When will I be seeing you. I need you.

She dropped the notebook back in her flight bag, checked her make-up, combed her hair, checked her stockings for runs, white shoes for smudges—she wet a finger and rubbed a smudge near her heel—and walked out of the lounge.

Miss Pahoa stepped out from behind her desk, smiled at Susan, gave her a quick professional once-over, head to foot.

You look good, Susan, a little tired, but always look good. Sit down. How've you been?

Fine.

Susan, let me say now, before I start, that you are one of my best girls. You have always been one of my best girls. When I first interviewed you, the minute you walked in the room, I saw you had it—the way you carried yourself, your voice, everything.

Miss Pahoa lowered her voice to confidentiality. Some girls are attractive enough, yes, and do the job well, but still, they don't have that something special. . . . She trailed off and picked up a folder.

Susan, I've been looking through your file. I'm amazed how good your attendance has been up until three or four months ago. And no warnings, no suspensions. There was that period where you took a leave of absence . . . that's been over a period of almost seven years.

She studied the file. But in the last three or four months, you've called in sick more times than you have in the last six years.

Miss Pahoa looked up over the file at Susan. Have you really been sick, Susan?

A few times, Miss Pahoa.

Miss Pahoa hesitated, perhaps she was going to ask her about the other times, that would be the obvious thing to do, but she didn't seem to want to press it.

Susan, may I ask you something?

Of course.

Are you happy?

Oh, yes, fine, Miss Pahoa, why?

You do like flying, don't you?

She wanted to say, no, I can't stand it, but she thought, what would I do? go to the mainland and be with him, but . . .

Suddenly she said, yes, yes, I do, why, what's wrong? Yes, I have been a little sick lately, but I'll be fine.

Miss Pahoa seemed to be asking her, Susan, for reassurance. After a moment, Miss Pahoa said, I just know it's a mistake.

Susan waited.

I had a call from Maui this morning—a gentleman who was on the Honolulu–Maui flight. He complained that you were rude to him—intentionally rude.

Oh.

He didn't want to be identified.

You don't have his name?

He preferred to remain anonymous.

Did he say what he meant?

He said you addressed him using filthy language. Susan, I know what you girls have to put up with at times, but it's part of your job. I don't believe you, of all my girls, would be rude to any passenger. He also said you struck him and spat at him.

She studied Susan. It's just not possible.

She couldn't lie to Miss Pahoa. The way she was looking at Susan. Impulsively, she said with conviction, I treat them the way they deserve to be treated, Miss Pahoa.

Miss Pahoa, again skirting doubt, then nodding.

As you know, these are grounds for immediate termination. I wanted to talk to you first because I have a meeting with Vice President Sullivan in a few minutes about this. We might have to suspend you, but, the company will give you a hearing in a week; you can grieve it, but I hope it won't come to that, Susan. Oh, Susan . . . I'll try to get the company to drop it before it comes to a systems board. But if you're suspended, don't be alarmed, I hope I can get the company to drop it before the hearing.

Miss Pahoa stood up and Susan stood up with her.

Susan, I'll do everything I can for you.

She came around the desk and looked at Susan a moment and then smiled. Don't worry, Susan. As long as I'm Chief Stewardess, they'll fire you only over my dead body. You have always been one of my girls.

After a moment, she said, I'm not sure I'm anyone's girl, but thanks, Miss Pahoa.

Back in the hall, Susan wasn't thinking much about Miss Pahoa or suspension or even losing her job. It would be a relief not to have to fly any more. She looked at her watch, but knew there wasn't time to drive back to the house, she was being stupid about driving back to the house to see if there was mail. And she still couldn't really make a picture of his face. Colors, that's what she could make of him, he was so many beautiful colors, on the beach, in the sun, his hair a bleached-out blond from the sun, speckles of sea salt crusted in his black eyelashes, so many colors in his eyes.

In the lounge, Gale asked, what happened? Everything okay? What did she want?

Oh, nothing, she wanted to ask me about my calling in sick the last few months.

Gale laughed. You get away with murder with her.

So do you. Not just with her. With everybody—giving boxes of candy to scheduling so you get a good bid. I'm on to you. Hoomalimali. Sweet-talker. Brown-noser.

It works, doesn't it?

That's the trouble.

Just I like to sleep late.

You want to walk over to United with me? I'm going to pick up some tickets.

You going to the mainland?

No, my father called me two weeks ago. They're going to San Francisco. You know, they never talk to me unless they want something.

They walked out of the Polynesian Air Terminal into the sun, walked slowly past the cabs lined up, past the lei stands.

Mickey's off the schedule for the rest of the day. She's gone home to start cooking. You still going to Mickey's house blessing tonight?

I don't know. It's one of those situations where Mickey's going to be hurt if I come, hurt if I don't come. Can't win with Mickey. Not supposed to, I guess. It's just she's so nosy, Gale. I don't mind showing her the note. I showed it to you. I just don't like her reading over my shoulder.

Gale nodded. Well, I know . . . but go. That's Mickey. She'll forget it. I'm going for a while.

Susan didn't say anything. A couple of pilots walked by and said hello.

Gale turned, don't you talk to him any more?

Who?

Who? That was Duke.

Susan stopped and looked back. The two pilots were walking on toward the terminal.

You're kidding?

No, that was Duke.

I talk to him, say hello to him. I didn't recognize him. He looked so old.

The drinking.

She looked after him. The drinking, she repeated. So old. The bags under his eyes. And the lines.

Then, abruptly, Susan laughed. I didn't recognize him. Well, there goes three years of my life. She snapped her fingers. He should be happy. He's a captain, now.

At the United counter, Harry had the tickets ready.

Susan took the tickets, stuck them in her flight bag.

Thanks, Harry.

Hey, no sweat.

Harry had recently grown a mustache, had puffy bags under his eyes.

I going see you tonight at da house blessing?

For sure.

Spa'k ya later.

Hang tough, Harry.

Susan switched on the microphone as the airplane began to taxi for the second round trip of the day:

Aloha, ladies and gentlemen, welcome aboard Polynesian Air lines DC-9 Royal Fan Jet Flight 181 from Honolulu to Kahului, Maui, then on to Hilo. In command of your flight . . .

The DC-9 took off a few moments later, and Susan gave the announcement for Honolulu:

Ladies and gentlemen, we're presently flying along the southern coastline of Oahu. In view now are . . .

She finished the announcement, then started serving cocktails.

Uncle William's face across the table from her. Your Aunt Jane . . . Susan looked down Tantalus. Susan watched the planes rising below her, their vapor trails slowly disappearing. And as she sat on the grass looking down at Honolulu, the air seemed to be filled with voices, voices that she had heard all her life, but now was hearing in a new way. Obachan, her mother, her father.

Obachan lying on the bed in the hospital, her head turning slowly on the pillow, looking at Susan, past Susan, dey be sorry for what dey done to you. . . .

Had she been talking to her, Susan? Or her own daughter Jane? She had wondered what she'd meant by that—there were so many things, now.

And after all, she was stupid, right? Her mother had always shouted at her, stupid! and half the time, she'd had the feeling that yes, because she hadn't understood something, it was because she was exactly what her mother had been shouting at her, stupid!

But then, too, maybe her mother had been really talking to her sister who got into the car with the GI and never came back.

Or, stupid, even herself, most of all, herself, for letting her sister go that day; it wasn't her fault, no, but she still had been the last one ever to see her alive.

Uncle William had said, Obachan had been afraid she'd gone off and gotten married, or else would do so, and . . .

Susan remembered her mother always yelling, you will get pregnant.

She looked down at the tight symmetry of the University of Hawaii buildings up in Manoa—she could make out the East-West Center. Manoa starting to fall into shadows on the western side and at the head of the valley.

She thought of the gold wedding band with someone else's initials in it and said to herself, what I really wanted was to go to the university but instead . . .

And what was her life now?

She thought of Duke. Duke and her waking up this morning. He'd stayed with her because his wife was away. Making love. Her not coming. Something too tense inside. She didn't think it was his fault. She usually didn't come. The closeness was enough.

But then Duke's getting up and making a gin and tonic.

And her saying, don't, Duke, it's not even ten o'clock, you could at least wait until one or two.

Duke raising the gin and tonic, laughing, and saying, somewhere in the world it's two o'clock, and drinking the gin and tonic.

154

After a while, he made another, and then said, aren't you going to put on some make-up? and she said, no, what for?

His eyes had darkened.

What for? How would you like it if I walked around here and didn't shave all day? Would you like that?

She'd said, it's not the same thing . . . not the same thing at all.

The hell it isn't. What kind of people have you been hanging around with lately anyway? Are you trying to look like a hippie?

Not wearing ten tons of make-up at ten o'clock in the morning isn't being a hippie. And it's a lot better than poisoning myself with gin at ten o'clock in the morning . . . even though it is two o'clock somewhere in the world. It's not two o'clock here. Can't you wait?

He turned his back on her to make another drink before she finished talking.

It's never two o'clock early enough for you, any more, is it?

She thought, the hell with him; he still wouldn't talk to her, he was just sitting there, drinking. After a while, she felt afraid and went into the bathroom, took a shower, washed her hair, put on make-up, false eyelashes, eyeshadow, and came out. He was making another drink.

Please, she said. She heard her mother's voice—bitchy—in her voice.

He ignored her.

She didn't want to be a bitch. And maybe he'd stop if she'd shut up.

She sat down in a chair, and watched him over there on the other side of the room, his back to her, feet propped up, staring out the window onto the lanai, and she felt afraid, but she wasn't going to say any more, she wanted to have something which would make her look busy, she wanted to be busy, so she started painting her nails.

After a time, he got up and kissed her, his breath smelling of gin, and she'd felt bad, and said, oh, Duke. . . .

She looked down at the pattern of buildings below—the university—and thought, how many of those people have a life like mine? She felt angry, angry at herself, angry that her life had somehow gotten like this.

Her sister—Carol—she was going to be a freshman there, her mother hadn't told her *she* was too stupid.

Her mother had tried to make her take secretarial courses in high school. Typing and shorthand. Something to fall back on. Typing. As though she didn't have a brain in her head.

She ran her hands back and forth over the grass. She'd wanted to go since she was eighteen . . . seventeen. She still wanted to go. Four years of flying. She would be twenty-two in a month . . .

She could quit the airline, just go. But how would she support herself? Nothing from her mother and father, that's for sure

Duke leaning over her, the smell of gin . . .

Kissing her, kissing her carefully, delicately, so as not to smear her make-up.

And then sitting in bars, Duke drinking and drinking until he could hardly talk, and her sitting there patiently, bored, quiet, sitting and sitting, not drinking her drink, his saying, drink, you still on that drink, Jesus, Susan. . . .

And her keeping her mouth shut, made-up, pretty and not saying anything, why? she knew she wasn't stupid.

And then, finally, getting up and leaving, Duke stumbling, bumping into chairs, into people, sometimes trying to draw himself up to fight, even a waitress.

One night, a haole GI had asked Susan something about what she was and then said without waiting—Japanese are Protestants, but then, turn a mixture of Japanese and Chinese inside out and you have a Korean. But if you're a Jap . . .

Duke almost killed the guy. It had taken two bartenders and a couple of busboys and waiters to pull Duke off him.

Other nights, stumbling, and his weight as she would finally help steady him out to the street . . .

Then the row over who would drive and his finally driving, a pilot who could land a DC-9 so gently she had once set a glass of champagne on the armrest and he hadn't spilled a drop, now weaving through the streets, rolling halfway through red lights, and ready to fight anyone who honked or pulled up next to him and made a comment.

Oh, she knew what Duke wanted. He wanted money. He was a copilot and he wanted to be a captain. But he wanted money more than anything. And she knew why he wanted it.

Because he was Hawaiian-Portuguese, and he would never feel good enough, light enough, haole enough.

He'd taken leave from the airline for ten months, gone to Thailand, oh, very secret, but she'd known what he was doing: flying for Air-America. And smuggling on the side.

When he'd come home, he had so much money, he didn't know what to do with it all. First, a new car. Then giving her presents. Dresses. Jewelry.

She said, what about the people you helped kill, Duke?

He looked at her, his eyes dark, and said, I haven't killed anyone. And fuck them. Fuck them all.

It's a CIA airline, Duke.

He looked at her. What the hell do you know about it?

Nothing, Duke. I'm just a dumb stewardess, I don't know anything about anything, goddamn you!

He gave her a jade necklace.

She threw it at him and said, who are you kidding, Duke!

He walked slowly across the room, picked it up off the rug, walked back to her, she was afraid he was going to hit her; he stopped in front of her with the necklace in his hand, looked sadly at her a moment, and said in a soft, almost helpless voice, keep it just the same . . . please.

And he reached over and hooked it around her neck. She felt the weight of the necklace.

She looked down, touched the necklace. This is really worth it. Worth everything. Worth what you're doing to yourself. I'll wear it when I follow you around while you play golf. Or the next time you stagger out of the Kaimana.

He looked at her and said, I'll tell you something, Susan, I don't give a shit who kills who. They all stink and I fly for whoever pays up. I'd fly for the Russians if they put up the money. I fly for myself, Susan.

I know you do, Duke. Keep drinking, Duke, and you won't be flying for anyone. Not even yourself. I'll tell you something, Duke, you feel sorry for yourself. You could fly from here to Saturn, you'd still never have enough money. . . .

Looking down at Honolulu, Susan knew it would just go on and on with Duke. She was always waiting for him. Waiting for him in a bar. Waiting for him to slip away from his wife and meet her somewhere. Waiting for him to come back from the Orient when he was with Air-America. Waiting to hear that he was safe when he delivered planes to Australia. They were single-engine planes and he knew and she knew that a single engine was a wild card, a joker, and could turn up anytime, and that was one of the reasons he liked to make those flights. Once she had looked at an atlas, all of that water between Hawaii and Australia, nothing between, and she despaired. A single engine. Duke alone out there. And then, waiting, waiting for him to cable, to call, to tell her that he was safe. One time it was a whole week before she heard from him. Then he called drunk to tell her he was safe. All of the time she'd been waiting. When she asked him when he'd gotten there, he said five days ago. She burst into tears and slammed down the phone. Susan knew that she would just go on and on waiting for Duke. That he would never stop drinking, never leave his wife. And that even if he did, was that what she wanted, a man ten years older than herself, who looked splendid in a pilot's uniform, never read anything, drank when he got out of bed in the morning? . . .

She wasn't eighteen, now.

Just that she loved him.

She thought about the university. In a month she would be twenty-two. Four years of flying and where was she? In the same place. No money saved. She knew she wasn't stupid. She knew there was time to start.

The seat-belt sign came on and Susan looked down through the windows. Oahu was fading into the dark, the Koolaus already a black mass, Punchbowl dark, Diamond Head Crater dark, Manoa, Waikiki, the airport, Pearl Harbor, all lit up. In the west, a faint red afterglow.

Susan pressed the microphone button and started speaking:

We'll be landing shortly at Honolulu International Airport. Please check to see that your seat belts are fastened and observe the No Smoking sign when it appears.

Her ears ached, she opened her mouth, wider, there was a release of pressure, they were descending.

A week before Susan's twenty-second birthday, her mother called. Gale held up the phone, hand over the receiver, she whispered, it's your mother . . . are you here?

Susan hesitated. Yes, I'm here.

Susan hadn't talked to her mother more than twice a year since she had left home.

She picked up the phone.

Hello, Susan . . . how are you?

Her mother's voice seemed high and mechanical. She didn't realize how much of an Oriental accent her mother had.

Susan hesitated again. How am I? Fine. I'm fine.

Her mother didn't say anything. Then, quickly—Susan, next week is your birthday. Will you come home for it?

Her mother's voice made her hands sweat, her stomach tighten. She hesitated, started wording an excuse.

Then she thought of Uncle William, she went in da car and nevah come back, your mothah da last to see her . . . she thought of the white silk scarf dark with blood, her mother, then only fifteen, sixteen, what her mother must have gone through . . .

. . . and she thinks the lady across the street is trying to kill her, kahunas, . . . if anything ever happens to me . . . Promise me you will investigate after my death! What was it like to live in a world like that? The phone ringing late at night, ringing and ringing. Trying to pick up the phone.

She knew what it was like.

Mother, she said.

Yes, Susan. . . . Her mother's voice sounded unreal, frightened.

All right, Mother . . . I will, I'll come home.

There was a long pause.

Her mother's voice sounded far away. Yes, Susan, I'll see you . . . on your birthday.

Susan hung up the phone. She wished she hadn't said yes. Just easier to forget her, forget it all.

Then she said, all right, maybe we can make a change; no, I don't like her, but I understand what happened. What she went through. At least it makes some sense why she treated me the way she did.

Susan wasn't convinced. She repeated it to herself. Some sense. Maybe we can make some changes. Maybe I can even help her, maybe she needs my help.

She thought of her mother hugging her. Maybe she wasn't stupid, her life would change, she could go to the university.

She bought a new dress—simple, well cut, modest in a way she hoped her mother would like. She made sure the dress was well to the knee. At the same time, while she was in the store, she noticed a blouse, something to give her mother, a present.

It was hot. The streets were bare, hardly any trees grew, the whole area was a development. Some of the streets still ended with surveyors' stakes and mud.

She pulled up to the curb, got out of the car, and was halfway up the walk before she had an uneasy feeling and realized she had the wrong house.

When she found the right house—she had to drive up and down several streets—she stepped out of the car, careful not to run her stockings or brush against the car door. She wanted to be faultless. She reached back into the car for her mother's present and walked toward the house. She could feel the heat of the sidewalk through the soles of her shoes.

There was a long silence after the doorbell rang. She was about to ring again when she stepped back and saw the curtains moving above the kitchen sink.

For a moment, she wanted to run, get in her car, drive away. She did not want to go into the house, see her mother. She looked at the present.

Suddenly, the door opened. Her mother. Her eyes moving quickly. Looking behind Susan, across the street.

Susan felt afraid. She didn't turn and look behind her. Hello, Mother.

Her mother smiled. Quickly. Hello, Susan. Happy Birthday.

Susan pulled at the screen door.

The door, Mother.

Her mother unlocked the door.

It was hot inside. The tv. Bookshelves empty except for some *TV Guides* and a set of encyclopedias.

She looked around. Where's Dad? Carol?

Her mother said, oh, they'll be back in a while.

Where'd they go?

Her mother patting her hair, the flash of the diamond, oh, they went to do some shopping.

Susan looked at her mother. She had plucked her eyebrows, then drawn them in a new line, too high and dark. Her make-up was too heavy, her lipstick too dark and red and too much bowed on the upper lip, but the effect was not of an older woman trying too hard, but more of a young girl dressing up to look older. Her mother looked vulnerable and girlish.

Susan wanted, then, to hug her mother, but she turned to walk into the kitchen and Susan walked behind her.

Then Susan stopped in the doorway, aware that the doorway framed her, she hoped her mother would notice her dress, say something about the dress, but her mother didn't.

Susan held out the present.

Mother.

What is this?

Something for you.

Her mother looked at Susan, then looked away.

Oh, Susan, how very nice of you.

Her mother took the present, ran her finger over the bow, curled and uncurled it, very nice, Susan . . . how have you been, you've stayed away so long.

I've been fine.

I'm glad you've come home, Susan. You look so pretty.

But her mother looked frightened. She ran her finger vaguely around the curled ribbon.

Susan wanted to say, oh Mother, don't look like that, I've talked to Uncle William, I know what happened, you could have told me, I would have understood.

Again, she almost hugged her mother. She took a step toward her. There was something so tormented in her mother's eyes, Susan was frightened and confused.

Susan saw her own face in a picture-size mirror on the wall. She looked down. A round white birthday cake centered on the kitchen table: it had her name on it in blue frosting: SUSAN. And candles.

Her mother placed the present on the edge of the table without opening it and said, I have something for you, too, Susan.

She turned, clicked open her purse, took something out, handed it to Susan.

It was a check.

Susan unfolded the check with a feeling of disappointment and confusion. She'd wanted something from her mother she could keep, a present, something she could wear.

Mother, thank you. . . . Mother, this is for three hundred dollars, what are you doing?

It's for you, Susan. She clicked her pocketbook shut.

But it's so much, really, it's not necessary.

Her mother started to say something, her mouth moved, she waved her hand, dropped it.

Susan stood for a moment, thought she would kiss her mother, but pulled out a chair, said thank you. She stared at the cake a moment. Thank you. She placed the check on the table.

Her mother walked to the other end of the kitchen table.

Susan?

Yes, Mother. . . .

Dad— She said the word and stopped. She closed her eyes. Susan saw her mother's hands clenched over the back of the chair. Her knuckles were white. It was hot in the house. Susan realized no windows were open. Were they permanently locked? The kahunas? Her mother opened her eyes and started again.

Dad—

Susan looked at her mother's face. Asked softly, what is it, Mother?

He's not your father.

Her mother looked at Susan, eyes wide, frozen.

Not your father, she repeated.

The room muffled and vague. Mother fading into the distance, the cake, the present on the edge of the table, the check a blur.

Susan felt herself gasping for air. Something hard had hit her in the middle of the chest, closed her chest.

She heard a voice.

Not . . . my . . . father?

Mother shaking her head. Not your father.

Dad . . . is . . . not . . . my . . . father?

Her mother shaking her head quickly.

Her voice still distant. Automatic and mechanical. Are you . . . my . . . mother?

She nodded her head quickly, yes, I am your mother.

Dad . . . is . . . not . . . my . . . father? She heard her voice, far away. What do you mean, he's not my father? She heard herself laughing. Who is . . . my . . . father?

Her mother shook her head.

You don't know who is . . . my father?

I know.

Then . . . who . . . is . . . my father?

Her mother shook her head quickly. Her necklace rattled.

Suddenly, Susan laughed. Mother, you are so funny. I didn't know you were so funny. Why didn't you ever joke with me before?

Again she shook her head.

Susan looked down and saw her hands holding on to the edge of the kitchen table. Susan heard her voice, why . . . why did you . . . wait . . . so long to tell me . . . this? She looked at the white cake. SUSAN. I'm twenty-two today. Isn't that . . . too . . . long?

164

Her mother went on staring at her. Holding on to the back of the chair.

Susan heard her voice going on by itself. You could have told me when you came back from the mainland. . . . I had a right to know. Her voice was so even, it frightened her. She felt herself starting to tremble.

Does Dad know I'm not his?

Her mother nodded.

Is Carol his?

Yes.

She felt as though she were making inquiries about someone else.

Did Obachan know?

Again her mother nodded.

Obachan knew?

Yes.

All that time . . . Obachan knew?

Again her mother nodded.

Abruptly, Susan stood up, knocking the chair backward. She heard herself scream.

NO! This isn't true. Why are you telling me this?

Her mother hadn't moved.

Why did you do this to me? Why didn't someone tell me? Suddenly she heard herself scream, Obachan! Why?

She began to sob. Why didn't you tell me! What's wrong with you? OH, God, Obachan! Why didn't you tell me! SOMEONE!

Then Susan heard her voice calm, but it's all right, all right, all right, it will be all right, I'm going to meet him, where is he? She approached her mother slowly, stepping over the legs of the chair, where is he, who is he?

Her mother shook her head slowly.

You must have a picture of him. I demand to see it! I'm going to see it! I'll tear this house apart! I demand to see a picture of him!

Her mother shook her head again.

You don't have a picture? You do! You won't tell me. Dad isn't my father? See, I can say it. Who is my father?

Her mother shook her head.

You won't tell me? Or you don't know? You don't know, do you, do you, you don't even know which one, do you?

Her mother slapped her.

I know, Susan. A serviceman. He wanted to marry me.

That's why you were always telling me I'd get pregnant, because you went out and got knocked up. With me! You and your don't-give-a-man-that-until-you've-got-three-carats!

Susan grabbed her mother's hand, wrenched it up in front of her mother's face, pushed the ring at her face. This! This! This! Look at it! You made me look at that ugly thing! Why didn't you tell me? Calling me stupid from the day you got me and took me home. Stupid! Why didn't you leave me where I was! I loved Obachan. I don't love you! You're stupid! Not me! You!

Her mother wincing. Susan flung her mother's hand at her, grabbed the check, tore it up.

Money! she screamed.

Susan—

Money. Why couldn't you have told me! Just the truth! The truth is all right. Why couldn't you have told me? Why did you wait so long!

She saw her face in the mirror. She grabbed the mirror off the wall with both hands. Held the mirror up close to her face. Her eyes, moving wildly. She turned.

Look, Mother. See me. See your daughter!

She held the mirror back in front of her. Her own face, light glinting wildly, look at me, Mother. Whose am I? How could you have waited? How? Whose am I? You don't know!

I know.

Whose? I demand to know!

She threw the mirror at the wall, it shattered, it doesn't matter, it doesn't matter, it doesn't matter what you say to me cannot matter any more, I'll never believe anything from you, it's hopeless.

She was at the door. On the walk, looking back at her mother up in the doorway. Then driving. Her leg felt slippery, she looked down, her calf was bleeding, a piece of flying glass had cut her leg, the glass cut my leg, she said out loud, blood starting to run down into her shoe, she wondered for a moment what was she going to do now that she had cut her leg and was bleeding. I was supposed to go over to Mother's for my birthday party. . . .

Then her heart started to pound, the road blurred, she pulled over. Her head in her hands, sobbing, her hands cupping a dark space, she cried.

She had gone drinking with Gale in the Bistro that night, and when the room seemed close and off-balance, she told Gale what had happened at her mother's. She started to laugh. Gale just stared at her, pushing her wineglass in circles on the white tablecloth, looking at the tablecloth, and then at Susan, and then back to the wineglass.

Afterward, Susan went home with one of the owners of the Bistro, Gale with the other; first, they were all laughing together—in one of the back tables at the Bistro, the Bistro was closed, that's why there were no more people; then, they were in a bed somewhere, he was making love to her, he had a beard, he was making love to her, she couldn't feel him at all, she hated men with beards, his beard smelled of veal scallopini, he was the one who supervised the cooking, I hate beards, she said, and started laughing.

When he was finished, she got up, staggered out of the bed, he said, where are you going? She was trying to get her clothes on, then she heard him beside her, the room was dark, there was some light coming in the window, she could see his face, get dressed and get out and don't ever set foot in my restaurant again.

Susan had been cooking for hours, the sun slanting in through the jalousies, stripes of white sunlight on the walls. Her hair was hanging in her eyes, she was sweating, the fan was on, food was piled on the counters, pots were steaming on the stove, the refrigerator was already filled with completed aspic molds, hors d'oeuvres, bottles of wine; now she was slicing vegetables, there was so much more to do, and there was still something she had to do, something at the store she had forgotten, she couldn't remember what it was, but it would come to her, the walls were white with sunlight.

Then Gale setting the table, putting out the new wineglasses and plates, Mickey and Harry and Nathan, she couldn't stand Nathan, but Gale wanted Nathan, so Nathan, and Gale and herself, just herself, here at the end of the table closest to the kitchen, so that she could get up and keep serving everyone.

Everyone ate in silence, stared at Susan, kept on eating, the fan blowing at their legs under the table, lifting the tablecloth, the front door was wide open, the sun had gone down and the lights of Honolulu were coming on against the fading blue sky and afterglow.

Susan kept getting up to take things out of the oven, turn up a burner, serve each person, pour wine.

Now Mickey was telling a Portuguee joke.

How does da Portuguee put on his pants in da morning? You know how?

No, how?

Da yellow spot going in da front and da brown spot going in da back.

Mickey laughing, stopping. Whats da matter, Susan? How

come you starin at me like dat? And smilin? What kine of smile is dat?

Harry reaching over and nudging Mickey.

Nevah mind. Very nice dinnah, Susan.

Susan looking at the empty dishes on the table, the bottles of wine, and suddenly getting up from the table, walking through the open door into the cooler evening air, lying down on the grass and staring up into the sky, a star was out.

Duke saying loud enough for the people around them—the bartender, the cocktail waitress, other customers—to hear, what the hell is wrong with you? What is it? You look awful. You're putting on weight, what's happening?

The sound of her laughter as she got up and walked out.

Each time Susan came home, Gale said, your mother called again. Whenever the phone rang, Gale answered it. When it was Susan's mother, Gale automatically said, she's not here; or, I don't know where she is, I haven't seen her.

One night, Susan and Gale went to Waikiki. The GIs on five-day R&R from Vietnam wandered up and down Kapiolani in twos and threes wearing new clothes, R&R clothes; they were sunburned, their noses peeling, hair cropped short, many of them self-consciously sporting mustaches and side-burns.

Gale and Susan wandered through Waikiki, through the International Marketplace, down to Hotdog Annie's, Gale groaned and said, come on, Susan, let's sit down and have a drink, my feet are killing me; they sat in a bar and had a drink. In the middle of the drink, Susan wandered out and Gale paid up in a hurry and followed her out, Susan was already on the sidewalk ahead of Gale, disappearing into the crowd, GIs and tourists looking at her; Gale caught up to Susan; Susan staring straight ahead, looking into the faces coming down the sidewalk, looking into the faces so that some of the people meeting her eyes looked away.

When Gale could walk no farther, she called up Mickey and Mickey came down and walked with Susan, until Mickey had to take her hand and lead her into a bar, put a drink in front of her, a hamburger; she ate some of the hamburger, swallowed some of the drink, and then stood up and wandered back outside.

At Queen Surf, the sea wall, stopping to stare out into the dark, listening to the waves slapping against the wall. Turning and walking on, sometimes stopping to listen to some sound, a bird in the zoo over in Kapiolani Park, a group laughing as they passed by, staring into faces, walking.

Then they would be taking off, Susan serving drinks, staring at passengers, staring into their faces until many of the passengers would look away. One morning, dressing, she noticed her uniform was so tight she could hardly move, she looked in the mirror, her face seemed full and heavy, her breasts too, and there was a bulge above and below her belt.

After the meeting with Miss Pahoa, Gale was driving home and saying, it's not just you; she wants both of us to take a leave. It's time for us to go somewhere—where should we go?

Susan thought about it for a long time and then said slowly, I'm not crazy, Gale.

Gale said, I know, Susan, no one ever said you were crazy, that's got nothing to do with it. Wouldn't you like to go to San Francisco?

Susan stared ahead through the windshield and decided the safest thing was not to answer any more.

Each time Duke called, Gale said, she's not here, honest, Duke; and finally, Duke came to the house right from his last flight of the day—still in uniform—and throwing open the door, he walked in and said, what the hell's going on here, what's wrong with you, where've you been and why aren't you on the schedule any more?

Gale said, you could knock, Duke!

I would if I'd thought I could get an answer out of someone around here.

He looked around the room. What is it, Gale, is she seeing someone?

She's sitting right there, ask her.

Are you, Susan? Susan? Why don't you answer me? Look at you—you've gotten fat, you've got no make-up on, your hair's a mess, this place is a pigsty, what the fuck's going on, you want to live like this? I'm not kidding, go look at yourself in a mirror.

Susan heard herself starting to giggle.

Duke crossed the room, sat down and took Susan's hand. Susan, what's wrong with you?

She smelled the gin on his breath.

What're you, a hippie? Are you turning into a hippie? Duke swung around and looked at Gale. Gale, is she stoned?

Why ask me, Duke, she's right there in front of you.

Are you, Susan? What are you on? Acid? Grass? Pills, what? Can't anyone tell me anything around here?

He squeezed Susan's hand hard. She saw he looked afraid.

Why are you smiling at me like that?

Leave her alone, Duke. Come back later.

I'm taking you to a doctor, Susan. You're sick.

No, Duke, I'm not sick. I'm . . . crazy. She smiled at him.

Stop giving me that stupid smile, Susan. What's wrong with her, Gale?

She needs a vacation.

Susan smoothed the epaulet on Duke's shirt. This is a nice uniform on you, Duke.

Duke pulled away and looked at her.

Leave us alone for a minute, Gale.

Gale walked outside.

Susan, Susan . . . I love you . . . you know that. . . . What's wrong, are you sick?

She heard herself giggling.

Are you?

She couldn't stop giggling.

What are you laughing at?

She stared out through the jalousies at Honolulu.

Will you come to a doctor with me?

What kind of doctor do you have for me, Duke?

Any kind, Susan. Whatever kind you need—I don't care how much money—

She started laughing. Do you have enough money, Duke?

Whatever it takes, I don't care.

He got up, lit a cigarette, looked at her. Sat back down.

Susan, if you could see yourself. This place is a sty. You look like hell.

She reached up and touched his face. She stared at his face. He took her hand. After a moment, she took back her hand.

Susan, will you marry me? We can live together, once we're living together, my wife will give me the divorce, she'll have to, you'll be the mother of my children.

They already have a mother, Duke.

Marry me.

One's enough.

Get your stuff together, we'll get an apartment . . . this afternoon . . . we can get a room in a hotel . . . we'll move in, she'll give me the divorce . . .

He opened the closet door. Grabbed a suitcase. The floor of the closet was tangled with clothes, shoes. . . .

Duke dropped the suitcase on the sofa. Come on, Susan, just tell me what you need, I'll pack.

She heard herself giggling. Duke in his uniform. So handsome, dirty clothes in both hands.

Those are Gale's, Duke.

172

These, then, are these yours?

Yes, Duke.

He started putting clothes in the suitcase, half folding some, then throwing them in.

What else, Susan? These things?

She could hear herself laughing.

She walked past him. Outside, she sat down on the grass beside Gale. They stared down at the city.

Duke stood beside her, the suitcase in his hand, eyes dark.

Susan, we can come back for the rest later.

Duke on the grass. In his pilot's uniform. White shirt. Black and gold epaulets shining in the sun. The suitcase. And a handful of her dresses.

Duke just asked me to marry him, Gale.

Susan. . . .

Doesn't he look beautiful in that uniform?

Duke dropped the suitcase on the lawn and walked out to the street toward his car.

I would have done anything to marry him.

He got in the car.

She waved once. He started the car and drove away.

Susan made lists of recipes, discarded them, made new lists from the stacks of cookbooks on the floor beside the bed.

Each afternoon, she spent hours in the supermarket, selecting vegetables, comparing prices. often slipping a gourmet delicacy into her purse—caviar, crabmeat.

Late in the afternoon, she would return to the house with two or three shopping bags, spread the food on the counters, wash yesterday's dishes, pots and pans, and then begin.

Veal Chops with Mushroom Stuffing: Spinach, butter, prosciutto, shallots, mushrooms, garlic, fresh bread crumbs, grated Parmesan cheese, salt and freshly ground black pepper, egg yolk, nutmeg, rib veal chops, vegetable oil, chicken stock.

First, trim and wash the spinach, place the drained spinach

in a saucepan with a tight-fitting lid—simmer until spinach is wilted. Drain. Let cool. When cool enough to handle, press between the hands, then chop.

Step by step.

Sweat.

Dice, chop.

Sweat.

Melt the butter and add finely chopped prosciutto. . . .

The sweat running down her chin:

. . . remove the saucepan from the heat and let cool slightly. Add the egg yolk and nutmeg and mix rapidly. Use the mixture to stuff the veal chops . . . add stock . . . bake . . . transfer the chops to a warm serving platter . . . high heat for two minutes . . . pour the juices over the chops . . .

The guests stoned. All but Mickey. Mickey won't smoke dope. Susan serving each of the guests until Mickey and Gale both say almost in unison, sit down, Susan, stop serving us, leave the plate, we can serve ourselves.

Susan, stop waiting on us!

Kahlúa coffee, Rémy Martin, Courvoisier . . .

The plates empty, a calm period for Susan, uneasy, but calm. Susan getting up, moving to the window, looking out, sitting back down, getting up again, walking to the door, standing in the doorway, looking out at the lights of the city, pacing.

Outside, the cooler night air, barefoot on the cool grass, something she had to do, the lights below, wandering back inside, the cookbooks, tomorrow, which one. . . .

Pork Strips Chinese-Fried with Red Peppers?

Susan wore muumuus now; her clothes no longer fit—her sleek chang san, her stewardess uniforms, none of them fit. Gale asking, you don't mind if I wear this dress tonight? and Susan shrugging, help yourself; often, Gale helped herself to a dress without asking. Eventually, she simply regarded the dresses as hers and wore them whenever she felt like it, leaving them draped over the back of a chair, or crumpled at the foot of her bed, where she had stepped out of them.

Susan opened her eyes. Gale's bed was empty. Sun was slanting in the room. Hot and still.

She heard the spitting of a suntan-lotion squeeze bottle. Gale, lying outside on a mat.

Susan rolled heavily into a sitting position, stood up with effort, balanced unsteadily, looked around. The cookbooks in piles. Scraps of paper stuck into their pages. Clothes everywhere. Unwashed dishes stacked in the sink. Ants streaming through spills on the counters. A gecko suddenly let out an arid sharp cry.

In the bathroom, Susan looked at herself in the mirror. Her skin shiny. The flesh heavy on her face. She took hold of her cheek, squeezed it between her thumb and index finger, pulled it away from her face, stared at the thick flesh. Her high cheekbones were buried in flesh. Her face had lost its fineboned definition. She had the feeling that if the flesh didn't stop now, her face as she had known it, might disappear altogether. She let go of her cheek and turned away. Stepped on the scale. Pulled up the hem of her muumuu so she could read the numbers. She was almost twenty pounds overweight.

She walked back out into the kitchen, opened the refrigerator, stared at the plastic containers half-filled with leftovers, some of them covered with bluish-mold, the Saran-Wrap beaded with condensation.

She pulled a stool up to the refrigerator, pulled up the garbage pail, and began dumping out the containers one by one.

When the refrigerator was empty, she sponged the shelves with boiling water, washed the dishes, scrubbed the counters, tied the garbage bags and carried them outside. Gale turned her head to squint against the sun at Susan. Back inside, Susan scrubbed the kitchen floor, moving heavily, pausing to rest, keeping on.

She shelved the cookbooks, sorted all her clothes from Gale's, threw some out, took a shower, washed her hair; then she made herself a cup of black coffee, drank it slowly and took her dresses and uniforms down to the cleaners. When she returned, Gale was still lying in the sun. Susan sat down beside her.

It's all over.

What is?

Whatever it is, it's over.

Gale turned and looked at Susan; Gale's face was covered with sweat.

Good. Your voice sounds different. Back to Susan. I hope so. What happened to end it?

Susan shrugged. I don't know. I just know it's over. I can't even blame my mother. I just feel sorry for her. Did I end it with Duke?

Gale nodded.

Susan said, Duke. She sat still a long time. She said, Duke once more, then got up and went in the house.

In the next few weeks she lost the weight; the high-sculpted lift of her cheekbones reappeared. When she made out her bid, and scheduling put her back on the line again, she was once again slim and beautiful, no traces of the weight remained visible, except for a fine, barely visible map of stretch marks over the curves of her pelvis and hips.

After she'd left the house that day, she hadn't spoken to her mother for another two years.

Then Susan came to the house one afternoon for something, and they both just ignored it, pretended it hadn't happened, none of it was real.

Her father didn't say anything either. Susan knew he had been told. But he didn't act any differently.

None of them acted any differently. They said nothing about it. Not a word.

Susan came to the house for something, stayed a short time and left.

Susan found the note in her locker.

Time: 4:15

Dear Susan,

As I mentioned to you, I did have the meeting with Vice President Sullivan. While he is favorably impressed by both you and your fine record here, it is more or less a rule of company policy to suspend individuals pending investigation in these cases of untoward rudeness. There is little either one of us can do to make an exception in your case.

As you know, there will be a hearing in which you will be able to grieve the charge. In the meantime, don't forget to file an appeal within seven days requesting a hearing—one letter to the airline, one letter to the union.

I will inform you of the date of the hearing and further developments. Until then, you will be off the schedule.

Yours,
Alice Pahoa,
Chief Stewardess

Susan reread the note. Angry, she still felt relieved. If they didn't fire her now, she wouldn't ever have the courage to quit. If she didn't quit, she'd end up like Mickey. What she wanted to do was to grieve and beat the charges—if she couldn't get them dropped—work on for several months, and then quit. But then again, fired, quit, what would she do without a job?

It wasn't so bad, day-to-day, the flying, but when she thought of it in terms of years—what do you do? I'm a stewardess, oh, how long have you done that? this will be my eighth year, when she heard herself say that, thought of it, seven years, then she felt panicky, frightened, as though there were something wrong or lacking in her, something she'd known she was going to do but hadn't done yet, and it was getting later and later, and she still hadn't done that something and still didn't know quite what it was.

She folded the note from Miss Pahoa and put it away.

Outside the terminal, Susan looked for Gale, didn't see her, and in the parking lot saw her car was gone. Remembered Gale was taking her car to be checked. A friend of Daddy's. Susan walked slowly through the parking lot, got in her car, sat for a moment, slipped off her shoes, rubbed her feet, and then started the car, put on her lights, and drove out of the parking lot.

On Nimitz Highway, she tried to remember if she had the United tickets for her mother and father, reached over, felt them in the flight bag, relaxed.

She drove back toward Honolulu wondering what she would do if there were no letter, deciding that maybe she would try to call him. It would be the middle of the afternoon there, that was another problem—they were so far away; he was awake while she was sleeping, she was awake while he was sleeping. But maybe she could reach him.

Susan got off the highway in Manoa, drove through the University of Hawaii campus. At a stop light, she saw some students coming out of an early-evening class. She watched them for several moments. They looked young. The light changed and she drove through Kaimuki, got on St. Louis Drive and started following the curves of the heights until the city lights formed a pattern of street and apartment lights below, and then she pulled up to the house, yanked on the emergency brake for the hill, turned off the engine, killed the lights, and then just sat looking at the dark house and mailbox.

She was still partially deaf from the jet engines and pressurization: the silence—just the crickets—and the coolness of the heights were nice. She sat for a long time with her head back against the seat, eyes closed.

Then she picked up her flight bag, her shoes, and slowly got out of the car. She crossed the street, opened the mailbox, reached in.

She pulled out several envelopes. Something for Gale. Bill. Bill. Bill. Bill collector. She reached into the mailbox again, felt around, went through the envelopes once more, walked slowly up the path toward the house.

Inside, she dropped the mail on the table, looked around. Everything as it had been left this morning when they'd left the house at sunrise. Her half-drunk cup of coffee, filmed over. The panty hose with the discovered run hanging over the chair. Beds unmade, counters covered with dishes, coffee grounds flecking the garbage bag.

It seemed so long ago that she'd left the house and coming back here made it seem so final in some way.

She ducked under a faded Japanese lantern. Stopped. Reached up. Touched it. The lantern had been in the beach house over their bed.

Susan unbuckled her belt, her body was still swollen from the cabin pressurization, she would take a shower, change, get out of this place, that was the first thing . . . she would stop at her parents, drop off their tickets—maybe there would be a letter at their house, or maybe he'd even sent the letter to their old house.

Anyway, she would take a shower, change, get out of here, maybe to Mickey's—

She unzipped her uniform, sat down, put her arms on the kitchen table, pushed back the dishes and laid her head down. After some time, she woke with a start. Jack! He was in the room. She could feel his presence. He was hiding in the room. He'd come back, but not told her—as a surprise.

Jack, she said, looking around.

The dream suddenly came to her. Something in the airplane. She'd been coming up to the cockpit . . . but not in her uniform . . . she opened the door to the cabin, but it wasn't the cockpit. It was their old room—a big white room. But no one had lived in it for a long time. Jack's shirt was on the bed. And a Japanese lantern on the floor.

She looked up and saw the Japanese lantern hanging above the kitchen counter. . . .

The back of her arm was warm with saliva. She wiped the side of her mouth.

Drifting. Jack . . . she wondered if she could at all . . . if Moon had done any permanent damage to her . . . she'd bled so much . . . eggs . . . a woman was born with all the eggs she would ever have . . . you carry them with you . . . from birth . . . they get older and older . . . weaker? . . . and if her mother was crazy, that could be in them . . . craziness . . . and the other one, what was he, who? . . . she remembered reading somewhere that at menopause a woman's ovaries turn to dust . . . could that really be? Dust? Horrible! She stood up suddenly, her heart pounding. She could smell the cigarette smoke, stale perfume, spilled booze on her. She looked down. The mail. She sorted through it once more, then stripped off her clothes, ran her hands over the creases in her skin from the uniform—the elastic crease at her waist from the panty hose, the pressure lines from the belt, the lines surrounding her breasts from the bra. She went into the bathroom and turned on the shower.

Susan looked through the closet once more, the dress wasn't there, she realized Gale must have taken it, it was the only dress she'd felt like wearing. A dress Jack gave her. She yanked a dress off the hanger, balled it up and threw it in the direction of Gale's bed. Why did Gale still insist on wearing her clothes, she never wore Gale's.

She found something else to wear, put it on, snatched a

piece of paper, pushed the dishes back to make a space at the table, sat down.

She thought of all her attempts to write during the day, felt like an idiot, said out loud, fuck it, I'll just write him what I feel; she hesitated a moment, thought—debating whether she'd tell him that she'd been suspended, decided, no, he might get scared, think I'm depending on him. She headed the letter and wrote:

Dear Jack,

I've been trying to write you all day. Why it's been so hard, I don't really know.

First, I tried to write you an innocuous letter, and then I tried to write you telling you how much I loved you and asking why you weren't writing. None of the letters seemed any good, but I think I was just afraid—afraid I'd write what I really felt and scare you off or something stupid like that.

I don't feel much I can't write in plain English. I love you and I'm angry that you haven't written. I don't know why you haven't written, but the only thing I can think of is that you don't love me any more, but don't want to hurt me and so you're letting me down slowly.

If that's what it is, I'd rather you just write me the truth— if you don't want me any more. It's better you tell me than leave me hanging. I wouldn't want you to feel guilty or responsible. I'll be hurt, yes, but it would be better than just being left in silence like this. I was so disappointed when I didn't get a letter from you today. Please tell me the truth. I always want the truth.

I've wondered if you haven't hesitated about me because I'm Oriental. This was something that was always on my mind while we were living together but I was afraid to talk about it. I guess that's my fault, not yours. But it's still on my mind. Is it because I'm Oriental that you don't want to go on with me? In the letters I tried to write you today, I mentioned this and then decided it might be something too close to the bone, but I don't want to—I can't—beat around the bush any more. I can't, I guess. Well, if it is because I'm

Oriental, I'd rather you tell me that, too. I wonder if you could even admit it to yourself.

Sometimes, I've had this fantasy that we were walking in a large crowd, a large Oriental crowd, we've been separated and we're wandering around looking for each other. Would you be able to find me, pick me out of the crowd?

I know that's a stupid fantasy because there actually were lots of times in large crowds—Ala Moana, Kapiolani Park— (remember the concerts?)—when you would walk right up and put your arms around me.

I wonder if my knowing you and loving you and the time we spent wasn't all something I dreamed, something which didn't really happen. Maybe it's just that you're on the mainland and I'm all the way out here on these islands. Sometimes this place is all like a dream anyway. But then, I know it isn't a dream—you and I—because I still feel the love I have for you.

Please don't leave me like this in silence, just write and tell me what's in your heart, that's all I want.

Love, Susan.

She stood up, found an envelope, looked the letter over quickly, and sealed it inside. She addressed the envelope. She looked at it a moment, decided it was a good letter and if it blew everything to bits, then it would, but . . .

She would mail the letter before she changed her mind. She looked through the closet once more for her dress, it wasn't there, suddenly, she yanked one of Gale's dresses off the hanger, started to put it on, looked at it, stepped out of it, kicking the dress aside, walked to the refrigerator, some leftovers, she looked at the mess in the kitchen, hungry, but couldn't eat, slammed the refrigerator door, grabbed a different dress, and pulled it on. Rummaged through her purse for some make-up. Pulled out a small jar. Romanoff Beluga Caviar. She looked at it a moment. Expensive. Slipped it in. Where? Remembered. So easy.

She was halfway out to her car before she remembered the letter and her parents' United tickets and went back for them.

She would stop at Gale's parents' place; if Gale was there, she would get her dress goddammit, take it off her if need be; she drove toward Pacific Heights, suddenly feeling confused, thinking, yes, maybe he had some feelings of hesitancy, of confusion, because I'm Oriental; if I'm confused, why shouldn't he be confused? Maybe it has nothing at all to do with my being Oriental, maybe I'm just fucked up, me, the way I am, and I'm blaming, no, not blaming, but using my being Oriental for that, just the way some of the girls when it's to their advantage—even Gale, who didn't look at all Oriental, but haole —used their Orientalness to play all their Oriental-mystique games....

Maybe, maybe, maybe . . . she felt confused. At a stop light, she jumped out, ran to a mailbox, mailed the letter, felt relieved.

She saw Gale's car wasn't in front of her family's house, was about to pull away, when she saw Gale's mother standing on the edge of a circle of white light thrown from the carport spot. Mrs. Lopez in tight-fitting red Bermudas. Mrs. Lopez hunched over a driver, swung, the practice golf ball hissed on its pivot, returned to position. Mrs. Lopez looked up, waved, walked to the curb. They exchanged a few words. No, Gale hadn't stopped home.

Susan turned around in the driveway and, still unhappy with what she'd been left to wear, started for Kahala, to her mother's and . . . father's.

Her father answered the door in his stocking feet and undershirt. He had more of a belly, it was round over his belt and stretched his undershirt tight; he was balder, the remaining hair grayer . . . his blues eyes paler.

He stood blocking the doorway, the paper hanging from one hand, a cigarette in the other. After a moment he said, hello, Susan,

He stepped back from the door.

Hi ... Dad.

The tv on loud, the color moving on one wall, reflecting in the glass doors of the lanai. Her mother turned her head.

The living room smelled close—of coffee, food, still air.

Susan took a deep breath, stepped out of her shoes, kicked them into a pile outside the door, stepped onto the thick rug. The overstuffed furniture, the porcelain lamps on the end tables, the overlarge lampshades, too much furniture, the still-empty built-in shelves. She was always afraid she would brush against one of the lampshades, knock the lamp off-balance, shatter one of the lamps, or china figurines.

Her mother turned her head. The light of the tv flickered on her face. Her eyebrows plucked, eyebrows still pencilled in too high, the mouth overly lipsticked.

Hi, Susan. She waved, wiggling the tips of her fingers two or three times the way one would wave to a child. She turned back to the tv.

Her face was almost the same, a made-up mask, the hair dyed perfectly black, bobbed; her mother's face reminded her of a doll's except the face had age in it, the bones were coming up, the skin seemed to be stretched too tight.

Her mother stood up and smoothed the front of her dress.

Eaten, Susan? Like something to eat? Some coffee?

Coffee, Mom.

It surprised Susan how small her mother was. Had her mother gotten smaller?

Her father sat back down in his chair, dropped the paper among the sections already on the floor, laced his fingers together over the roundness of his belly. He looked at her, but didn't say anything.

I've got the tickets. She reached into her purse and fished them out.

Let's see. He held out his hand. Let me see the tickets. He wagged his fat fingers. The faded tattoo on his forearm.

Susan handed him the tickets.

Any mail for me here, Dad?

Mail? Why would there be any mail for you here? We haven't even seen you for six months. Why should there be mail?

Oh, I just wanted to check.

He put the tickets down on the arm of the chair and looked at her.

No, really, why would there be any mail for you here, Susan? Be logical.

Oh, forget it, you're right, there shouldn't be.

Well, don't go getting annoyed at me because you didn't get any mail here. You've got to control that temper, girl.

Forget it, Dad.

Don't look at me like that.

Her mother brought out the coffee, set it beside Susan, fussed over it for a moment, returned to the kitchen, brought back a napkin, folded it once, looked for a place to set the napkin, set it under the coffee, debated, went back to the kitchen, returned once more with some turkey on a plate, cole slaw, potato salad, then sat down on the sofa, spotted the tickets.

What're those, dear?

The tickets. Susan got us the tickets. He held them up. The tickets.

Oh, very nice, Susan.

Susan took a sip of the coffee. She half-stood, reached over and turned down the tv. She looked at the turkey. She was hungry.

Her father opened the tickets, read them, nodded once,

stopped, looked from one ticket to the other, held them up close. Susan broke off a turkey leg. Raised it to her mouth.

Susan, what's this, you mother's ticket is on a different day than mine?

She put down the turkey.

It shouldn't be, I told them to make them on the same day.

Never mind it shouldn't be. These tickets are on different days. Would you like to look for yourself?

No, I believe you, they must have made a mistake.

Same flight numbers, but *different* days.

What's that, dear?

Nothing. The tickets are on different days.

What?

Different days! He shouted and glared at her. Shook his head from side to side in exasperation.

Susan was surprised to see the tv light glint on the flesh-colored button in her mother's ear. Her mother balanced on the edge of the enormous sofa as though she might fall off the edge.

Her father slapped the tickets against his open palm. Sighed. Lit a cigarette. His lips moved for a moment, there was a tightness around his mouth. He inhaled deeply.

Susan, I don't know how you can let a snafu like this happen. You were right there at the ticket counter when they gave you the tickets. Didn't you take the trouble to check them? Check details? He tapped his head. If you don't pay attention, people dope off on you. You've gotta check details.

Her mother looked at her. Susan felt the two of them staring at her, she rubbed her hands together, sure-I-check-dem, the voice floated, she cut it off quickly, felt confused, smiled, the smile was wrong, found the words, careful.

Yes, I did check them. All right, it's a mistake, what's so bad about your flying on different days?

Susan, he shook his head from side to side, Susan! This is

your mother we're talking about. I can't even let her drive to the store alone, how am I going to let her fly to San Francisco by herself?

Susan saw her mother's eyes flash to her father's for a moment, he didn't notice, Susan suddenly felt that her mother didn't need the hearing aid, that she knew what was going on, knows what's going on, she's always known, she's . . .

Her mother's eyes met hers. They were bright and stared into Susan's, they both looked away.

. . . crazy.

Her father saying, what a snafu, so typical, will you tell me, Susan, how am I going to let your mother fly to San Francisco on her own?

Susan stood up.

Will you stop referring to Mother as though she were a package tied up over there on the sofa!

Sit down, Susan.

She's sitting right here. How can you talk that way about her while she's sitting right here? She understands. Stop treating her like she's a child! A moron!

Sit *down*, Susan.

Give me back the tickets.

And *calm* down young lady.

I was doing you a favor.

Sit *down*, Susan. And don't talk that way to me in my house!

Her mother stared at the tv set.

Give me the tickets, I'll have them changed—Jesus!

And don't use that tone with me!

They glared at each other.

After a moment he handed her the tickets. See if you can get it right this time.

She jammed the tickets into her purse.

Shouting? I see you've found Mother and Father in their usual mood.

Susan looked toward the stairs. Her sister's voice, but . . .

Carol?

Hi, Susan, welcome home.

She made a mock gesture of welcome. Carol. She had that elaborate, slightly ironic way of speaking, mocking, that university way of speaking.

But there was something different about Carol. Her eyes. Her eyes were large and seemed darker now. Only takes a few minutes, local anesthetic, can do it in the doctor's office, just cut the lid to make the fold, scrape out a layer of fat....

Carol walked toward her.

Can't be changed back again. Susan hadn't seen her since.

Yes, her eyes were large and seemed darker now, the ridges and hollows hidden beneath the folds visible, but, looking at Carol, the eye operation hadn't made her beautiful; she was more overweight than she'd ever been, her long hair, instead of being luxuriant in it's fullness, struggled down her shoulders and back in a mass of broken ends and tangles.

Susan didn't know what to say. After a moment, it's ... nice ... to ... see you, Carol.

Likewise. Nice to have a breath of sanity in the menagerie.

Carol padded toward her, her finger marking the pages of a book. Her eyes had the slightly out-of-focus look, her movements the vagueness of a person who read too much, spent too much time alone.

Things, as you can see, are as usual around here, high-pitched.

Her father picked up the paper. That's enough, Carol.

Yes, Father dear, tra la la—

That's all!

It was cooler on the lanai, a breeze was clicking the palms.

Carol's voice had the mockery in it.

You're lucky, they're not too bad today. Now it's slow torture. They sit there in front of that tv night after night. They don't say two words to each other. Some kind of contest. Hard to say who's winning. I really think they're in the final stages of trying to kill each other.

Susan looked back into the living room through the glass door, the color tv flickering, the two of them sitting there, her father in the easy chair, a look of sullen anger in the lift of his chin, her mother balanced on the edge of the sofa like a doll.

Is she better about the kahuna thing?

Carol shrugged. Who knows? She's cagey; since we've moved, she can't say the lady across the street is trying to kill her, but I'm sure she'll find something. I still go through the paper and find little holes cut out and we know who cuts articles out of the paper around here, don't we now? Mother dear. Mother and her darling kahunas.

Carol lit a cigarette, the match flared up for a moment.

Really, she's off somewhere in her own world. By the time Dad gets home, he's usually in one of his moods and between her not hearing, and his shouting. . . .

He looks a lot older suddenly.

Well, either they're walking around screaming or else they're ignoring each other for days. I don't know which is worse, but it's not healthy. Personally, I'm going crazy here. I'm going bald. Carol laughed. Really. She grabbed her hair. I've been losing hair by the handfuls. I went to a doctor and he did a workup on me and said it's all psychological.

Carol returned to her mockery. Yes, I'm bald, folks.

Susan's eyes were getting used to the dark. Looking around, she could begin to make out the submarine plaques—the enameled wooden shields—coming out of the dark. He had taken them all, hung them up on the lanai.

Susan listened to the tv coming from inside, the palm fronds clicking.

Why don't you move out, Carol?

Oh, I would, I would, if I could find a job. With my big B.A. from the U of H, I could almost work as a checker in Safeway. Maybe when I'm bald, I'll be able to work in a sideshow. Even then, probably have a lot of bald ladies, not much demand for me.

The mockery suddenly went out of Carol's voice. I don't know what I'm going to do, they're driving me crazy, Dad's after me to go into life insurance. He said he'd get me a car if I ... At least you've got a good job, Susan....

Susan said, distractedly, might not have it much longer, I just got suspended ... as of four-fifteen today, as a matter of fact. The airline strikes swiftly. She heard the mockery in her own voice.

Carol waited, asked, what happened?

Susan shrugged. She was tired. I'll give you a detailed report some other time. It's too stupid. And I'm too tired. I'm going to grieve it. What really happened is that I've been smiling too long, I'm tired of smiling.

What if you lose the hearing?

Susan shrugged. I don't know. Then I'm fired. I won't die. I'd rather quit. I'm going to the mainland sooner or later. I've had it on this rock anyway.

Susan's eyes had become more used to the dark, the submarine shields coming out of the dark, the bright enamel on their escutcheons glinting in the light from the tv.

After a moment, Susan said, well, Carol, if it gets too bad for you, come stay with Gale and me once in a while—she was going to joke, if you don't mind Gale wearing your clothes, but realized Carol was much too heavy; Gale couldn't wear her clothes. Carol might feel hurt, Susan stopped. Tried it differently. Although Gale and I will probably be just as bad....

Carol had the mockery back in her voice. She gestured toward the living room. Nothing could be as bad as those two.

They didn't say anything. The tips of their cigarettes brightened several times.

Suddenly, Susan asked, did it hurt?

What? You mean ... my eyes?

Yes . . . your eyes.

Very little. It was a simple operation. He just cut the folds. . . . No, there was very little to it, really.

Does it . . . make . . . any difference to you?

Carol didn't answer. Her cigarette brightened, faded. Brightened. Faded.

Any difference? It makes some difference, I can't exactly put it into words, Susan. I'm not really happier or anything. But around here, in this house, who can tell?

Susan said nothing.

Then Carol said, a little defensively, you mean, did I fall over the first time I looked in the mirror and the swelling and bandages were gone? No, I recognized myself. I'm the same person.

Carol sounded unsure. And then Susan knew she would never have anything like that done on herself, give up that part of herself, knew it for sure as though there had been part of her asking a question she hadn't known she was asking, but now she had the answer.

She said to Carol, you look nice, Carol. Don't worry, you'll find a job.

Susan stood up.

I better get moving. I have to go to Mickey's. She's having a house blessing for her new house tonight.

Oh, where is it?

Over in Aina Haina. I forget the street name. I know the place. Carol? Does Mother ever . . . say anything . . . about me?

Mmm, not much, but she doesn't say very much about anything. I know she was worried when you and Jack were living together.

Oh, yes, Mother thinks no woman should ever give that away to a man. Charge them, I guess. Never mind what we get from men, we're supposed to be in a position to charge.

Carol laughed. Susan knew her sister was still a virgin, long past the time most of her friends; she knew that her sister was lonely, but for some reason, was also keeping herself unattractive to avoid men, maybe the hurt in loving them. Still, Carol laughed and it was nice to hear her laugh.

In the brightness of the living room, her mother and father hadn't moved. She saw her cup of coffee still on the table, cold now, or lukewarm. The plate of turkey still there.

Her father ducked his head to one side impatiently as Susan and Carol walked in front of the tv.

Bye-bye, Dad.

Just when she thought he wasn't going to say anything, he said without looking at her, on your way, Susan?

On my way, Dad.

He turned his head but didn't look at her in some kind of embarrassment. So long, Susan.

Bye, Mom.

Her mother didn't turn her head.

Bye-bye, Mom!

She turned her head, looked startled, fear in her eyes.

What's that, dear?

Susan's saying good-bye, damn it!

Oh. Bye, Susan. Her mother stood up, smoothed the front of her dress.

Again, Susan was surprised by the feeling, but she's so small. Her mother followed behind Susan and Carol.

Stop by, Carol.

Maybe sooner than you think.

Fine, I meant it.

Thanks. Carol turned and started up the dark stairs. Susan noticed her finger still marking the pages of the book.

Outside, Susan stepped into her shoes.

Bye, Mom.

Bye-bye, Susan. Come again sooner next time.

She would kiss her on the cheek, she wanted to, hug her, now.

Susan stood motionless a moment, looking at her mother.

Mom. . . .

Her mother looked startled.

Yes, Susan?

Susan took a deep breath. Bye, Mom, walked toward the stairs.

She turned at the head of the stairs. Her mother waved, then stepped back and started to close the heavy wooden door. Susan walked down the stairs and crossed the parking lot to her car.

Halfway across the parking lot, she felt panicky. She looked back at the condominium, then thought she'd drive on to Mickey's.

She drove along the Kalanianaole Highway, but after several traffic lights, she wasn't sure she should go on. The light changed, the car behind her honked, she pulled over to the curb, sat with the blinker flashing.

She thought of what it would be like at Mickey's. The house would be filled with people, airline people, Harry's family—brothers, sisters, his old father and mother, Mickey's old mother would be there, Gale, lots of stewardesses, everyone would be talking, children would be playing, crying, Mickey's voice would be loud through it all; everyone would be fair play for everyone else's needling, there would be the need to laugh at stupid jokes, make more stupid jokes, there would be complaints about the airline, gossip, old gripes aired by Mickey, the world never treated Mickey right, people were out to get her. . . .

Maybe Mickey wouldn't even let her in at all.

Susan turned off the blinker. Always fighting with Mickey. Gale, too. But mostly Mickey. Just that Mickey didn't understand the need for privacy—or had such different ideas of privacy—or space. Reading that note over her shoulder this afternoon. And then being angry when she, Susan, was annoyed. Even when she talked to you, she talked so loud. And stood so close. Mickey didn't seem to recognize space and privacy. Maybe they could never really be friends beyond a certain point. Some chemical disagreement.

Susan put the car in drive, stepped on the brake, slipped the car back into park.

All right, I don't go, she never speaks to me again. I do go, she's insulted I had the nerve to show up; she won't let me in.

Susan thought of the new house, the smells, the noise. Took a deep breath. On New Year's Day, it was the custom to drive from house to house, stop a while, visit and eat, move on. She had done that with Mickey and Harry once. Rooms full of people. Sitting on sofas, in folding chairs. Sitting on the floor. So full she had to look for a foot-sized space on the floor, step from space to space off-balance, all the time dizzy, hot, the rooms close with food, bodies; then, driving on to the next house, all the time Mickey keeping up a nonstop stream of chatter, Mickey getting more and more excited, and anxious, turning to Susan, you having a good time, eh? And Susan, dizzy, feeling more and more drained, oh, great, Mickey really; and smiling, smiling.

Susan pulled away from the curb, hit the green light; drove on, Hawaii Kai, she started up the hill at Koko Head. Came to the top of the hill, passed the turn-off for Hanauma Bay.

The moon was half-full and ahead she could see the whitecaps in the Kaiwi Channel, feel the wind hit the car. During the day when she would come to this part of the road, just before the top of the hill and turning onto the windward side of the island, she would always anticipate the sudden opening up ahead, right and left, blue, the ocean blue, and the surge of wind; driving farther on and, taking the first curves, there would be the deep iodine smell of ocean, seaweed, tide, the air heavy with moisture, the sense of sea surge.

Now in the dark, under the half-moon, the breaking seas glowing, the dark channel seemed endless. All the time growing up in Hawaii, she had never lived near the ocean until she'd lived with Jack. Strange that there had been a whole side of Hawaii she'd never known or really even felt firsthand, or cared about until she lived with Jack, a mainlander and a haole. She hadn't even known how to swim. Jack had taught her. She'd had a fear of putting her face in the water.

She drove down the hill and started into the curves, the road winding along, the dark lava of Koko Head on her left, the sea below on her right. There were several cars pulled off on to the narrow shoulder, and, looking off the road, down the rock ledges and into the dark, she could see the Coleman lanterns of the fishermen—usually older Japanese men—the lights glowing like fireflies on the rock ledges. At different hours of the night, driving this road, she'd see the men in light windbreakers, with their long surf-casting rods and lanterns, climbing back up onto the road, or starting down, stepping over the guard rail, always a man going down to fish in the dark, as though it were the same man in a constant state of migration....

Jack had had the same things, the Coleman lantern, the surf-casting rod. She'd been frightened, she read in the paper of the men who would go down on these rocks to gather opihi, disappear, afterward, a friend might tell the police all he had seen was the wave receding from the spot. They rarely found the body. The thought of the body in the black canyons of ocean between the islands . . .

But Jack had been confident, comfortable with the sea.

When they climbed down onto the rocks, he would light the lantern, coax and pump until the mantle had an even white glow. The light spread over the rocks and ledges. He showed her the rusting iron rings. They'd been driven into the rocks so the fishermen could lash themselves to the rocks in heavy weather. There were other lanterns on other ledges. They sat there half the night, the constellations rising in the black sky, the Southern Cross, the Scorpion, the mantle of the Coleman glowing, the sea surging and echoing as the breaking waves rushed against the rocks and trapped air in lava tubes with muffled explosions.

With Duke, it always seemed as if they were in a hotel, a bar, on a golf course, always with a lot of people, always Duke drunk. With Jack, they would go up into the mountains, pick guavas, climb the ridges up into the clouds, their hair getting chill and wet....

Susan drove, the road winding alongside the ocean, Sandy Beach was coming up; here, just ahead, was the beach where Burt Lancaster and Deborah Kerr had played the love scene in *From Here to Eternity*. The only way down was a steep path twisting through the rocks and lava. Susan peered down into the dark.

... From Here to Eternity ...

Frank Sinatra had once given her mother a fifty-dollar tip....

Susan was winding down the hill now, level, Sandy Beach rough tonight, mist from the breaking surf blowing across the road in her headlights, misting the windshield, she put on the wipers and spray for a moment.

Looked up into the dark of Kalama Valley on her left, developments going up now, the old Hawaiians said the land was cursed here. There was little rain in this pocket of the island; a Hawaiian legend told how Pele had been thrown through the air by Maui, the indentation in the land, the valley, was the place where Pele's cunt had hit.

Kalama Valley was also supposed to be one of the paths to the sea; at any rate, Hawaiian rumor had it that the valley was full of unhappy spirits. Rumor or no, it had, in fact, not long ago, been full of unhappy flesh and blood people, poor Hawaiians who were being evicted from their shacks because Bishop Estate had decided to develop the land.

On the morning of eviction, the Kalama Valley residents had gone up on the roofs of their shacks. The police had been ordered to get ladders, climb up, and carry them down, one by one; once on the ground, the police fingerprinted and photographed them, right there, from the back of a truck.

The last man on the roof had been the kahuna, Lono, and when it had come to arresting him, going up there on the roof and laying hands on him, the police had balked. He was a kahuna.

Lono had stood on the roof of the shack, the mountain ridges behind him, Lono, a bald, plump, fifty-year-old, coffee-colored Hawaiian with thick glasses, bad teeth, and an odd way of moving his tongue. He had gone on chanting his old Hawaiian chants and the newsmen had taken pictures, the tv camera crews had recorded it for the news, the police—nisei, Hawaiian, Portuguese, no matter—had stood back and refused to touch him.

When he had finished chanting, he had come down off the roof, climbing carefully down the ladder; the police had stood clear of him, no one wanting to touch his hands to take fingerprints, no police photographer wanting to photograph him. One of the newsmen asked what he had been chanting and he said in a heavy Hawaiian accent, death, old Hawaiian chant for death, death by fire.

Then, chickens scattering, he crossed the dusty road, got into a rusting Ford pickup with a couple of poi dogs drooping their heads out the window, and drove away.

Two weeks later, the wife of a Bishop Estate Trustee had been burned to death in her hospital bed. There had never been a fire in the hospital before. An official investigation could find no cause.

Susan thought of her mother, in some suspended state of terror, in her condominium, thick walls, thick carpet, the electrical appliances, the overstuffed furniture, her mother, when her father was at work, her sister out somewhere, alone in the

197

house, waiting, secretly clipping the articles out of the paper, secretly arranging them in her scrapbook, wondering, waiting . . . never safe. . . .

Susan stepped on the gas, starting up the hill to Makapuu.

At Makapuu, reaching the top of the hill, rounding the curve, the surf coming in, far below, white on the black ocean, farther out, Rabbit Island, stark and rocky, like a chunk of lunar mountain in the moonlight. Makapuu Point light flashed from the rocky point.

Here, the Koolaus sheer and close. Loose rocks occasionally thudded down across the road. She drove past the beach park, turned, drove down a short street toward the ocean, could go no farther, the ocean, turned and followed the street, saying to herself, it's a mistake to do this.

In her headlights, a couple of poi dogs sleeping in the street slowly got up, stretched, mooched out of the way.

She slowed at the mailbox, parked.

The sandy driveway lined with tall ironwood trees blowing in the wind. She passed the red barn, looked in the doorway, the gray flicker of a tv.

The yard a litter of broken surfboards, junk cars up on blocks, windshields smashed, bodies rusting; poi dogs snoozed in holes they'd dug in the sandy grass.

She looked around. Roy's car was pulled up under the hau tree in the middle of the yard.

Susan walked to the back stairs, put her hand on the rusting rail, stepped out of the shelter of the stairs onto the sandy path leading to the beach, felt the blast of wind. Makapuu light flashing. Halfway up the stairs, she looked down into the dark. Somewhere near the fence aloe plants grew.

She climbed to the back door, knocked, knocked again, touched the door, moist, she turned the knob, called, pushed open the door.

The kitchen.

The same.

She walked to the door of Roy's room, knocked. Roy? Looked in. A big white room.

Sat on a stool in the kitchen. The coffee cups they'd left. She picked one up. This one had a chip along the rim. Here. She touched the chip with her finger. Here.

The cupboard doors creaked in the wind, back and forth.

She walked to the other end of the kitchen, the house was always full of wind currents, right here was one, she walked into the center of the house, felt the cool air moving, looked into the dark room, walked back toward Roy's doorway. Roy? Went up and into Roy's room, this had been Jack's room, but they'd changed rooms, she stepped up into the room, walked slowly across the lauhala mat into the center of the room, stopped, closed her eyes, the sound of surf through the windows, air moving, she raised her arms, opened her eyes, drifted toward the bed; she stood by the bed. The hook still in the wall. The Japanese lantern, used to rock in the wind. She reached down and touched the bed. Jack's bed. A sudden sense of pressure over her body, darkness and falling, the sound of the surf fading, and pressure tighter, a place and the weight, this part of his shoulder over her chin, this part, the curve of his shoulder and neck, a beautiful curve, a soft curve, soft to the hand, too, but powerful; release, then, coming apart, the closeness, the sound of the sea again in the windows, his breath against her cheek, his breath getting deeper, the sea, a stillness in his body, his hand on her back, breath getting deeper, the sea ...

Susan stood by the window. The rush of the sea through the jalousies. Dark palms heaving at the edge of the window light. The windows fogged with mist drifting in from the breaking waves.

She walked along beside the window ledge, touching the

glass floats. Japanese net floats. They'd find them tossed upon the beach, crusted with barnacles.

Here, the avocado plants. Trim and green. Susan pinched off several dead leaves with her nails, smoothed the stalk with her fingertips.

She walked slowly around the room, the wind blowing hard through the jalousies, the wind always blowing, papers fluttering; always a sense of movement, motion, wind, but order, as though the house were a ship steaming ahead.

The leaves of the plants shook, the back door slammed, Roy walked in, sand on his bare feet.

He was startled.

I knocked, but there was no answer . . . the door was . . .

He waved his hand. That's okay, I was just surprised.

Roy waved at a chair.

Tea? or I've got some wine. . . .

Wine.

Susan looked after him. A long blond ponytail caught loosely at the back of his neck. Nice gray eyes. A light-blond mustache. He'd always looked small next to Jack.

Roy returned with two glasses of wine.

It seemed strange to be drinking out of glasses which she had used every day, which had grown familiar, now strange again.

The wind shook the roof. The floor vibrated, several of the glass balls clicked together on the window sill.

Roy nodded at the wind shaking the roof, it's rough out on the beach. Stars are out, but there's a lot of wind. Rough flying weather?

A little bumpy today—clear air turbulence—but not too bad.

Susan looked around the room. Things look the same.

They pretty much are.

You've taken good care of the plants.

I can't really go wrong. Everything grows here, there's so much sunlight and rain. I had the avocados out on the stairs, but last week it got pretty windy. How's the weather been on the other side?

Oh, dry and sunny, dry and sunny, never changes on the leeward side.

They sipped the wine, the palm trees moving beyond the pale reflections in the window.

Have I gotten any mail here, Roy?

Roy went into the kitchen, returned with several envelopes. Bills.

Oh. She laughed. You can keep those, you don't know where I am.

Right. Roy smiled and threw them on the table. He went out again, returned self-consciously with the wine bottle, offered Susan a cigarette, took one himself.

You've been working on your pictures. . . .

They looked at one hanging behind Susan, Roy nodded, crushed out a cigarette, held up a finger, wait a second, and getting up, self-consciously, walked into the closet. Susan again noticed the bed, how neatly it was made, Roy returned with a large folder.

He undid the strings, carefully drew out several of his pictures, started going through them, the two of them nodding, commenting.

He stopped, looked at one a long time, focused the light, drew on his cigarette.

Susan stared at the painting. It seemed to be a pattern. Hard-edged. She looked closer and she saw it was jungles and volcanoes and the ocean and flowers and a jet leaving a vapor trail, and then, through the jungle leaves, in between giant flowers, there were faces, and she recognized Jack's face, and her face, and Jack's face, and her face, they were peering through the leaves over and over again.

Finally, Susan said, is that the way you see me, Roy?

I took the likenesses from a picture of you and Jack up at Manoa Falls.

It looks like Jack. But you've made me look so . . . romantic . . . so Oriental.

Roy leaned over the picture, his ponytail fell off to one side and brushed her cheek lightly.

Her purse was on the floor beside the chair, she caught sight of the letter from Miss Pahoa, felt afraid, Miss Pahoa would help her, I'm behind you, Susan, yes, but Susan knew it would come to a hearing, she would have to grieve it, it would probably go to a systems board, might even go to arbitration.

After a moment, Susan said, have you heard from Jack?

Roy slid the picture away from the rest.

He sat back down.

Shook his head. No.

Really, Roy? You can tell me the truth. You'd tell me if he had written you?

Really, Susan, not a word, hasn't he written?

She shook her head, started to say no, shook her head again harder, swallowed, looked away.

Oh, you know how Jack is, he'll write you, Susan.

She looked at Roy, got her voice back, it was tight, do you think so, Roy? He was writing every day. Now, he's stopped.

He'll write, Susan.

She rubbed her hands together.

It's a nice painting, Roy. I didn't mean I didn't like it before. I think it's beautiful. Do you think that's the way Jack sees me, too—so Oriental?

He lit another cigarette, drew on it deeply, watched the smoke. I think he just sees you as Susan.

After a moment, she stood up.

Wait. Roy returned with two sections of cardboard, placed the picture between sheets of clean paper, placed the cardboard above and below the picture, and carefully taped them together with strips of masking tape.

In the kitchen, she turned, hugged Roy, he hugged her, he smelled of cigarettes, sour, too, he didn't change his clothes enough, she didn't like his smell. She took the picture and stepped outside into the wind.

As Susan drove back toward Makapuu, her stomach started to growl, she realized she had last eaten this morning, been sick during the flight, and had not been able to put anything solid into her stomach since. She'd been hungry several times, but she hadn't been able to eat.

She drove back toward Mickey's, debating . . . Sandy Beach, the mist blowing across the road, Kalama Valley dark on her right, winding along through Koko Head, the fishermen's lanterns hovering in the dark out beyond the road and swinging headlights.

Again, the lanterns made her think of Jack, his face a smooth mask of white light in the Coleman lantern, a pleased smile on his lips. The sudden thud of the sea against the lava rocks. A moment later, the echo.

There had been so much passion between Jack and herself. Then, somehow, it started to slip away. It had been there, but it had become hard to get hold of. It never seemed to be the right time. Or neither of them could initiate it. Always, she could feel it there. The desire. But their love-making had changed from a heated journey to . . . something more restrained . . . then careful, and slightly embarrassed. Polite. Just the sight of him turned her on, made her want him, made her want to touch him, hug him, kiss him. . . . And she did, he wasn't one of those men who didn't like touching, thank God. Duke had been that way. He didn't like to hug and kiss. Sometimes, Duke would turn, irritated, and knock her hand off his shoulder or arm. Hugging and kissing for Duke was just a perfunctory hello and good-by before and after screwing. Jack wasn't that way. But something had changed. She just didn't have words for it.

Gale had been getting into encounter groups, gestalt therapy, all of that here and now, Rollo May, Fritz Perls, Esalen shit, and one day, Susan had surprised herself—she'd always looked at therapy as self-indulgence—and asked Gale for the name of a psychotherapist. Gale was able to recommend one— he's expensive, though—and Susan went to see him.

Susan followed the curves of the road, occasionally looking out into the dark channel. The sea out there. Black. Moving.

After several visits, he had asked her something about her mother, she couldn't remember what, but she remembered suddenly saying, facetiously, oh, I'm a slut, don't you know, my mother used to tell me that, Susan, you're a slut, a worthless, stupid slut. She used to say that I'd never amount to anything, that I'd get pregnant. . . . All sluts get knocked up . . . the first time I can remember her calling me a slut, I was eleven or twelve . . . I didn't even know what the word meant, and there she was calling me a slut. . . .

Susan lit another cigarette. She chain-smoked when she talked to him. He'd sit across from her in jeans or baggy khakis and a coffee-stained aloha shirt. His glasses were always smudged. He chain-smoked, too, listening to her, nodding, encouraging, his hair—long on the sides—flopping on his shoulders as he nodded. He was balding on top. She was touched by his attempt at long hair.

She shrugged. She just kept on calling me a slut.

He nodded.

Susan shrugged again. Well, so what . . . I don't know where that gets us . . . so my mother called me a slut . . . oh, I can just hear myself. This sounds so typical, this must be what everyone tells a shrink. . . .

He sat up in his chair. Never mind what people tell shrinks, Susan! Stay with it. Don't avoid it. Stay with it. You've got something here. You love Jack. You had passion with him. Passion's important. Where did it go?

I don't know. Maybe I'm just not sexy to him any more. I don't know.

Oh, yes you do!

No, no, I don't.

You don't think you're sexy, is that it?

I don't know.

Are you sexy or not!

I don't know.

He was sitting on the edge of his chair.

Do you feel sexy?

Sometimes.

And how do you feel when you feel sexy?

Good.

He threw up his arms, spread them out, nodded, smiled, repeated, good, good, wonderful!

She nodded, smiled. Wonderful.

Could you seduce me now if you wanted?

I don't know.

Yes, you do. Let me see you be seductive. Try to seduce me.

I couldn't.

You couldn't? You're not sexy? You couldn't seduce me? A girl with a face like yours, with a presence like yours—you couldn't seduce me?

No.

Why not?

I just couldn't.

He nodded for several moments, thinking. Suddenly, said, all right, I'm your mother. He glared. Stood up out of the chair. Pointed his finger.

You! Susan! You're a slut!

She sat, blank.

Get into it, Susan. React! You're a slut!

She sat motionless on the edge of the sofa. Took a deep drag on the cigarette. She smiled at him. I see what you're trying to do, but I can't get into it.

You cheap little whore! Do you always smile when you're called a slut!

She flushed. Was he kidding?

He came closer. Stood almost right over her. Pointed his finger at her.

You're a slut! A worthless slut!

She flushed again.

He bent over her, his face closer. His own face flushing red. He really looked furious. You're a slut! I mean it, Susan! This isn't a game. You *are* a slut! And you know it, don't you? You've kept it a secret, but I know it. Slut!

His face closer.

A whore, Susan! You know it! And I know it!

Her heart was pounding.

Susan. I *know* you!

She felt her head getting blurry.

You're a slut!

Shut up, she flailed at his face. Just shut up! Shut up! Stop it!

He pushed his face closer.

I won't shut up. You are a whore! You really are a little whore! A cheap little whore!

She grabbed at his head, knocked his glasses off, she had hold of his hair. Shut up, SHUT UP!

No, I won't shut up! YOU SLUT! SLUT! SLUT! You'll get pregnant, slut!

She grabbed at him, tore his shirt, he lurched away, she yanked at his hair. Shut up!

SLUT!

He staggered backward, Susan up now, after him, clawing at him, he covering his face, still shouting SLUT SLUT SLUT.

She fell to her knees, bowed her face to the floor, she was

sobbing, he was on his knees beside her, his arms around her.

He was asking questions. Between sobs she could hear herself gasping. What did you feel, Susan, before you came at me?

Nothing, nothing, nothing.

And when you finally said, no. What did you feel then?

Angry, crazy, powerful.

And—

Too powerful!

Too powerful?

Like it would never stop now that it was out!

It?

It!

And now?

Calmer ... tired ...

She went on sobbing. Calmer and sad.

She cried a long time. He kept his arms around her.

And toward me? How do you feel toward me?

Closer, closer.

After a time, he said softly, well, that's the idea, isn't it? To feel ... angry ... powerful ... closer ... sad ... to *feel*. ...

When she looked up, she saw she had scratched his cheeks, torn his shirt. She became aware of hair—his hair—under her fingernails, between her fingers. His glasses were lying in the corner.

Oh, God, I'm sorry. She reached up and touched the raw scratches.

What do you feel now?

Oh, sorry, sorry I hurt you.

And what else?

Tender.

He smiled sadly. Ah, tender, he said softly, almost to himself.

Then he'd been back in his chair, she on the sofa, smoking, talking quietly. He'd been talking for a while, he was saying, do you see, you've been so busy being the not-slut to prove your mother wrong . . . anger, fury, they're a turn-on. Look, a man—the man in all of us—likes the slut, the bitch, the whore. . . . It's in all of us, there's nothing wrong with it. Can you see that, that there's nothing wrong with it, that it's exciting?

She nodded, I think so.

Can you stop trying to prove your mother wrong and put those feelings back into your love for Jack. He needs them. Your anger! Your slut! He needs all of you! Not just your sweetness. Can you give those feelings to him?

She was trying to answer yes, she was shaking her head, no, she was crying again. He was out of his chair. He had his arms around her and she was sobbing into his chest and far away, she could hear his voice, go ahead, Susan, go ahead.

The lanterns drifted and floated away behind her as she drove up the hill toward Hanaüma Bay, came to the top, coasted slowly down the hill; she thought once of going back to her house and going to sleep, she thought of the mess, she wanted to be alone, to lock the door and read something beautiful and orderly, but she didn't want to be alone either. Susan drove on to Aina Haina, turned up the street to Mickey's, drove over the bridge, pulled up behind Gale's car. She was surprised to see Nathan's white Mercedes parked across the street. Both sides of the street were lined with cars.

Then she stood in front of the house. The first time she had seen their new place, Harry and Mickey had just moved in. The front yard was overgrown with flowers,—bougainvillea; ginger; bird of paradise, brilliant orange and blue flowers, torch ginger—the back yard, the same, ti, ginger. But the most beautiful part of the yard had been an enormous, twisted old hau tree that had grown up right beside the house. Some of the branches grew across the roof and yard, and cast a wide dark shade, shade that was so deep and cool, it almost felt as though you could kneel and drink from the shadows.

Mickey had led Susan into the house. First, the lanai. Then, the high-ceilinged living room with its high glass windows. The windows full of the green hau tree. Susan looked up at the green in the windows and said, how beautiful, its like being in a tree, it keeps it so cool in here.

Mickey looked vague, you tink so? Come look at da rest of da house, and led her down the hall to the bedrooms.

Shortly after, Susan came to visit and found the hau tree cut off inches above the ground; the only traces remaining were some sections of the trunk lying on the ground waiting to be hauled away. The yard glared white, the flowers and grass had been cut, the sun had shriveled everything. With the hau tree, the house had seemed part of the valley; now, it seemed isolated.

Inside the rooms were sweltering.

Mickey wiped her neck with a handerkerchief, said, yeah, hot now, but we going get da air conditioning put in tomorrow.

But why did you cut down the tree? It takes years for a tree to grow that big, Mickey.

Mickey waved her hand, wrinkled her nose. Oh, make da yard look like hell, dat tree, all disorganized; we going grade da yard, put in one garden, plant nice grass, nice flowahs, you see.

Harry spent several afternoons digging the stump out of the ground, standing out in the sun in a bathing suit and workboots, a red bandana around his head, his back gleaming with sweat; he patiently dug around the stump, then stepped down into the surrounding hole to hack with an ax, then, cut off the roots with a chainsaw; finally, he poured gasoline on the stump and set it on fire; when the fire burned out, he chopped, cut some more, poured on more gasoline. Once, the chainsaw glanced off a root and cut into the toe of his boot. Harry kept going. Finally, he dug out the blackened remains of the stump.

Then, Harry had several truckloads of earth brought in, he

and a friend who worked for a construction company, surveyed the yard, then graded the earth, using shovels and hand rollers until all parts of the yard, from the house to the edges of the property, were exactly level.

Next, Harry got hold of another friend, and the two of them worked morning until night on several weekends digging postholes, setting the iron pipes in concrete and then stretching chain-link fence all around the yard.

When the fence was finished, Mickey introduced climbing pikake to all parts of the fence, carefully tying the thin vines to the fence, weaving them in between the wire where she could.

Then they planted grass, leaving two sections of the yard unplanted. Where the hau tree had been, Harry poured a concrete patio. Behind the house, a similar square, this a dog run.

The dogs, two enormous Dobermans, were to be watchdogs. Both of the dogs stood waist-high and could easily crush a person's wrist in their jaws. Mickey grew to have very tender feelings for the dogs. She gave one of them a birthday party, a five-pound steak and a cupcake; and got furious when Susan and Gale laughed at her. The dogs were fairly well trained, but still somewhat unpredictable. Occasionally, they would growl at Mickey; once, Mickey had been alone in the house with one of them. Mickey in the bedroom. Each time she turned the doorknob to come out, she could hear him growling outside the door. She would talk to him; he would quiet down. And then she would put her hand on the knob and the dog would start to growl again. She had not been able to call Harry because the phone was in the other room.

Finally, when Harry returned home, the dog calmed down. Still, Mickey wouldn't let Harry into the bedroom, or let him unlock the door until Harry had reassured her the dog was back in the run, finally shouting, okay, look out the window! When she'd seen the dog outside, Mickey had unlocked the door, fallen into Harry's arms and burst into tears.

Now, as Susan stood on the sidewalk, she looked at the house, the grass growing evenly in the front yard, the chain-link fence covered with the fragrant pikake so that it formed a screen.

Above the fence, the bare roof, under the half-moon, the houses down the street, and far above, and beyond, the dark walls of the valley.

Susan hesitated at the gate. The valley was still. She could hear voices inside the house, hear sudden laughter. There was never any wind in this valley. For a moment, she smelled something stagnant, something rotting.

There were piles of shoes, sandals, sneakers on both sides of the door. She could smell cooking. Her mouth watered. She swallowed, rang the doorbell.

Mickey opened the door, she was laughing at something, she turned, saw Susan, stopped.

Hi, Mickey.

After a moment, Mickey answered, yeah, hi, Susan.

The tone was supposed to convey coldness.

Mickey pulled the door half-shut behind her. You've got your nerve, you know, comin here tonight aftah da tings you say to me today. Not once. Twice! She held up two fingers as Harry pulled open the door.

Hey, Susan! Howzit, come in.

Mickey turned on Harry. How you know I like have her in, eh?

Harry laughed quickly. Sure sure, nevah mind, she come in, come on, Susan.

Harry, Mickey whined, she say so many tings to me today, call me one tita. . . .

Harry laughed again. I know, Mickey, and you one big angel all da time.

Harry reached over Mickey and waved quickly several times at Susan. Come on, Susan, we want you here, no more quarrels in dis house, tonight, plenty to eat, plenty to drink. Harry spread out his hands taking in the house and yard. We mortgaged up to da eyeballs, we going to work till we ninety, but nevah mind, da kine . . .

Harry took Susan's hand. Come on!

Mickey shrugged. Okay, Susan.

Hey, come on, Susan, forget it, come on in, no stand dere.

Susan stepped out of her shoes, toed them into the pile, entered the house.

The living room was filled with people, the lights were bright, everyone was talking, laughing, babies were crying, people were sitting on the floor, leaning against the walls, five or six people were cooking in the kitchen.

Fix one plate!

Mickey gave Harry a sullen look.

Oh, that's okay, I'll get it myself.

Mickey shook her head, looked as though she felt bad. No, 'as okay, I'll fix one, Susan.

Harry waved his arms around, moved Susan into the room. Knots of people, some of them waving to Susan . . . Gale, yes, wearing her dress, the dress Jack gave her, Gale gesturing come on over, join us. A moment of anger at seeing Gale in her dress, then, nothing.

Gale with Nathan and Nathan's haole wife sitting on the other side, staring ahead with a sullen look, she didn't look as though she had the brains to object, Nathan holding Gale's hand, Nathan's other hand rested on Gale's thigh, she held his hand; Nathan had a look of quiet spiteful contentment on his face.

He smiled at Susan. She turned away.

There were Harry's mother and father holding several grandchildren between them, a lot of Harry's friends were there—from United, from his real-estate days, Harry's three brothers, the one who married the haole girl he met at USC, their hapa kids were playing, one of Harry's uncles, who was always getting into gambling debts, and his too young girl friend. Stewardesses. Ramp agents. A couple of guys Harry had once unsuccessfully tried to fix Susan up with a long time ago.

In the kitchen, Susan could see Mickey walking around a table, carefully picking things off platters, bowls, dishes, and arranging them on a plate. Mickey's old mother was standing there, impervious to the noise, quietly frying shrimps and carrot slivers and onions, watching them from behind her thick glasses. Occasionally, Mickey turned to say something to her, her mother kept on cooking without glancing up, and then Mickey would shout at her in Japanese.

Mickey's mother was afraid of black people. She believed black people smelled bad and was sure it was because they were cannibals. There was no telling her otherwise. She was full of superstitions. Susan couldn't tell if it were the Japanese, her mother, exasperation, or all three, which made Mickey shout so loud.

The room was so crowded, so warm, so heavy with food and sweat and perfume, Susan could hardly breathe, but there was something comforting about it, too.

Mickey handed her the plate and cup of warm sake with a look which was hard to gauge, a look both sullen and understanding.

Susan felt her mouth water so quickly she could hardly thank Mickey. Mickey turned to go. Mickey, wait!

Mickey turned.

I want . . . need to talk to you. . . . Can we talk for a minute . . . in there?

Susan pointed to the hallway, and Mickey led the way toward one of the bedrooms.

On the bed, Susan sipped at the warm sake, felt the heat spread through her, decided to take a bite from the plate, started eating quickly with the chopsticks, unable to stop, hating herself.

Mickey watched her. You hungry, eh?

Susan couldn't stop, just nodded.

Mickey sighed. Go ahead, Susan, eat.

Susan ate for several more moments, took a deep breath, looked at Mickey, sighed.

You ast me in here to watch choo eat?

They stared at each other, laughed.

Here. Mickey handed her a napkin, wipe your mouth, you dumb tita.

Mickey shook her head. You high-strung, you crazy. Her voice rose higher. I train you back in da beginning, you nevah used to be like dis. Susan, you going get yourself in trouble someday!

Susan swallowed the rest of her mouthful, wiped her mouth, nodded. Someday is today, that's what I wanted to talk to you about, Mickey. I *am* in trouble. I've been suspended.

Mickey sat up, her eyes widened, she gaped at Susan. At the look on Mickey's face, Susan laughed. To Mickey, trouble with the airline would be bad enough, but being suspended would be like death. The airline owned Mickey, owned the house, owned the next twenty years of Mickey's life.

Mickey just stared.

You suspended? What happened?

Susan dug out the note from Miss Pahoa, went on eating, suddenly calm as Mickey read the letter.

Once she glanced up to see Mickey's eyes moving quickly over the page and Susan wondered, can I tell her the truth? there were no witnesses, it's his word against mine, Mickey is the union representative, but she's in it for the airline, she's not even on her own side half the time . . . unless she thinks someone's slighted her.

Mickey finished the letter, looked up. Suspended? What choo did, Susan?

Nothing. Some guy called in a complaint. He doesn't even want to be identified.

How you know it's one guy?

Susan laughed, balled up the napkin. Oh, I just said that, figured it must be a guy.

Mickey read the letter again. You do anyting, Susan? Really?

Susan shook her head. No.

Mickey said, okay, Susan, don't choo worry. We gonna fight it.

Susan staring at Mickey. All that nonspecific fury, fury at being Japanese, fear at feeling the airline might dump her because she was getting older, wasn't so great-looking any more. . . . Maybe Mickey would be the right one to tell.

Harry stuck his head in the door. Where you been? Priest ready, now.

Mickey got up. We going talk bout dis more. You come in, now, Susan, but we going talk bout dis aftah.

The living room was quieting down, everyone had stood to face the center of the house, which was one wall of the living room with built-in cabinets and shelves; the shelves half-filled with books—*The Reader's Digest Condensations*, Book-of-the-Month Club books. The lower half of the shelves were built-in cabinets. The tv had been pushed to one side to make an altar. On one side of the altar, there was a banyan branch with a strip of lightning-shaped white rice paper. The holy sakaki branch. The white rice paper represented the food and clothing offered to the deceased, the purity of one's heart. The other side of the altar was piled up with food, several fish on a plate, mochi, a bottle of sake, flowers—the many things God had to offer man, and which man, at this moment, was offering back to God.

Susan recognized the Konkokyo priest from his picture on the kitchen calendar, Insurance & Real Estate, he was a dignified older Japanese, with a full head of silver hair, neatly parted. He wore a gray suit, stood in stocking feet. He pulled on a full-length gray robe, a black-crowned hat. He faced the altar and the room quieted. After a moment, the priest began to chant in Japanese. A baby started to cry, Harry's mother shushed the baby, holding him, rocking him, patting his back, talking softly. The chanting went on.

Susan watched Harry's hand rise tentatively from his side. Reach for Mickey's hand. They stared at the altar, heads slightly bowed, Mickey's hand slid into Harry's. When the priest finished, the room was silent for several moments, then people began to talk again in hushed voices.

Susan looked out through the kitchen window at the dark shapes of the Dobermans. They moved back and forth in the run. She turned. Mickey waving at her from across the room, pointing down the hall.

Then Mickey and Susan sitting cross-legged, opposite each other on the bed, and Susan, moved by the house blessing, the closeness, starting to talk, to tell Mickey what had happened, what had really happened today. But telling about Dr. Moon involved telling who he was, how she knew him, the abortion, which required telling about Richard, running away to Idaho. . . . She found herself doing just that. Telling everything.

All of the time Mickey just stared at her, mouth falling open, eyes wide, sometimes putting her hand over her mouth at something Susan said, making quick comments; no, no, cannot be. Doctor did dat to you? You let one man do dat to you? Oh, no! You were pregnant back den? I was trainin you and you were pregnant? Mickey shaking her head. . . . And he keep you comin back to his office every night. . . . Oh, Susan! Didn't choo know any bettah?

Susan went on talking, unable to keep herself from telling Mickey everything, knowing she should stop, but unable, finally coming to the part where Dr. Moon had passed her, on his way down the stairs, turned, came back up. . . .

Touched me. Here. Susan reached up and lightly touched the mole. He was almost by me. He *was* by me. Then he came back. If only he'd kept going.

Susan told the rest.

Mickey just shook her head. So dat was da noise I heard.

Susan nodded.

Mickey shook her head. Hit him. Spat at him. Susan . . . Susan . . . What happen to you?

I don't know. It was just so fast. One second I was all right. Then I kind of . . . I don't know, Mickey.

I knew I heard someting funny.

They sat silent for several moments. Then Mickey looking shrewd. Were dere any witnesses, Susan?

No.

You sure?

Absolutely sure. Just you. And you weren't really a witness—with your eyes.

Mickey leveling her finger at Susan. You swear dere were no witnesses?

Yes.

Susan! So stupid! How could you do such a ting! Hit a passenger! I train you myself! I break your ass. I sorry now, I know what choo going through at da time, but I teach you, first ting, nevah let da passengers get to your feelings. Always gotta keep control of yourself! I break you ass cause I figure you put up wit me, you no lose your tempah at me, you be okay wit da passengers. Always! I drill it into your t'ick skull jus for dat reason! To save your job! Susan, how many times a day, I feel like tellin one passenger to fuck hisself? Once? Twice? One tousand! Fuckin! Times! If I lose control of myself, den what happen? No, Susan! Nevah! Dere's dat time always waitin, just dat one time, 'as it, da end! Da passengers break our asses, we lose our tempah, we da ones dat pay, not dem!

Susan, you one good stew, you one professional, you look good, you know how to make people feel nice, people like you . . . Susan, we professionals, we trained to be nice to people when dey nice, smile, and we trained to take dere shit and still smile when dey assholes! We not paid to react!

I know, I know, I know.

Mickey was angry now, not at Susan, just angry. You lose your job, what's gonna happen to you, eh? Eh, Susan?

I don't know, it's not the end.

You not know. It's not da end. What choo gonna do, Susan? You nevah go college, you not married, your family no give you nothing, what choo going do?

It's not the end of my life, Mickey!

Okay, Susan, tell me it's not da end of your life! Mickey sighed, made a fist, shook it. Oh, Susan! I could hit choo! Now you tell me one more time, you sure dere were no witnesses?

None, Mickey! He was the last guy off the plane. If only he'd kept on going instead of coming back. . . . I'm only sorry I didn't push the bastard down the stairs when I think what he did to me. . . .

Nevah mind, you done enough already. Okay, Susan . . . Susan! You tell Gale what happen?

No. . . .

Anyone? You tell anyone?

No.

Mickey nervously pointing. Okay, I tell you what choo going do, you going keep your mouth shut, you no say another word to nobody! Nobody! You and I, we da only ones dat know. Susan, I gonna stick my neck out, risk my job, too, I da union rep. You know what I gonna do? I gonna get up dere in da hearing and lie my ass off for you. Dey find out, you know what happen to me? I finished, too!

Mickey shook her head. But dey got no way of provin you said anyting, you got one good record, Miss Pahoa, she likes you, we just going stand up and face da fuckahs down! Dey got no airline witout us! We gonna fight dem, we gonna grieve it!

Mickey reached over and put her hand over Susan's mouth,

squeezed hard enough to hurt, and said through clenched teeth, and you gonna keep your fuckin mouth shut from now on!

The living room was even more crowded now, people were setting off strings of firecrackers outside the house, the house was filling up with the acrid smell of gunpowder, Harry was drunk and shooting off a Roman candle in the street. Susan leaned over the phone, put a finger in her ear to hold out the noise, she gave the operator his number, she would call Jack—if only she could get some word from Jack. . . .

After a moment, the operator said, you can dial that number yourself.

No, no, I want to charge it to my own phone; that number is . . .

But that's not necessary. The number you gave me is a local exchange.

What? Suddenly, Susan realized she had given the operator Obachan's old number in Kalihi. She felt a chill go through her; she hung up the phone.

Sudden flashes of white, acrid clouds . . . On the doorstep, exploding firecrackers had filled her shoes with shreds of red paper. . . . The Dobermans were barking . . .

People stood in the street dodging firecrackers, laughing; Harry and his friends were shooting Roman candles over the house, the yard, the palm trees. . . . In the flashes of white light, Susan saw Gale hugging Nathan, her face buried in his shoulder.

Susan drove back to Honolulu, back up to the house. She sat on the cool grass looking down at the lights of Honolulu. The ocean was luminous but not bright under the half-moon, slippery and viscous-looking, like an old broth, she could make out the black shape of Diamond Head, the bright lights of Waikiki.

Susan knew it had been a mistake to trust Mickey. Mickey

would tell them what had happened to solidify her own place with the airline.

Susan wondered how she could have been so stupid. How could she have forgotten, that once, after she'd made out her bid for the month's schedule, Mickey had overbid her on the basis of her seniority? She'd said to Susan, hey, Susan, tough shit, I nevah put friends before job.

An airplane rose, the moonlight shining on the fuselage and wings, red lights flashing. Susan watched the airplane. I nevah put friends before job. . . .

Work. Suddenly she thought of the therapist, again.

The therapist saying to her, all right then, Susan how do you feel at work? Wait! Don't tell me. You're at work now, you're in your uniform, made up, you look great. . . .

He stretched back in his seat.

I'm a passenger. Come on, now.

He handed her a coffee cup.

This is a drink. You're serving me. Here. Do it.

Good afternoon, sir, may we offer you . . .

They went through it.

What do you feel?

I feel lonely . . . alone . . . you know, I don't want to turn into a certain kind of person at work. Hysterical . . .

He nodded, nodded. Right, right, the bitch-slut fear . . .

She shrugged. So I don't feel anything at all. . . .

He nodded. Until you explode.

Until I explode, she said to herself.

He had gone on to say, if you could just find ways of letting the anger out a little bit at a time so you wouldn't explode.

She watched the red lights flashing, getting farther and farther away in the air.

Until I explode, she said to herself.

Going somewhere in a car . . . late in the day. Somewhere. Where? The car so big. Someone in the front seat. Her father. Driving. Taking Mother to work in the bar; then, starting home. The turn-off. To Obachan's. Straight ahead, home. Turn-off. Obachan's. Waiting for the turn-off. The turn-off coming. Passing. Going straight home. Starting to whimper. Cry. Crying. Her father looking over at her. Glaring. Next time, looking away. Trying not to cry. Sobs. Her father. Glaring. Then the turn-off coming up. Coming up. Heart pounding. The turn-off. Passing. Lip quivering. Staring. Don't cry. Staring. Straight ahead. Neck tight. Don't turn right or left. Straight ahead. Don't cry.

Susan stood up abruptly, went inside, the house a mess, she debated cleaning up the place, decided no, threw the piles of clothes off her bed onto the floor. . . .

She woke to the sound of a Mercedes, far away, rising around the curves of the height. She turned over, drifted off.

The voices, low, close, across the room.

Nathan and Gale.

The creak of the bed. Gale's soft pleading gasps.

Susan pulled the pillow over her head.

Later, the Mercedes starting up and drifting down the hill. In the pale light, Susan saw her dress—the dress Jack had given her—lying over the back of a chair in the middle of the room.

On the other side of the room, she could hear Gale softly sobbing. Susan wanted to say something, anything; Gale, are you all right?

The sobbing went softly on and on, fading into periods of silence, then new sobs.

Finally, Susan got up, crossed the room, kneeled on the floor next to Gale's bed.

Gale, she said softly. Gale.

Her head moved on the pillow. She burst into new sobs and pushed her face against Susan's shoulder. Susan could feel the tears on her skin. She put her arm around Gale's head and held her until the sobs became softer, faded, her breath deepened.

Gently, Susan moved her arm, Gale's head rolled back on the pillow; her knees were stiff when she stood, walked to the door a moment, looked down at the city, and got back into bed.

In the morning, Susan lay quietly in bed and thought of all she would have to go through just to get herself back where she had been yesterday morning—if it could be done at all.

She'd have to grieve the charges against her, beat them, get reinstated in her job, just so she could turn around and quit. And even if she could get reinstated, would she have the nerve to quit? Or would she just go on and on, another year, two years, five years more, just getting older. . . . If she had wanted to free herself from the airline, once and for all, well and good, but she should have just quit. This way, she'd put herself in the hands of others—Mickey, Miss Pahoa, the vice president—well, she was stuck with it now.

Susan saw Mickey sitting up on the bed. . . . I train you myself! Always gotta keep control of yourself! I drill it into your t'ick skull jus for dat reason! To save your job!

. . . I don't want to turn into a certain kind of person at work. . . .

Give him your bitch! It's all right!

Susan saw the expressions, fear, fury, on Mickey's face, and knew that for Mickey her job was her life, the only thing she knew, she had, her only real way of belonging, and Susan could just as easily have heard Mickey, instead of saying, to save your job—to save your life!

Susan got out of bed, made a cup of coffee, looked over. Gale's bed was empty. She hadn't heard her leave, Gale had a week of early flights.

. . . Gale sobbing, the warm tears on her skin . . .

Susan picked up the dress Jack had given her, smoothed it, and hung it back in the closet.

Susan sipped her coffee and thought how yesterday morning

she had served Dr. Moon, the shock of seeing his hands on the tray, placing the drink between his two hands, actually smiling at this man who had . . . Remembering coming back night after night, the silence in the examining room, the humiliation. And it wasn't her alone, it was any girl, eighteen, scared, someone she once was, had been, but still was; then, yesterday, how she had waited at the aft door, dry-mouthed, heart pounding, waiting for him to come out, still afraid, afraid of what? after all these years? She didn't know.

Always gotta keep control of yourself! Susan . . . you so stupid!

So stupid!

Hesitating, stalling her mother with a smile, while she translated, rephrased, pidgin, back to English, stalling for time, smiling, did she have it right, yet, the words, pushing the words around, back and forth, a hollow feeling of terror in her, her mother's voice loud, stupid! Mickey placing her hand over her mouth last night, squeezing her mouth, hard, and you gonna keep your fuckin mouth shut from now on!

Susan opened the door, sat in a chair outside looking down at the city, squinted in the bright sun. The coffee was hot and pleasant to swallow.

Susan tried to think what had been happening to her, what had happened to her, what she had been feeling at the exact moment, or at the moment just before she had . . . reacted.

She didn't know.

She knew she had felt terrified, dry-mouthed, shaky; afterward, calm—calmer—and peaceful. Or maybe just empty.

Grounds for immediate dismissal.

They were right, of course. Stewardesses couldn't go around slapping passengers faces every time they were insulting.

She swished her coffee around in her cup.

No, not that the airline was wrong. Or even that Mickey was wrong.

She saw Mickey's face again. Always gotta keep control of yourself!

She remembered a time she had reacted without thinking, lost her temper. Hadn't even had time to lose her temper. She had been nineteen, twenty, walking beside the Ala Wai Canal, she was wearing a short dress, flowers embroidered across the collar and sleeves, a white dress, she'd hardly noticed the big Hawaiian approaching, a moke, greaser, another step and he'd pass, his hand, suddenly grasping, he'd reached under her dress, grabbed her between the legs, she'd pulled away, screamed something—she'd been carrying a leather purse with a shoulder strap, she swung the purse by the strap, hit him in the face, hard, splattering her things all over the sidewalk, into the canal, he'd been blinded for a moment. Fucking bitch! she ran, dropped the pocketbook and ran, dashing into the street, running between cars, she reached the other side of the street, apartments, ran down a street, she could hear brakes screeching, knew he was coming across the street after her, she ran behind an apartment, no place to go, a small yard, no one around, a hedge, she heard his footsteps, she broke through the hedge, dropped down on all fours behind the hedge, he came running up the walk, stopped, she heard him panting, cursing, through the hedge she saw his pants, he was looking right at her, didn't see her, his pants moving away from her, down the hedge, he spun around and ran down the walk. She lay on the ground behind the hedge for a long time after he'd gone....

Always gotta keep control of yourself!

Maybe, yesterday, for the first time in her life, she hadn't lost control—trembling, dry-mouthed.... Maybe she'd gotten control.

She finished her coffee. Now she could be melodramatic and try to rub everyone's face in it, stand up at the hearing, beat her breast, and say, oh yes, it was me, all right, I stood up to a passenger who was treating me like shit, I'm proud, fire me.

But there was no point in that. None at all. She'd put in too much time at this airline for that. She didn't need it. The moment had served for her. Had shown her there was someone else still in her who—

Who would what?

Susan didn't exactly know yet, just who.

The airline was going to make her pay. She thought of Mickey. Mickey was right. Now was the time for her to keep her mouth shut. She would grieve it.

Susan went back inside, made herself another cup of coffee, sat down at the kitchen table, and wrote identical letters, a formal request for a hearing, one to the union, one to the airline. She sealed them in envelopes, cleaned up, put on a bathing suit, put a dress on over it, waited for the mail . . . nothing.

She walked back from the mailbox making up her mind she would move out of Gale's place—on what money?—something, somehow. And she wouldn't write again or call Jack until she heard from him.

At the airport, she dropped off each of the two letters, then went over to the United counter at the main terminal.

Harry waved as she approached. His eyes were slightly red • and puffy.

Hey, howzit, Harry, hung ovah, ey?

He nodded, held his head.

Good party, Harry, worth it.

He nodded again.

She showed him the tickets, explained without making the error seem like his fault. He wrote out two new tickets. She checked them over. Thanks, Harry. Spa'k ya latah.

Now what would she do, bring them back?

She thought of her father sitting in the armchair, her mother balanced on the edge of the sofa, tv on. No.

She folded the two tickets in a blank piece of paper, placed them in an envelope, hesitated as she looked at the paper, wrote nothing, sealed the envelope, and mailed it.

Call Carol? Her eyes. So round. Staring. Staring at what? Walking up the dark stairs, her finger still marking the page in her book. Decided not to call.

At Queen Surf, Susan waded out, stopped for a moment to watch a mother gently leading her baby into the water. Susan waded out until the water was deep enough, she stopped, looked back at them, the baby, lifted her feet off the sandy bottom, turned over on her back, and closed her eyes . . . baby

. . . if I want to . . .

She floated.

An IUD. After starting to live with Jack. Before that, pills, but taking them too long. The day the IUD had been inserted. . . .

Coming from the doctor's office, feeling fine, stopping in Safeway. . . . Cashing a check and suddenly, hot and cold sweats. Lightheaded. The cashier studying her. Calling the manager.

Thinks I'm forging a check. Sees me sweating. Thinks I'm nervous.

Susan leaned against the counter, nauseated.

Next to her, the woman stared.

Susan explaining about the IUD and the woman asking, oh, how many children do you have?

Susan's ring hand in her pocket. Taking it out to let her see.

None. I don't have any children. I'm not married. But if I wanted a baby, not having a ring wouldn't stop me.

Rising and falling in the gentle swell.

. . . a ring wouldn't stop me. Said it just to see the look on the woman's face. Just to see it.

The woman had looked away.

The sun shining on her face, her body cool in the ocean, rising and falling. . . .

. . . a ring wouldn't stop me.

The hearing date was set, and after several breathless calls from Mickey, where she seemed to do nothing more than say over and over again, you sure you no say nothing to no one? You sure? And a discussion of strategy—we not drivin to da hearing togethah—meet you dere, I not seeing you for a few days, important dat dey tink we not conspirin.

And after a sad call from Miss Pahoa, who apologized for not being able to get the charges dropped, the hearing date came up. After Susan's long anticipation, the first hearing seemed to be a memory before it had even begun.

They had sat in Miss Pahoa's office, Mickey, the Grievance Chairman; Susan, the Grievant; Miss Pahoa, the Chief Stewardess and Vice President Sullivan, both representing the airline. The atmosphere was informal, the office as it had always been. The DC-6 on the desk, the photographs of Miss Pahoa in her military-looking stewardess uniform of the forties.

They all sat down immediately. No one had had a chance to get emotional or do much else. Vice President Sullivan was affable, calm, the charges were reviewed, and he'd said, let's look into this further.

Miss Pahoa said, but why? this girl couldn't have done such a thing, been rude, much less slapped anyone . . . look at her record, except for one leave of absence and some sick days, she's had a perfect record. . . . She held up a handful of letters, I have had letters from passengers for as long as she has been flying, asking who this girl is, saying that she was so nice to them, made them feel wonderful. . . .

Mr. Sullivan nodded. I know, I agree, that's why I say we have a full hearing so she can have her record properly cleared.

Miss Pahoa flushed a little. But what can be done at a full

hearing that can't be done here? What more can be found out?

Vice President Sullivan remained firm; I know your feelings for Susan, Miss Pahoa; you and I have discussed this at some length and I'd like to see this put through the proper channels. I'm sure Susan would agree with me. He turned to Susan and smiled. She has nothing to be afraid of.

That had been the end of the informal hearing. Mr. Sullivan had seemed to be in a hurry, and maybe he had something he wanted to do—golf, take his son to the beach. . . .

Afterward, Mickey and Susan stood out in the bright sun, Mickey trying to interpret every gesture, what it all meant, what this smile meant, that gesture, until finally Susan said, never mind, Mickey, there's no point in second-guessing, we'll find out soon enough. You act like you're the one on trial here.

Hey! If it happen to you, can happen to me, too! I know what dey up to, you tink dey want an old Buddha-head like me, thirty-seven-years-old, flyin?

Susan suddenly realized she was afraid of Mickey's temper, that maybe at some time during the hearings, Mickey would lose control of herself, blurt something out. Or come through for the airline to make herself look good. She should have kept it to herself, faced the charges alone.

Mickey said, okay, Susan, now dey going set da date for da four-man board, bring in da lawyers, and cut out da nice-guy shit. Don't matter how much of your life you give to dis company, one false move and you're out!

When Susan got home, there was a telegram stuck in the door. She opened it.

PLEASE COME.
LOVE, JACK

She read it several times.

She wanted to ask, for good? Are you asking me to come for good?

But she knew she would just have to go, take a chance, leave whatever she had here in Hawaii, good and bad, to see.

He did sign the wire love, but that was easy to do.

She decided to take her own sweet time in answering him.

Mike Gold, the ALPA lawyer, showed up several days before the four-man board and listened to Susan's story. He was about three years older than Susan—twenty-nine—but he had the heavy body, the gestures, the gravity of a middle-aged man.

He heard Susan out, then paused a long time. He still looked a little tired, pale, and out of focus from the long flight from Washington.

Finally, he said, Susan, I want to tell you, I think there's something else here that you're leaving out.

Mike—

Wait. He held up his hand. Wait. I don't know what it is, but I don't want you to tell me anything more—if you understand me. I have never lied under oath. Last time you and Mickey were in Washington negotiating new contracts, I saw your temper . . . and your stubbornness . . . so I know you've got it in you.

Mike—

He shook his head again. No, don't say any more.

He hesitated, frowned. I don't want to worry you, Susan, but you might as well know everything. I guess our irate passenger thinks the airline has been dragging its feet a little on you. . . .

He reached into his pocket. This is a Xerox of a letter our anonymous passenger had his lawyers send to the airline. It still doesn't give the passenger a better case, but they're trying to show the airline they mean business by going the legal route. You'd be surprised how many people are scared by the letterhead of a law firm. Most likely, it's a bluff to get some action, but they are definitely upping the ante.

Susan looked at the letterhead. She recognized the name of one of the big local law firms. She glanced at the letter:

My client, who prefers to remain nameless. . . .

She handed it back to Mike.

Read it?

No, don't want to; just explain it to me.

Mike studied the letter a minute. Okay, their client, who prefers to remain nameless, he repeated in a mocking voice . . .

He took a deep breath. Look, what it says in essence—it's really not so subtle blackmail, though they've worded it pretty circumspectly, is that their client, who they're trying to make us believe is a big wheel, has a controlling interest in a large travel agency. . . .

His voice was mocking.

They state that their client has always had a good relationship with Polynesian Airlines—and would like to maintain that relationship. He has always believed the personnel at Polynesian were of a certain high quality and would like to maintain that belief, but if Polynesian fails to do its duty—i.e., dump you—then he will have no other choice but to recommend that his travel agency's clients be booked on a more hospitable airline—like Inter-Island Airlines. . . . And—

Mike hesitated.

And file suit against Polynesian.

File suit against Polynesian? For what?

Mike pressed his lips together.

For assault.

Assault!

He nodded. Look, they're trying to put the pressure on. They know—so do we—how nervous airlines are about lawsuits.

Don't get alarmed. I didn't want to worry you and I don't now. But you're a big girl and I want you to know what the stakes are. So stay cool.

Assault charges, she repeated.

He reached out and squeezed her hand. Now relax. It's a game and they've made their next move. Even if they do bring the charges, which I don't think they'd ever do, they don't have much to back them. They're still just testing to see what they can get away with. Stick to your story.

After a moment, Susan asked, what kind of a case do you think we have?

Mike paused. He thought for a moment. Started to say something. Then changed his mind. We'll see.

The night before the four-man board was to meet, Mike Gold took them out to dinner—Gale, Susan.

Gale sat next to Mike and after a couple of glasses of wine, leaned against him and rested her hand on his thigh. She would sometimes laugh, then get quiet, remote, and her eyes would look vacant, then sad. Then she would tune in for a moment. Her eyes were dark, the lids heavy, her lips dark with wine.

In the lua, Susan said, you don't seem to be having a good time. Are you okay?

Oh, I am, Susan. What makes you say that?

I don't know. Your eyes.

No, she shook her head. I like Mike. It's good to see him again. There's something about Jewish men I've always liked. . . . He's so sure of himself.

After dinner, they went for a short walk, and then back to his suite at the Ilikai. They sat out on the dark lanai sipping brandy and looking down at the lights of the Yacht Basin and the line of lights following Waikiki. There were some lights, too, from boats on the dark horizon. Gale laughed and groaned, oh, I ate too much.

Susan put down her glass and got up. Well, next time I see you, we'll be in the hearing. . . .

Mike stood up and followed her into the living room. Don't worry, Susan, just go in there, be yourself, stick to your story, and we'll win. He considered for a moment. I don't think there's anyone at the airline that really wants to nail you . . . not that badly. . . . Yeah, Inter-Island has been competing pretty hard with Polynesian lately. Management might figure this is a good chance to shape you girls up a little. He thought for a moment. Maybe Sullivan's trying to make an example of someone, but we won't let him make it you. I don't see that they've got much of a case. No witnesses. No matter what they say or do, no witnesses . . .

Mickey, Susan thought, Mickey heard the slap, she heard it, told her the whole story . . . I can deny . . .

. . . no witnesses. Really, all they have is Miss Pahoa's testimony of the complaint. She took the phone call. Unless Miss Pahoa really wants to make you look bad . . . and even then, it's still arbitrary.

Mike again thought for a moment. Now, if the airline wants to be arbitrary, fine, but we won't let them get away with that, either.

No witnesses, Susan said.

Mike nodded.

No witnesses. Just our nameless passenger and his complaint and threat of suit, but . . . All of a sudden Mike Gold looked pissed. . . . He's not going to get to first base with that.

You think not?

We'll take care of it.

Thanks . . . thanks for dinner, Mike.

She kissed him on the cheek. He patted her on the back, kissed her lightly.

Gale kissed Susan on the cheek. Don't worry, Susan.

As Susan stepped out into the hall, she looked back. Gale

was reaching behind her neck to unfasten her dress. Mike set his cognac down. Susan pulled the door closed.

Back at the house, Susan watched part of a late movie, then tried to sleep. After a while, she turned the light back on, read a while, turned off the light, still couldn't sleep, turned the light on again.

Got up. Looked at Gale's empty bed.

She sat at the kitchen table, took out a piece of paper, wrote the date at the top, started a letter to Jack.

My dear Mr. Clear Air Turbulence,

Wish you were here with me tonight. I feel so alone and it makes me sad not to see your beautiful eyes. There are so many things I want to say to you. All day long I have thoughts for you. Thoughts like flowers. I put them in a vase called Dear Jack. Some are fragile and don't last long. Jack, you are so far away. A letter takes four days to get to you from here. We can send a man to the moon in that time. Oh, Christ, Jack, I'm being so stupid.

Susan stopped, looked up at the Japanese lantern, looked around the room. Wrote:

There are too many things here to remind me of you. Everything, my life here, seems to be a blur now, happening somewhere out there, in a distance. I feel as if I'm in a cable car, suspended. Everything is moving by very silently and swiftly.

Susan stopped. Wrote:

Sometimes the silence frightens me.

She looked around the room again.

As usual, I'm alone with my constant companions. Me and my tv. Me and my book. Me and me.

Suddenly, she thought, he just doesn't want Oriental children. She put down the pen.

She got up, paced around the room, sat down again. Wrote:

You know, Jack, it's so strange, when I was being raised by my grandmother, the haoles were the other people, but when I was taken back by my mother . . .

She paused, reread the last line:

. . . but when I was taken back by my mother . . .

Paused again, wrote:

. . . and father, then Orientals became the other people.

She paused a long time:

I don't know what it was that kept me hanging on so long here. Something I wanted. I just never had the courage to let go of whatever it was I thought was here, but never really was. Hawaii, my lush fragrant vacuum.

Jack, there are so many things I want to say to you. What do you do when you're not with me? What *are* you when you're not with me?

Jack, I'm fucked up, I know it, there are so many other women you could have, all I want to know is do you really want me?

She sat a long time, then stood up, one of her knees cracking softly. She folded the letter, got back into bed, read it over once, then placed it in the pages of her book. She turned off the light. After several moments, she could see the windows glowing softly in the dark. She lay still a long time. It was so quiet.

The informal atmosphere of the preliminary hearing was gone. The airline sat on one side of the long conference table— Miss Pahoa, Vice-President Sullivan, and their lawyer; the union sat on the other side—Mickey, Susan, Mike Gold. A stenotypist sat at the head of the table.

Susan looked over at Miss Pahoa on the other side of the table. Miss Pahoa tried to smile, looked away.

She's going to do it to me, Susan thought. And I can't blame her, I've done it to myself.

Feeling Mickey at her elbow.

Or, if not Miss Pahoa, Mickey. Mickey hasn't looked me in the eye since we got here.

Mike was on the other side of her.

Susan looked back at Miss Pahoa. Circles under her eyes. This time, Miss Pahoa managed a quick smile. Susan remembered the first time they had met. The hiring interview. Years ago. Literally years ago. Her knees had been shaking when she'd walked into the room. But Miss Pahoa had been so nice to her. And at the door, calling her back, and saying, you look just lovely, Susan. Susan looked at Miss Pahoa again, looked away. It made her sad.

The airline lawyer was still questioning Susan. Just what exactly had happened on that flight? You had been airsick? Did this happen often? Wasn't it unusual for a flight attendant to be airsick? It had been necessary for you to spend some time in the lavatory. Was there something special that day which might have made you sick that day? Were you upset? Nervous?

Mike Gold standing up. While this isn't a trial, that is a leading and pointless question and I object. We're not here to determine the grievant's moods.

The airline lawyer continued his line of questioning:

On landing at Kahului, where were you stationed while deplaning passengers?

The aft door.

And you are unaware of any such incident, any gestures on your part, any words, which might have incensed this passenger who has complained and who prefers to remain anonymous?

Nothing.

In other words, in your mind, there was no incident of this kind; you have no idea who the passenger might have been or why he might have made such a complaint. A very specific complaint. To you it was just a routine flight?

Yes.

What do you suppose might be the motivations of a passenger in making a detailed complaint of this nature?

Mike Gold stood up.

I object. That's a leading and irrelevant question and you know it. We're not concerned with what the grievant thinks the passenger's motivations might have been. Did she or did she not do what the passenger has accused her of doing?

The airline lawyer continued: Why should a passenger go to the trouble of making a specific charge—that the flight attendant in question struck, spat at, and cursed him?

Mike Gold remained standing. You know that what she thinks might be motivation is not the question. Did she or did she not perform these actions? Yes or no?

The airline lawyer repeated: The actions of slapping the passenger. Spitting at the passenger. And cursing the passenger. Correct?

Mike Gold glared at him. Correct.

The two lawyers stared at each other. Sullivan sat quietly, elbows on the table, palms pressed together and the tips of his fingers touching his lips. He was staring at Susan. Susan stared back. After a moment, Sullivan looked over at the airline lawyer.

Mike Gold was speaking: These kinds of complaints are made against flight personnel all the time. If you are going to make more than the most arbitrary case, if you want to be fair, produce some witness.

Susan looked at Mickey out of the corner of her eye. The

airline lawyer was looking at Mickey. Miss Pahoa and Sullivan looked at Mickey.

Mike continued: We haven't come here today to make assumptions about Susan's mood on the morning of the flight in question—Honolulu–Kahului—or pass judgment on her character. As it now stands, all you have is a single phone call. . . .

And a letter threatening, among other things, to sue Polynesian Airlines— The airline lawyer held up the letter.

Mike held up his own copy. And a letter threatening Polynesian Airlines—which has nothing at all to do with the issue of whether or not the flight attendant in question is guilty of the alleged actions.

Of striking a passenger, slapping his face, spitting at him . . .

Sullivan shifted in his chair and made an expression of disgust.

. . . and of using certain four-letter words.

Miss Pahoa looked at the table.

The airline lawyer held up the letter.

Mike Gold threw his copy on the table. Polynesian Airlines doesn't fire its personnel because they are threatened with letters of this nature, does it? Who manages this airline—he looked at Sullivan—the whims of the passengers or management? Do you want to start a policy on terminating your personnel whenever a passenger threatens you with a lawyer and needs placation?

Sullivan spoke for the first time: This isn't a question of placation. She struck a passenger.

The airline lawyer turned quickly to look at Sullivan, started to raise his hand toward him.

Mike Gold's voice rose as he slammed the table: Strike that from the record! She *allegedly* struck a passenger. ALLEGEDLY! Mike Gold looked down to the end of the table. Strike that from the record!

Sullivan and the airline lawyer exchanged glances.

The airline lawyer nodded and spoke quietly: Strike that from the record.

Sullivan sat back with a look of disgust.

Mike Gold glared. What is this prejudicial attitude? Is this a hearing or a passing of judgment? I see some among us have their minds already made up. Can we have a fair hearing?

Sullivan sulked.

Mike picked the letter up from the table. Waved it. One phone call and this letter. And you have her guilty of the charges. But no witnesses! Not one! Prove that she's done what she's been accused of, and fine, he spread out his hands, well and good, I'd be the first one to say she should be terminated. But give me some witnesses, give me some proof, something more than these accusations. This so-called nameless passenger hasn't even bothered to show up, wants to remain anonymous. Have you considered that?

Miss Pahoa was being questioned. How long have you known the grievant?

Seven years. I hired her myself.

The questioning dragged on, Mike Gold objecting. What about her character, her record. Had there even been any complaints before?

On the contrary, passengers often wrote letters to Miss Pahoa asking about Susan, telling how gracious she had been, how welcome she made people feel, how lovely she was.

After a while, the airline lawyer said, what do you think of the complaint against Miss Wilson?

I was shocked. Susan's always been one of my girls. I was shocked.

The airline lawyer shifted his ground. Tell us about the phone call. You took the phone call, am I right?

Miss Pahoa nodded. She sat quietly for several moments. She looked down at the table. When she looked up again,

Susan saw her lips quiver. She wanted to reach across the table, do something, say something, I'm sorry.

Miss Pahoa started to say something and looked down again.

Miss Pahoa? The airline lawyer looked at her. Sullivan was staring at her.

Miss Pahoa raised a hand to her lips. Then her other hand. She touched her lips with her fingertips.

Susan looked down and swallowed.

Sullivan spoke softly. Miss Pahoa?

Miss Pahoa was starting to shake her head from side to side. Her voice shook. Susan wouldn't . . .

Susan took a deep breath. Her hands were sweating. She wiped them on her skirt.

Miss Pahoa's voice quivering, Susan seeing she was going to cry, wanted to hide her eyes, oh God, not here, don't cry, not in front of everyone.

Miss Pahoa barely managed: I have nothing more to say.

The airline lawyer and Sullivan were looking at Mickey.

Mickey stared at the table. Susan glanced at her. Mickey's face had a frozen expression. Susan had seen that expression, recognized the expression, when? Where? Sometime, several years ago . . .

They'd been cooking. Mickey's kitchen. Some grease had suddenly flared up in a sheet of flame. Mickey let out a scream, her hands went to her mouth, she stared, face frozen, as it was now, then she'd thrown herself into Susan's arms.

Susan had held Mickey as she cried, sobbed. The fire out, calmer, but with the same expression on her face, Mickey told Susan about the bombs.

Bombs?

Some bombs. Up near the Pali.

You mean Pearl Harbor?

Mickey nodding. Mickey had been five or six. Holding her

mother's hand. The story seemed incoherent. Just phrases. Mickey's face frozen while she talked. Bombs . . . the flesh was hanging from the trees across the street . . . fire . . . she'd wet her pants, cried, held her mother's hand. Her mother had led her somewhere, up some dark stairs, her pants were wet, the flesh, Susan, I saw it, flesh, hanging off the trees. . . .

Mickey's face had been the same then as now.

The airline lawyer spoke her name, softly, supplicatingly. Mrs. Chun?

Mickey looked up, face frozen, said in too-loud a voice, Yes! What!

Mrs. Chun, you were on that flight. Honolulu—Kahului.

Yes!

What did you observe of Miss Wilson's mood that day?

I object. Come on, do we have to keep going back to material you know is irrelevant?

Mrs. Chun, will you answer the question?

What did I observe of Susan's mood that day?

Yes,

I object.

Nothing.

Susan looked at Mickey, I nevah put friends before job.

Nothing? You have known the grievant for several years. Miss Pahoa tells me you even helped train her. Did you?

Sure, I trained her.

Was she a good trainee?

Objection. What the hell does this have to do with the charges?

She was good. I trained her myself!

So you do know her?

I know her.

Mike Gold was standing. What's the point of this line of questioning?

The airline lawyer paused. Asked quietly, would you say the grievant is capable of the alleged actions?

Mickey stared at the table.

Mike Gold turned to Mickey. Mickey, this line of questioning is wholly irrelevant.

Mickey looked from Mike Gold to the airline lawyer. The question is irrelevant like he says.

But is she capable of it?

Mickey stared at the table.

Mrs. Chun?

Hey, I said it's an irrelevant question! Didn't choo *hear* me?

Miss Pahoa said, could we lower our voices, please?

Mickey flushed.

Everyone looked over at Miss Pahoa. Mickey stared at some point high on the wall. Her eyes were bright.

The airline lawyer paused. Then, after a moment, made a decision, started again: All right, Mrs. Chun, you were on the Honolulu–Kahului flight. First stewardess. Where were you standing as the passengers were deplaning in Kahului?

First stew stands at the forward door. That's where I was.

With whom?

Gale. Gale Lopez.

And Miss Wilson?

She was at the aft door.

Alone?

Alone.

You and Miss Lopez stood at the forward door, and Miss Wilson was at the aft door until the passengers had deplaned, am I right?

Right.

Miss Lopez was with you the entire time?

Right.

Did either you or Miss Lopez leave the forward door for any period of time and enter the cabin?

No.

And after the passengers had deplaned, where did Miss Lopez go? Did she enter the cabin?

No, she followed the last passenger down the stairs.

And where did you go?

I went back into the cabin.

What did you do in there?

I stopped in the buffet to get my flight bag.

Then what did you do? Did you leave the airplane?

No, I stayed in the buffet to comb my hair.

Sullivan looked at the airline lawyer.

Were there any other passengers left in the cabin?

Mike Gold looked at Mickey.

No, none that I saw.

None that you saw. Then there might have been passengers still in the cabin?

Ey! What's dis! If you no see someting, it ain't dere, is it? Jesus!

Sullivan looked at Mickey. Mickey glared at him.

The airline lawyer continued: Then what did you do after you finished combing your hair?

I walked back through the cabin to get Susan.

Did you see or hear anything unusual?

Mickey turned pale. Her eyes were small and black. Unusual? Like what?

Anything.

Susan aware of Mickey at the corner of her eye, but not daring to turn her head to look.

No, nothing unusual!

Nothing at all?

Nothing! I said.

Sullivan and the airline lawyer exchanging glances.

Sullivan spoke quietly, are you sure, Mrs. Chun?

Mickey glared at Sullivan with fear and hatred. I am sure, Mr. Sullivan!

You didn't hear a sound? No voices raised? No sound of commotion? Nothing at all?

Mike Gold was up. I object! She said she heard nothing.

Nothing is nothing. Stop trying to intimidate the witness.

Mickey glared. Nothing, she repeated.

The airline lawyer continued: You walked aft, then and found Miss Wilson?

Yes.

What was she doing?

Standing there.

Where?

Just inside the door.

Just standing there?

Well, what would you expect her to be doing?

How did she look? Was there anything unusual about her appearance? Her uniform?

Mike Gold was up. Come on, what's that mean?

Was there, Mrs. Chun?

Mickey shrugged. No, just looked like Susan.

How would you characterize the way Susan looks?

Mike was sitting again. Susan heard him mutter, asshole questions, asshole questions.

What do you mean, how she looks? She's a good-looking wahine. Here she is, look for yourself. She looks like she looks.

Susan felt herself being studied. She stared at a point slightly above the heads turned toward her.

Mickey sighed in exasperation.

The airline lawyer and Sullivan looked at each other. Sullivan looked at Mickey a moment, then looked away, suddenly stood up, glared at Susan, Mickey, and Mike Gold, and said, we can't run an airline around the private lives of our personnel! He turned to the stenotypist. You can damn well enter that into the record. He picked up his briefcase and walked out.

In the hall, Mike, Mickey and Susan stood together. They were silent for several moments.

Then Mike said, you're off the hook, Susan.

Lucky thing for her, too!

Mike shook his head, we could have grieved it successfully. An arbitration would have let you off.

Mickey shook her head. I not know, you one lucky wahine, I seen dem get rid of girls for lot less den dis.

Mike said, never mind. There are a few details to be taken care of—I'll make sure the charges are removed from your record. Your lost pay will be restored. . . .

Susan turned to Mickey. Thanks, Mickey.

Yeah, tanks yourself! You tink I was going to squeal on you, didn't choo. Mickey shook her fist at Susan. Should have! Jus cause you tink so. Oh, you make me mad, Susan. Mickey had a crazy look in her eye. If I get canned . . . she shook her fist at Susan.

Mike looked around, Keep your voice down, Mickey.

She turned on Mike. Keep your voice down, she echoed. She turned back to Susan. Get away wit murder, you! Always! Good-looking bitch!

Mike looked at Mickey. Good-looking bitch? What do looks have to do with this? It's got nothing to do with looks. They had no witnesses.

Mickey and Susan looked at each other.

No witnesses. Ey! If it had been me, you tink I get off, eh?

Whose side are you on anyway, Mickey?

My own!

She stabbed at her chest, wheeled, and quickly walked away.

Mike and Susan looked after her a moment, looked at each other, Mike reached over, put his hand on her shoulder once, squeezed lightly, turned, and walked down the hall.

Gale burst out laughing. Something in Johnny Carson's week-old monologue.

The laugh came to Susan as she dozed, face turned away from the tv. The monologue went on, faded away.

244

After a time, Gale said from far away, are you going to quit now and go to the mainland . . . Susan? . . . Susan?

Susan opened her eyes. Rolled over. Lay silent. The monologue went on. Gale laughed.

Go to the mainland? I don't know. I think I'll get back on the schedule and make some money first. Then I'll see.

What have you written Jack?

What do you mean?

About going to the mainland, Susan?

Oh, that I'm thinking about it.

Are you thinking about it?

Susan nodded. Yes, I'm thinking about it.

You know, Susan, you leave the airline now, that's it for you. Pau. Specially after the grievance.

I know.

Susan?

What?

Tell me—I won't say anything—did you really do it? Hit a passenger? Slap him? Slap a passenger, Susan? Spit at him? Did you really do that? Everyone at the airline wants to know.

And you want to know?

Yes.

What do you think? What does everyone at the airline think?

What do I think?

Yeah.

I think you did it!

And people at the airline?

They think you did it, too!

Why do you think that?

Gale considered seriously, then said in mocking pidgin, cause you one tough tita, tita! Susan looked over at Gale. One tough wahine!

The monologue went on. Susan laughed softly at something. What an asshole Johnny Carson is. She laughed again.

You aren't answering me!

Susan turned, studied Gale. Said simply, I did it. Keep your mouth shut, too!

Gale smiled. She looked happy. And curious.

I'm glad. Of course, I'll keep my mouth shut. I'm glad you did it.

I don't recommend it. It's the long way around no place to no place.

I'm still glad. What made you do something like that—I mean, after all this time?

Susan didn't want to go into the business about Moon, the abortion . . . After a moment, she said, why did I do it? I don't know. It had been coming for a long time. It just happened to arrive that day. She knew it was the truth, even though she was leaving the details out.

They were quiet for a while. Then they talked about different things. Jack. Nathan. The airline. Gale said she had signed up to take a course with Werner Erhard. EST. Gale explained Werner Erhard and EST. Wanted to know what Susan thought of it. Of Werner Erhard and EST? Yes. Bullshit. Save your money. No, I'm going to do it. Susan closed her eyes. Gale's voice and the tv started to blend. Werner Erhard. EST. Farther and farther away.

Susan woke to a groan, the room dark now. Another groan. Susan pulled the pillow over her head. Nathan.

After a moment, another groan, louder.

Susan!

Susan moved the pillow. Gale? Gale? Are you all right?

Oh God, Susan!

Susan turned on the reading light, saw Nathan wasn't there, crossed to Gale's bed.

What's wrong, Gale?

Gale looked up, her eyes dull, lines pinching her mouth.

Pain, Susan . . . my stomach.

Susan touched her forehead. You're soaked.

I feel like I'm burning. Bring me a glass of water.

Wait until I take your temperature.

Susan returned with a thermometer, stuck it in her mouth.

Suddenly, Gale stiffened with pain.

Don't bite the thermometer!

Gale's hand groped, squeezed Susan's arm, her forehead wrinkled. She relaxed after a moment.

Susan took out the thermometer.

What is it?

Susan hesitated. A little over normal. Then decided not to lie. No, Gale. It's a lot over normal. It's a hundred and three.

Can I have the water now?

Susan brought her a glass of water, lifted her head up, Gale gulped it quickly.

Gale suddenly convulsed with pain; spilled the water.

I'm taking you to the emergency room.

No, Susan, not the hospital.

What are you going to do, lie here all night?

Susan found some clothes, helped Gale sit up, swung her legs over the side of the bed, pulled off her nightgown, and helped her into a muu-muu.

Can you stand and walk?

I hope so. God, I hope so. . . . I'm scared, Susan.

She stood unsteadily and Susan helped her to the door. Outside, she dropped to her knees, and grabbed her abdomen.

Okay, come on, Gale.

Susan knelt, helped her back to her feet.

In Queen's Emergency, Gale disappeared into a room, a curtain was drawn, Susan waited. Across the parking lot, a driver and ambulance attendant were making up a gurney—folding back the sheet, tucking in the blanket. They slid the stretcher back into the ambulance, got in, and drove out of the lot, the tires screeching on the curve.

At a quarter of five, Gale walked unsteadily toward Susan, holding her abdomen. Her eyes glazed.

They're not sure what it is, but they gave me some painkillers and told me to call my gynecologist first thing.

In the morning, Susan called the doctor, helped Gale into the car. Her arm around Gale's waist, she supported her into the doctor's office. The nurse met them at the door, and Gale disappeared into an examining room.

Then Gale was on the phone, her voice was far away.
Susan?
Are you ready for me to come get you?
Susan . . . I'm in the hospital. I'm going into emergency surgery in forty-five minutes. He says it's an ectopic pregnancy. . . .
Gale. . . .
He said if it had been another two or three hours, it could have ruptured and . . . killed me. Gale said it almost as a question.
Do you want me to call anyone for you? Your parents?
No, don't call them. Can you call Nathan?
Gale, not Nathan.
Please.
Okay, Gale, all right. I'll call him.
I better hang up now. The nurse is here with a needle.
You'll be all right.
Susan . . . the doctor said . . . you saved my life.
I'll see you when you wake up.
Thanks, Susan. Susan?
What?

You better call scheduling for me and tell them.

Okay, Gale, don't worry. See you in a while.

Susan had never seen Gale so thin, her cheeks and eyes were hollow, her shiny black hair framed her face on the white pillow, the plastic name tag slid easily from her wrist to her elbow when she raised her arm.

Susan cooked her an entire dinner, brought it down to the hospital on a tray, carried it in to Gale, but Gale could only pick at the food.

She seemed off somewhere.

The doctors said she was going to be all right.

Gale told Susan, they say I've lost the ovary . . . but . . . I'm alive. She tried to laugh. She held up a thin finger. Don't count me out, I've got one left. You can do a lot with one ovary.

Nathan sat quietly by the bed, either hanging his head and staring at the floor, or just looking embarrassed. Occasionally, Gale slipped her hand through the stainless steel bars of the bed and stroked his hair. Glossy black hair like her own.

Susan usually cut short her visits when Nathan appeared at the door. Once, as she was arriving, Nathan was about to leave. He was leaning over the bars and whispering to Gale, his long black hair hanging over her face; her thin hand rested on his cheek. He leaned closer to her, his hand on her stomach, suddenly, Gale screamed, a single loud, piercing scream, and grabbed at her abdomen. Nathan jumped back.

Tears filled Gale's eyes.

She whispered. The stitches, oh God.

Nathan looked from her stomach to her face.

Gale . . . Gale?

After a long time, Gale sniffed, and said softly, I'm sorry, Nathan, I didn't mean to scream.

This time Nathan leaned carefully over the bars. Gale turned her face to his, he kissed her.

Susan bit her lip, turned quickly, and walked out.

Susan wrote Jack that she would be coming. She didn't write that she was quitting her job. He would know. And she didn't want to make him feel as though she were depending on him.

She was surprised at how little there was to do, how little anyone had to say—or could say. It was so easy just to resign.

Miss Pahoa had looked up from her letter of resignation, stared at Susan for a long time. She started to say something, then stood up slowly, came out from behind the desk, and hugged Susan hard. When she pulled away, she was blinking quickly. Susan tried to say something, couldn't, walked to the door, hesitated, wanted to say, I'll write, but instead just managed to say softly, Good-by, Miss Pahoa.

Mickey's look was one of sadness, confusion, fright.

Susan, long as I live, long as I know you, I nevah understand you. Nevah. You always a little differen. Susan, how come you fight to keep da job if you know all da time you going turn around and quit? What choo going to do now? Go to the mainland? Marry Jack?

Going to the mainland. Don't know if I'm going to marry Jack.

What's da point go all dat way if he no marry you?

I love him—that's the point.

Harry came out of the side door of the house. Inside the dog run, the Dobermans bounded toward Harry.

Leavin us, eh, Susan?

Susan nodded. She looked around the yard. The grass was coming up. The flowers. The pikaki had started to spread out on the fence to form a fragrant screen.

Looks pretty, Harry.

He looked at the yard and smiled, then turned back to Susan. When you going?

250

Not sure.

When you sure, give me da date. I get you one flight, first-class.

Susan looked at Mickey. Remembered her when they'd been training. Young. Bright. Tough. Now the toughness had turned to an air of permanent agitation.

Mickey reached over, pulled Susan to her, kissed her on the cheek. I sorry to see you go, Susan! Nevah thought I'd see da day. You really leavin us. Hey! Write to me, you little bitch.

I will.

Oh, I bet choo will! Once you get to da mainland, you forget us all!

Mickey gave her the finger. Susan laughed. They hugged again, pushed apart, Mickey slapped Susan lightly across the cheek.

Spa'k ya later, tita!

Her mother was on the other end of the phone. Susan was explaining. She was leaving for the mainland. There seemed to be some confusion, she had to repeat everything twice, three times, shout, her mother kept saying, what, Susan? What? Oh . . . very nice. What?

There was a long pause. Susan didn't know if her mother had understood or was even still on the phone.

Hello? Mother?

Yes, Susan.

Did you hear me?

Yes, yes . . . the mainland. How long are you staying? When will you be coming back?

I don't know.

You don't know?

No.

Oh. You don't know when you will be coming back?

No, Mother. . . . Can you come to see me off?

What?

I said, can you come to see me off at the airport?

Then her mother seemed confused again. Something about Dad having the car.

No, not today. . . .

And Carol had gone off on a camping trip to the Big Island. Mother. . . .

Everyone's away.

I'm not going today, Mother. If you have a pencil and paper, I'll give you the flight number and date.

Yes.

Susan read off the flight number and date.

Did you get that?

What?

Did you get that?

Yes, Susan. When are you coming back?

I don't know, Mom. I have to go take care of some things, now. Bye, Mom.

Bye, Susan.

A couple of weeks before Susan's flight, Gale's mother decided to drive to Haleiwa for the Bon Dance—the Japanese celebration of the dead. Gale packed a dinner, invited Susan, and the three of them drove up to the North Shore. As it got dark, they stood on the shore with hundreds of others. It was calm, the surf had glassed off. From somewhere in the distance, a church across the road? the sound of music, and the Bon Dance. Each of them, Gale's mother, Gale, Susan, lit candles in the Bon lanterns and set them adrift on the darkening water. Susan turned, saw an old woman staring out over the water, saw she was too old to wade out, Susan took the Bon lantern for her, waded out, set the lantern adrift. The stars were coming out, one by one. Susan watched the lanterns drifting out into the water, dead souls crossing to another shore. She stood in the dark, looking out at the beautiful lighted candles, like stars, hundreds of them, flickering and shining on the black ocean, washing away in the slow slippery waves.

Susan gave most of her things to Gale. Pots and pans. Knives. Her wok. Cookbooks. Her tv set. Lots of dresses.

Gale accepted them in an uneager way. She had a forlorn look.

At the airport, Gale left Susan at the United counter and went to park the car.

Harry was there at the counter.

Oh, Susan, you looking so pretty. I got choo up dere in first-class, champagne all da way to New York. Where's da rest of your baggage?

This is it.

Dis it? No more? You traveling light? I was getting ready to load everythin you own!

No need.

Mickey say aloha again. She come see you off, but she on da schedule.

When Susan turned from the counter, Gale had a pikake lei. She lowered it over Susan's head. The white flowers were beaded with water and cool on Susan's shoulders and through her dress.

Susan looked at Gale. She was still painfully thin, her cheeks gaunt; there were thin lines at the corners of her eyes.

How do you feel, Susan?

Scared. Happy.

They sat down to wait for the flight to be called. Susan kept scanning the floor, watching the doors, expecting to see her, but knowing she wasn't really coming. Mother. Her face made up, her eyes searching into the corners of empty rooms, voices. ... The mainland. Winters. Snow. Covering ...

———

Check-in.

The line slowly moving toward the ramp agent to board. Gale moving alongside the line next to Susan.

As the ramp agent took her ticket, Susan looked back. She looked around once more.

Gale looked at Susan. Gale put her arms around Susan. They hugged each other hard, kissed.

Write, Susan.

I will. Take care, Gale.

We'll see each other again . . . soon.

You'll come visit.

I hope so. I will.

They hugged again, pulled apart. Susan stepped past the ramp agent.

She turned.

Gale waved. Aloha, Susan! Aloha!

Aloha!